Praise for the novels o

The Vani

"Seraphina doesn't let up this time. In her ... you off a cliff, hits you with red herrings and suspects at every turn, and takes your breath away with her final startling twist."

—Katie Tallo, internationally bestselling author of *Dark August* and *Poison Lilies*

On a Quiet Street

"Welcome to the 'burbs...except you won't find much peace and quiet here. A fast-paced, highly-enjoyable and compulsive read that may well make you look at your entire neighborhood a little differently."

—Hannah Mary McKinnon, internationally bestselling author of *Never Coming Home*

"A writer to watch."

—Publishers Weekly

Such a Good Wife

"Seraphina Nova Glass's twisty...thriller plunges the reader into a dark, compelling world of lies, adultery and murder. Bold, racy and masterfully plotted, *Such a Good Wife* kept me guessing from the very first page to the scorching, jaw-dropping conclusion."

—Rose Carlyle, #1 internationally bestselling author of *The Girl in the Mirror*

"In *Such a Good Wife*, Seraphina Nova Glass weaves a deliciously dark tale... A sly and pulse-pounding murder mystery set in steamy Louisiana."

—Kimberly Belle, internationally bestselling author of *Stranger in the Lake*

Someone's Listening

"Glass weaves a taut web of suspicion, murder and revenge in this chilling tale. Sinister characters and blind ends increasingly heighten the tension until the harrowing final climax. Add *Someone's Listening* to your must read list!"

—Liv Constantine, internationally bestselling author of *The Last Mrs. Parrish*

"Unputdownable. I found myself suspecting everyone at some point. Twisty, original and a must-read—highly suspenseful and cleverly written."

—Karen Hamilton, bestselling author of *The Perfect Girlfriend*

Also by Seraphina Nova Glass

THE VACANCY IN ROOM 10

SERAPHINA NOVA GLASS

GRAYDON
HOUSE

GRAYDON
HOUSE®

Recycling programs
for this product may
not exist in your area.

ISBN-13: 978-1-525-80980-4

The Vacancy in Room 10

Graydon House
22 Adelaide St. West, 41st Floor
Toronto, Ontario M5H 4E3, Canada
www.GraydonHouseBooks.com
www.BookClubbish.com

Printed in U.S.A.

For Shelly Domke

1

CASS

There's a Shell gas station across the street. That was the first thing I noticed when I moved here because I arrived at dusk and the sign's *S* was burned out. As I approached the motel, the only thing I could see on the dusty horizon was the word *HELL* lit up in orange and yellow, which seems appropriate once you get to know the area. I only saw the sad *S* hanging off the billboard by a hinge and swinging ominously as I got closer, and I wish to God that I took it as an omen and turned around.

There are a few other landmarks on this desolate stretch of two-lane highway between The Sycamores apartments and the good side of town—an Arby's, a Motor Inn, Larry's liquor store, some strip malls with hand-painted signs, and Teaser's Gentlemen's Club.

I shuddered when I saw this dump that's now my home. It used to be a motel, and they didn't even change the name. It's three strips of two-story building connected in a U shape, with a dumpy pool in the middle. They renovated the motel rooms to be apartments...sort of. They are now slightly-better-than-a-shitty-motel-style apartments with a couple bedrooms, but they didn't even change out the paisley carpet or burgundy drapes. I literally gasped when I first laid eyes on the semen-stained bedspread in my fully furnished oasis.

Room 10. It used to be apartment 100, but one of the zeros is missing, and in its place is a gash that looks like someone once took a machete to it, but I don't ask questions. It's the smallest apartment and sits adjacent to the boiler room, so now I'm Cass from room 10. It's so pathetic the others don't even consider it an apartment.

I'm used to it now. The shock wore off weeks ago, and here I still am, just after Christmastime, curled up in front of my window with a Brandy Alexander, watching sleet tap the icy pool water's surface with a backdrop of Barry from number 206 trying to jump-start his pickup in the parking lot.

I think I'll start to cry again, so I close the hideous drapes and sit in front of my laptop at the table. The tears don't come. Today is one of those numb days, as it turns out.

I can't really predict what I'll get from day to day. Sometimes it's the impossibly sad version of myself who will sit for half a day scrolling through my ex's social media sites to torture myself with images of him and my replacement, Kimmy. What sort of grown woman calls herself Kimmy? Sometimes the Diazepam works, and I feel the emptiness of it all in a different way—the pain presents as a dull ache around the edges, but I can function, put one foot in front of the other, offer a thin smile when I pass people, sometimes even a nod hello so I appear relatively normal. Whichever version of myself shows up from day to day, I don't forget for a second that Kimmy is living in my four-bedroom house in Santa Fe, and I'm in this dumpster fire of an apartment complex outside town. With nothing.

It all unfolded too fast for me to explain why I'm even here. I was being kicked out. I wasn't just being cheated on and left but was actually displaced from my home with nowhere to go, so in my desperation, and after scrolling through dozens of cheap short-term apartment ads that someone with no job can't afford, I answered a want ad for this place because they needed someone to do the apartment cleaning and light repairs in exchange for free rent.

In my old life, you couldn't pay me to stay here for one night. But that life is so far away it's like it never happened—like left-over wisps of a dream you try to hold on to and remember when you wake up, but they float through your fingers. When I saw the ad, I took it, because what choice did I really have?

A red flag, my dad said. "A man who doesn't believe in marriage but will live with ya and play house. Reddest of all the reddy-red flags, Cass."

I argued it was noble because Reid thinks marriage is a sexist construct and we don't need a piece of paper to prove our love. My dad sprayed his sip of beer out through his nose on that one.

And he was right about it all. I have no protection now. I didn't work the last few years because that was how we both liked it—I was able to volunteer and cook my way through Julia Child's cookbook like someone in a movie.

He liked the way it looked, that he was a bigwig Realtor who could support us both, and he liked his crêpe suzette and quiche lorraine ready to eat when he got home. It worked. *There is nothing wrong with that*, I told myself.

And then it stopped working. And I have no job or money, and although I think I had every right to punch him in the back of the head when I discovered them at a restaurant together— discovered he was cheating—with my own eyes, I made it worse because there were no late-night crying arguments or discussions about how we'd get through this—no sobbing apologies or denials on his part, begging me to stay and telling me it didn't mean anything. Just an eviction and a cold shoulder. After six years together, it was over just like that.

I usually have to sit with my head between my knees for a minute to avoid hyperventilating when I think about this too long, but today is a numb day, so I don't have the energy to look at Kimmy's Instagram. Well, okay, I peek at it for just a few minutes, to see if there is anything new.

The numbness turns into a tapping up my spine that feels something like rage when I see her in her white puffer coat and ice skates laced up, standing next to my person. My Reid. Not hers. How is this possible? They're holding two candy canes together making the shape of a heart. Gag. They're smiling at the camera, rosy-cheeked and glittery-eyed. She looks more like his daughter than his new lover.

Okay, I'm being an asshole. I'm sure she's at least legal because Reid is very informed on legal matters of all sorts, which is why he was so prepared to screw me out of everything and even write up an official eviction letter from his house with thirty days notice when I refused to leave.

Fun times at Deer Head Lodge the caption reads. I vibrate with fury, but before I can do anything, like maybe drive to the lodge like a psychopath and push Kimmy from a ski lift and watch her plummet to her death—maybe get impaled by a candy cane if I'm lucky—my phone buzzes.

It's a tenant. Mary Hidleman from 109. And I have to take the call and fix whatever problem she has this time, because as much as it pains me to say, I need the job.

Where else can I go? I quickly run over all my options in my mind the way I often do and always come to the same conclusion. I lost touch with my actual friends years ago when I met Reid, and they're married with families for the most part; they don't want some loser on their couch. My father's a drunk who rents a room in his buddy Oscar's basement, and our mutual friends sided with Reid. He was expert at making me look like this was all my fault, from the crumbling of our relationship to the restaurant "assault." So, I'm here now. I'm somehow the caretaker of The Sycamore apartments, and I'm trapped.

Mary calls for me to come in when I knock. Her apartment is mostly dark, lit only by a droopy string of Christmas lights loosely draped around the front window and flickering light from the television. The Shopping Network is selling adult onesies that look like giant creepy gingerbread people. Mary's in slipper socks and a threadbare housecoat that, in her braless state, leaves little to the imagination.

She sits in her rocker recliner with her legs spread open, chatting to the TV about the economy and the ridiculous prices they're charging for adult pajamas.

"I see London, I see France, Mare," I say matter-of-factly, and she closes her legs and gives me a dismissive wave of her hand. A cigarette hangs from her lips, and she points in the direction of the tiny kitchen.

"I saw him under the sink, but I don't know where he got off to. Little fucker."

I notice a small pistol, sitting right out in the open on her table that's cluttered with ashtrays and junk mail.

"What's that for?" I ask.

"Well, I was gonna try to shoot it, but I thought I'd call you first. See if you got any of those traps that snap their heads off. Or poison, I guess, but I poured some antifreeze on a clump of peanut butter last time I saw a rat, and it didn't do nothin'." She leaps up and starts bending down in search of one.

"You can't shoot a gun in your apartment."

"Well, goddammit, the building keeps gettin' fuckin' rats. What if it gets in my bed? My grandson's coming to visit. I can't have rats in the beds." She steadies herself on the counter, dramatically, at the very thought. "The owners have to do somethin'."

I peer around at the open cans of Hormel chili tinted with a bluish mold, macaroni and cheese left in a pan on the stove that looks like it's congealed into an orange brick, and oil-stained pizza boxes scattered around on end tables and overflowing out of the trash can.

I've never seen a rat in my unit, but I don't say that.

"All I can do is put down a trap—a live trap. Not the kind that snap their heads off," I tell her, and she shrugs. Then I see the smoke alarm on the kitchen wall has been pulled off and is dangling by a couple of wires. I point at it and give her a questioning look. She pushes the butt of her cigarette into a Sprite can.

"Kept going off," she says.

"Hmm."

In the short time I've been here, I can already see that Mary's troubles are more in the loneliness department than the rat infestation department. Maybe a little of both to be fair, so when she finds out I'm staying for a bit to lay traps and fix the smoke detector, she beams and offers me a plate of cookies that look like Santa hats with marshmallow trims and puts the kettle on for tea.

It's a funny thing, loneliness. It's something I'm only learning about recently—the might of it—the things it makes one do.

It's dusk now. "I'll Be Home for Christmas" hums from behind the door of unit 106 as I walk back to my empty studio apartment across the lot. The sleet has turned to a soft snowfall, and my body aches with a grief I can't articulate.

Before I open the door to my apartment, I see the light on in the small rental office next to my unit. It's where I give poor new saps rental agreements to sign and where most of the paint and cleaning supplies are stored. Besides the owner, I'm supposed to be the only one with a key, so I must have left it on or left it unlocked.

When I push open the door, a man is there. I leap back with a frightened yelp, but then I see that he stumbles and falls against the wall and then laughs.

"There's my Kitty," he says. "I was looking for you. Meow." The guy is so drunk I can smell him from the doorway, and he clearly has no idea where he is.

"You can't be in here. Get lost."

"Aw, Kitty isn't nice anymore. Your hair's different, too," he says and grabs me, pressing all of his weight against me.

I try to pull away, but he kisses me, holding the back of my head with both his hands and sticking his tongue in my mouth before I can even react. I scream and try to push him, but he's huge—a head taller than me with a thick neck and a beer belly the spills over the waist of his oily jeans. He starts to shove a hand down the front of my pants, but he loses his footing. I sidestep him, and he falls to the ground in a hard thump.

"The strip club's across the street, dude. I think you got lost. Out. Seriously." I kick the bottom of his boot with my shoe.

"Show me them titties again, Kitty cat. Titty cat." He laughs hysterically at his attempt at a joke, and then…silence.

"Really!?" I yell and kick his boot again. He's out cold. Son of a bitch. I think of how badly I want to crawl under my heating blanket with the rest of my brandy and not have to call the cops and stand in this freezing office explaining it all to them before they haul him off to detox or whatever they do these days. Maybe I just leave him. But the file cabinet and tenant records… I can't have some crazy have access to everyone's credit card info and unit numbers and all the spare keys if he wakes up, and it turns out he's a total creeper.

I sit on the office chair and blow out a hard breath, thinking through my options. And then I notice the wedding band on his finger and feel the tips of my ears go hot and my heart speed up. He's married. This married guy is out trying to get laid during the holidays.

I think about his wife. Is she home with their kid, playing Chutes and Ladders at the coffee table with *Home Alone* on in the background? Are they eating popcorn balls and peanut brittle? Is the floor still littered with wrapping paper from the day before? Is she looking at her phone every ten minutes wondering when he'll be back from a holiday party at the Mad Hatter to join them—the one that she was supposed to be at with him until the sitter canceled, never knowing he was actually with the sitter at a Holiday Inn instead.

Maybe she threw a Miller Lite at his head and told him to get out of her face and go to the strip club for all she cared, like you see on an episode of *Cops*, but it doesn't matter because either way he's a cheater. And I want to punish him with all my might. He shouldn't be allowed to get away with this.

I don't know what makes me think to do what I do. First, I take out his wallet and look at his ID. John Bradwick. Forty-seven, lives on Ashbury Court across town. A few small photos are tucked inside. A big-haired blond woman with round cheeks is all gums as she smiles at the camera with a scowling toddler on her lap...and this man, John, posed behind them like a sort of weird Glamour Shots photo. On the back in faded ink it says John, Peggy, and Levi 2011. A phone number is actually written in pen inside the leather of the wallet. I could call it, but it would probably ring to the cell phone in his pocket, so there's no point. There's eighty-seven dollars in cash. I take it.

Then, I don't know, I just do it. I dig through the drawer for a tube of lipstick I've seen rolling round in there—not mine, but whatever—and dab the hot red hue onto my lips. I take off my top, but I keep my bra on because I'm not a pervert, and I lay down next to the giant on the floor. I leave lip marks on his cheek and swing my leg around him and take a few selfies of us. I roll his head my way, and it heavily falls into my neck, looking like he could be kissing me, and I snap another.

Then, I go next door to my apartment, drag over my heating blanket, and curl up in the office chair. I look up Peggy Bradwick, and after I find enough of what I'm looking for to set my plan in motion, I watch Netflix on my phone until the idiot wakes up.

At 5:13 a.m., John sits up with the terrified look of a man who has no idea where he is. I calmly explain that he was hammered and must have stumbled over to The Sycamores from the bars across the street. He blinks at me, then holds his head a minute before standing.

"Uh…you just let me sleep here?"

"Yep," I say.

"You should have probably called the cops. I mean…"

"Probably."

"Well, uh. Thanks, I…"

"I do charge a fee, though," I say.

"I'm sorry," he says, feeling for his phone and wallet, which I did place back in his pockets.

"Yeah, I thought it would be terrible if you ended up in jail, or I let you wander off and get a DUI, or if your wife found out you were with some chick name Kitty…"

"Hey, whoa, whoa. What? How do you—"

"Peggy would wanna know where you've been. I'm sure she's worried sick. Your phone's dead by the way, but she probably called all night."

"Wha… Who are you? Seriously? How do you know my wife? I…"

"Listen, John. I had some time to look Peggy up. She's a nurse. Good work, nursing. And you live on Ashbury Court, and Levi's what, eleven or twelve now? I'm sure she doesn't want to see this," I say, and even as I show him my phone, displaying the photos I took of us with my lacy green bra and his lipstick-smeared cheek on my shoulder, I feel a wave of nausea for what I'm doing and have to remind myself he's just like Reid. He deserves this.

His eyes go wet and glossy, and I can see him swallow. "We? What did we…"

"Oh, God no. Really, stud? You think you fall on my office floor in a drunken heap, and I have sex with you? Is that how it usually goes for ya? No, I just took these for insurance," I say, and barely recognize the forced confidence in my voice.

"What? What does that mean?"

"It ensures that if you give me what I need, I don't ruin your life. I hate to do it. I really actually do, but you're a cheater, so…"

"What do you want!?" he says as spit flies from the corner of his mouth, red blotches beginning to dot his face.

"A thousand."

"Dollars!?"

"Yeah. Dollars. I thought about a figure, and that seems reasonable."

"What makes you… Are you insane? What makes you think I have that kind of money to give you?" He's moving toward the door, but I see the hesitation—the knowing that he's stuck.

"You're a plumber. They make good money. A nurse, too. Not bad. I'm sure you can spare it."

"I…" His mouth opens and then closes.

"Next time, you'll think of Peggy before screwing strippers named Kitty. Only assuming there—the stripper part, but the name is telling. A name says a lot."

"What is the matter with you? You did all this for… You did this fo—"

"I know you're confused and probably have a wicked hangover, but I have Pegs's email from her Facebook site. Can I call her Pegs? Looks like people do. You should tell her she shouldn't have her info public like that. She looks nice—like the kinda person who would trust people, but still. Not a good quality these days. If you bring cash by the end of today and slip it under the office door—I mean, not loose cash, right? That would be silly. In an envelope or something—then I don't send her the photos, and you go back to your delightful bungalow with Pegs and little Levi."

John's face is pale as the moon now. It seems to change color with every new revelation, and he feels for the doorknob behind him to leave.

"What if you send it to her anyway? How do I know you won't?" he says in an almost whisper.

"You don't know me, John, but I'm not an asshole. I'd have no reason to do that if you do what I'm asking. I hate to even do this to you at all, but…" *But I was left with nothing*, I almost say but don't say. "I need the money. That's it. Nothing personal. And you did a shitty thing, so…"

"If you send this photo out, people might see it—like anyone—people you know! Your family. I could show it around here for…revenge, or I don't know. You're not safe in this, either. You would look just as bad screwing a stranger, it could ruin…"

"John. Look around. Does it look like I have anything left to lose?"

After a few silent moments, he gives what might be interpreted as a tiny nod and then walks out into the icy morning air and across the street to whatever bar or club his car is at, I assume.

I'm shaking. My hands are trembling. I can't believe what I just did. I don't even know who I am right now.

Three hours later, I'm in my apartment eating canned ravioli and trying to get the satellite TV channels to come in when I see a Ford truck pull up on the side of the building. A large man in a hooded raincoat pushes something under the door of the office. My heart leaps. When the truck is far enough down the street, I push my feet into slippers and run next door. I let myself into the office and grab a manila envelope from the floor.

Back in the warmth of my apartment, I sit on the detested plaid sofa and spread the crisp cash-machine bills out on the coffee table. A thousand dollars. Oh, my God. I can't believe it worked. I never would have sent those photos. He could have called my bluff. He also could have not taken it as relatively well as he did and attacked me instead…or worse.

I can't do something like this again. I must have been out of my mind last night. I promise myself that I won't do something like this again.

I wish more than anything that I kept that promise.

2

ANNA

Seven months later

A steamy July rain sizzles and pops off the hot pavement of the Gas 'N Go parking lot, and I know something bad is coming. It's his silence that rattles me—the tremble in his voice when we spoke this morning. Why won't he answer my calls?

A bearded trucker in a Pabst T-shirt places his Dr. Pepper on the counter, and I tap my foot impatiently as the cashier says they're turning over shifts and he has to wait for the night guy to come in and switch registers. He nods outside, where a young man in a mullet, who must be the night guy, takes his time getting inside. I watch him flick the butt of his Winston Light behind the Polar Ice chest and eat the slimy end of a Slim Jim while he sits on a propane tank under the store awning and scrolls on his phone.

"Are you kidding me?" I mutter, but the trucker doesn't make a fuss. He just lays a couple bucks in change on the counter, adjusts his ball cap and covers his face with one arm as he rushes back to his rig.

I check my phone. It's seven minutes after five, so I assume

Slim Jim guy is officially late, and I don't have time for this. I put down the gas station wine and Henry's favorite powdered mini donuts and sprint to my car.

I turn on the ignition—the pounding of the rain on the metal roof is deafening. I feel tears spring to my eyes, and I don't know why, I just know something's happened. It's not like him to miss my calls. Ever. Certainly not all day. I punch the call icon under Henry's name on my phone. It rings through. *Shit*.

I speed through glossy two-lane roads toward our house. I know things haven't been good lately. He lost his teaching job. I'm between journalism jobs, but we're fine. It's a rocky patch is all. We're not broke. We have prospects. He has more time for his own art, we're spending more evenings together— dinners, right? It'll be fine. I go over the pep talk in my head, so it's ready when I find him.

When I get there, I take the stairs two at a time and fling open the door, rain soaked and breathless, and…nothing. I don't know what I expected. An empty wine bottle is still on the coffee table and last night's curry sits in greasy take-out boxes on top of the trash, and it's so quiet the tick of the wall clock is startling.

I try to think of any reason Henry would not be picking up the phone. There could be a dozen reasons. It died, he lost it, he has it on silent by accident. Sometimes when he's painting he'll put it on silent, and I get that.

But it was the way he sounded before I left for work this morning. It wasn't the same as his usual depression I've come to grow used to these last few months—it was a hollow sound— an emptiness when he spoke. And it's not that he said anything alarming, just *goodbye*, *see ya tonight*, but something about it rattled me.

I check every room, and then I decide he must be at The Sycamores. Over a year ago, his friend suggested he rent one of the shitty apartments there that was sitting empty forever so he could use it as a painting studio, as we quickly ran out of room at our place for his work. He pays next to nothing for it and has spent most of his time there since he was laid off. I tell myself that has to be it. He took advantage of the rainy day, put headphones on and is lost in a painting. My gut feeling is just paranoia.

Before I can grab an umbrella out of the closet and run back out the door to set off to The Sycamores, my phone rings.

"Henry!" I say, breathless. Anger meeting desperate relief.

But he doesn't say hello. I just hear the hiss of falling rain through the phone and then…sobbing.

"Oh, my God, honey, what the hell? What's wrong?" I've known Henry since we were in college and heard him cry maybe three times in over fifteen years. I can't imagine what's happened.

There is silence on the other end again.

"What is it!? I've been trying to call all day, what's happened?"

"Anna," he whimpers, and then hiccuped cries stop him from speaking. "I can't do it anymore."

"What? What does that mean? Do what?"

"I've ruined everything. I messed up."

"Henry, where are you? I'm gonna come and get you, and we can talk about it. It'll be okay, just tell me where you are."

"I'm so, so sorry. I love you, you know that. I did something, Anna. I need to tell the truth now. I fucked up our whole lives, and I'm so sorry, but I just can't…I can't do it anymore."

"No, you didn't… You… We can figure out whatever this is, okay?" I try to use a calm voice, but I'm so confused. This is coming out of nowhere, and I'm afraid he'll hurt himself—that the last few months were worse than I ever knew, and he was this bad off. "Babe, please. It's gonna be okay."

"I did something unforgivable," he sobs.

"Whatever it is…"

"No." He stops me. "You don't understand." The saddest, most desperate cries I've ever heard escape his lips, and my heart breaks.

I sit on the edge of the couch and run a hand through my hair, trying to quickly figure out what I'm supposed to do—how to help.

"I...killed someone," he says. "I did. It was me." And then I hear a deafening bang, and the line goes dead.

3

ANNA

The body of thirty-six-year-old local artist and teacher, Henry Samuel Hartley, was found in shallow water on a bank of the Rio Grande just south of the Santa Fe city limits early this morning. Authorities are ruling it a suicide.

The papers told the world only hours after I found out and before most of his family were informed. The photo next to the story is the one he uses for all his professional sites and business cards—his sandy blond hair hanging ever so slightly over one eye, his smile meeting his blue eyes and beaming at the camera in his shirt and tie that look out of place on his body. Maybe because I've only seen him in formal attire a handful of times in my life. He's usually in paint-stained jeans and vintage T-shirts—The Smiths, Tears For Fears—that's more his style. They should have chosen one of the photos that showed who he really was.

The shock hasn't subsided. In the two weeks since his death, the funeral has come and gone, the life we shared together snatched out of thin air. My things are packed in boxes, and the house is going on the market next week because I can't stand the emptiness and the memory of him haunting every room. I can't be here without him. So now here I am. At The Sycamores.

I feel close to him in a different way in this eerie place because his work is here. Some boxes of belongings and all the hours of his life he spent inside these walls are all I physically have left of him now. And maybe there will be clues inside these boxes or on his computer or even in his paintings—something to help me understand what was happening to him.

I need to know. Why was he so desperately sad over the last months—who the hell does he think he killed? That can't possibly be true, but something made him take his life. I never told the police or his family that part—I mean, of course I told them he called, crying and saying he's messed up and was so sorry and hysterical. They needed to know what preceded the suicide—his fragile state—but the *I killed someone* part? No. Because it can't be true.

I pull a suitcase across the concrete between the parking lot and the external stairs up to Henry's studio. My new home. I pass the pool where a few women sit at a white plastic table playing Go Fish and drinking 7-Eleven jumbo Slurpees. I notice the brunette because her excess girth spills through the shell shaped cutouts in back of the plastic chairs. She's yelling at a kid floating in the pool with water wings and a dinosaur squirt gun.

I struggle with the broken wheel as I tug my bag past them.

"You got a seven, Rosa. I saw it!" one of the women hollers.

"Go Fish, Jackie." The other one, Rosa, I guess, giggles.

"Don't tell me you ain't got no fuckin' seven. I saw that shit." Jackie stands to snatch Rosa's card, but the plastic chair is stuck to her backside, so she sits back down. Jackie pulls the chair off her butt and stands and lights a cigarette with a scowl. "Whatever."

"This is why no one plays with you, Jackie," the unnamed third woman says.

"You play Monte, lady?" one of the voices asks, and then I realize they're talking to me.

"What?"

"We ain't playin' Monte, Crystal. We're playin' Go Fish. Plus, she ain't gonna answer you. Chick looks beat up," the other says. I don't know who's who anymore.

"You okay, chick?"

"Uhhh," I start to reply, but they've forgotten about me and continue arguing among themselves. So I gratefully continue on and heft my bag up the stairs, one at a time, until someone appears behind me. I begin to apologize in a daze, a knee-jerk reaction to being in the way, and I try to shift to the side to let them by, but I realize it's a face I recognize.

"Sorry," I say, masking my surprise as he picks up my lop-sided suitcase.

"Can I help you with this?"

"Oh..."

"I mean if either of us are getting up the stairs," he says with a half smirk, and I think I offer a semblance of a smile back, but I'm so numb every day that it's hard for me to really be sure if my face matches my intentions anymore. The man is Carson, maybe. No... Callum...something. He's the guy who told Henry about the apartment here.

I only met him once, at a school play. They teach at the same place; well, they *did*. And I met him and his wife at intermission. They were putting on *West Side Story*, and Henry and I were at the concession stand eating bake-sale blondies and wishing they sold stiff drinks instead to get us through the second half. Callum and his wife came up.

I feel bad I don't recall her name, but she looked so thin I instantly judged her, and on the way home in the car, I joked to Henry about needing to bug Callum for her diet plan. He told me she was terminal—I don't even remember the kind of cancer—a bone cancer, I think. But I do remember that I felt like the shittiest person on earth, so her beautiful, frail face and thinning chestnut hair and tiny frame is etched in my memory forever.

He told me Callum and his wife only lived in this shithole because they didn't have medical insurance and the bills destroyed them. I guess he was only part-time at the high school, and she had to stop working, and the debt buried them. She finally passed a few months ago, according to Henry.

When I look at Callum, I feel the weight of his grief mirroring my own, right back at me, and it's hard not to look away and run from this additional reminder of pain. The realization happens in a moment when I meet his eyes. We both lost everything we care about, and life has dumped us here, like a further punishment.

He has the case at the top of the stairs before I snap out of my catatonic moment and say anything at all. I climb the rest of the concrete stairs and nod at him.

"Thank you," I quietly say, and I pretend not to remember who he is before slipping safely behind the door of 203.

Inside the apartment, the stagnant air steals my breath. I try to turn on the air-conditioning unit in the window, but it just makes a rattling noise and putters out. I open the windows and stand a moment, taking in the room. Dust particles dance in the slanted beams of light peeking in from the open curtains.

Many of his easels look like ghosts, covered with drop cloths in the still space. The small kitchen is mostly unused except for a scattering of mugs and a few IPA bottles. The bed is covered in stacks of empty stretched canvases and coffee cans stuffed with used brushes. It looks more like a painter's studio than an apartment.

I don't want to move anything. I want to keep it all the way he left it, but I'll need to at least carefully clear the bed. I move a box of oil paints to the floor and sit, and then the tears come.

I am doubled over in a pain I didn't know was possible. I sob uncontrollably until my ribs ache. *Henry. Why?* I curl up in the fetal position, and I replay all the arguments over the last months. All of the bickering that was an obvious facade for the weighted issues behind it.

After years of agreeing we never wanted kids, one day after he'd been laid off, he sprung on me that he changed his mind and he'd been wanting to tell me for a long time. I told him it was a midlife crisis, and it would pass, and he was being ridiculous. We wanted to travel the world and drink great wine and read the *New York Times* together from our high-rise condo's balcony in the city on Sunday mornings and follow our big dreams, but we never made enough money to do any of that. Fine. Fair, but we don't just go back on everything we ever said—ever wanted—all of a sudden.

That was when he started changing: six months back. But I thought he was having a moment—thinking we gave up a life that was still in our grasp because the one we were chasing our whole lives was feeling pretty out of reach now. We officially failed, but kids were still possible. A little cottage outside the city could happen if we wanted it, he said. But I didn't want it. I still wanted to move to a Costa Rican beach or Ibiza and not be a slave to a 9-to-5 or kids—like we always said we'd do.

God, why didn't I just say yes? *Yes, baby. Whatever you want. Anything you want.* I'd give anything to go back and say yes.

I see the sun reflect off a white triangle near the front door, and I sit up and look at it. I didn't notice it when I came in. It's an envelope. I could have stepped over it, or maybe someone shoved it under the door since I've been inside.

I walk over and pick it up. I turn it over to see my name on

the front. Anna Hartley. I think maybe it's from the rental office. Some general info, a bill, something like that, but when I
open it, my hand flies to my mouth, and I drop it.

The scrap of paper feathers gently to the floor, and I look
down and see the two-word note looking back up at me:

GET OUT.

4

CASS

I stand in the doorway of 108 while she's screaming, pointing across the floor at something.

"Sylvie, for real, I don't know what you're freaking out over."

Sylvie stands on a kitchen chair in slippers and a T-shirt, and all three of her kids are huddled on top of the modest kitchen table that looks like it could buckle at any moment.

"*Hay monstruos!*" she cries.

"Hey what? Monsters?" I was gonna guess cockroaches, but my patience is wearing thin, and the very word will just induce more screeching from the huddle of children.

"*Ratas!*"

"A raccoon?" I ask, inching into the muggy apartment.

"A rat," one of the smaller kids says softly, hiding behind his sister. I look over to see not a rat but a tiny mouse eating a crumb near the stove. I try not to laugh, for the kids' sake. The mouse looks like he should be wearing a little fedora and starring in an animated movie.

"Oh. Gotcha. Well, you gotta shut your door. They can just walk right in. Why doesn't anyone shut their doors around here? It's like a dormitory."

"*Gato,*" she says, and I look to the kid for a translation.

"Cat," the kid says shyly. "She wants to know if you have a cat."

"Not on me," I say, and pick up a colander from the counter and try to trap the little bugger, but it only makes the entire family scream in terror when I miss and he scurries under the fridge.

"Borrow cat from Mr. David. 106!" she says, and I open my mouth to question this when the mouse makes a run for it and disappears into the back of the house. Sylvie fans herself and looks like she'll pass out.

"Fine, yeah. Okay," I say, backing out of the front door and walking to knock on David's door.

Before I do, I see a woman. She's sitting on a wrought-iron chair on the strip of shared balcony—that's really just a walkway to get to the stairs rather than a balcony—and she's in front of Henry's door. She doesn't see me, so I continue on to David's door, and before knocking, I take a deep breath and shake my head the way I do multiple times a day, still in utter disbelief that this is my life.

David's substantial weight and breathing problems make him immobile, so he calls for me to come in from his recliner that squeaks and sighs under the girth of him as he shifts his body to greet me. The units are all small, so when I open the door, he's only feet away from me. I've never seen him in any other spot before. Over the last six months or so, I've come in for a clogged toilet and a couple HVAC problems, and it's like he's actually welded to the chair.

There are nine cats visible when I step inside. David is playing *Call of Duty* on his Xbox. He pulls his headphones down and looks at me without saying anything.

"Uh. I'm supposed to ask you about borrowing a cat?"

"Is the cat for your own use?" he says, oddly formal and without hesitation, as if this is an everyday request.

"Um…108."

"Does Sylvie have a mouse? She never shuts the front door. They can walk in."

"They can. Yes," I say, and he nods as if we understand one another about a very important subject.

"I prefer if you take Sister Christian. I usually give out Clawdia for such things, but she has a sour stomach," he says.

I look around wondering how to figure out which cat to grab.

"So just…?" I give a confused twirly gesture with my hand, looking for which cat to snag.

"She's the beautiful black Siberian in the sink."

I go into the kitchen and see four cats on the counter. One fat black one curled up in the sink. I pick her up like I'm holding Simba over a cliff and walk to the front door.

"She can bring her back tomorrow. Sister Christian likes to take her time, but she'll get it."

After I drop the cat off, I see the little mouse scurrying along the concrete pathway on the side of the building, which is lucky because I never planned to let Sister Christian massacre the poor thing anyway. I was going to come back with a hunk of Gouda and a butterfly net, but instead I take off my Thunderbirds ball cap and scoop up the would-be cartoon mouse and release him into the wooded area behind the building. I name him Fig and wave goodbye as he stitches his way through the leaves and brush until he's gone.

On my way back to the office, I notice the girl in front of Henry's door is gone. I wonder if it's his wife.

Everyone's heard about his suicide, of course, and the whispers in a place like this travel quickly and come with many versions. It doesn't matter that the papers posted that he was found in the river. Around here he was found "hanging from the rafters," forget that there are no rafters, or he was "found in his bed with a gun in his hand," although no gunshots were reported. And of course, there are a few that refuse to go in the pool now because they say he was found face down floating in his own blood, and they fished him out in the middle of the night, which is why no one saw it.

It makes sense, though, the crazy gossip. The Sycamores is where the broken people live. Everyone is a bit off in their own way. Everyone seems to be filling a void or mourning a deep loss of some kind. Since I'm the one they call to fix leaky toilets and clogged pipes, I hear more than I want to. Maybe they tell more than they want to, too—a knee-jerk reaction that accompanies their loneliness, and I'm just the person who happens to be there to absorb it all.

There's Babs who glides around the pool all day in a unicorn floatie drinking gin martinis, who calls me to reach things in high cupboards in her apartment on a weekly basis even though we're the same height, and then she forces me to sit and eat a lemon Bundt cake or apple crumble and drink powdered Lipton tea—and I always do.

There's the guy in 119 with the face tattoos who's been spotted eating SpaghettiOs out of the can on the balcony on more than one occasion, who tells me that Gwen in 201 has the herpes. Gwen in 201 tells me that Leonard in 111 got his dick stuck in the vacuum and had to go to urgent care, and Leonard tells me that Gordon in 104 steals Amazon packages, so look out. Then there's Rosa. She's one of the "pool girls" along with Crystal and Jackie. They're a permanent fixture at the plastic poolside tables while their kids beat each other with pool noodles and eat Flamin' Hot Cheetos all day. Sometimes Letty and Tina join them, but Letty and Tina have jobs, so they have less time to chain-smoke and argue over cards and who owes who change from the 7-Eleven Big Gulp run, and which contestant on *The Bachelor* deserves love and which ones are just whores who are trying to grow their Instagram accounts.

Rosa's quiet. She's one of the people who doesn't air her

dirty laundry and who I know little about. A few others keep to themselves, too, but most folks are like Crystal with three young kids and another on the way—but no father in sight—who spends her days poking at her phone with her long corn-chip fingernails, perpetually FaceTiming God knows who. And there's her partner in crime, Jackie, who doesn't seem to possess an inside voice. She's rarely seen without a blue Big Gulp and a pack of Camels in hand, and her voice can be heard far and wide, arguing about who's cheating at Go Fish and gin rummy, who can "fuck off" and "suck her dick" because she ain't gonna be disrespected.

I walk across the concrete patio, wiping cat hair off my denim shorts, and pull up a chair next to the pool girls. A giant box of malted milk balls and Junior Mints are melting in the sun. Crystal must have taken her kids to the movies. I take a sticky milk ball and pop it in my mouth. The girls stay focused on their game of Crazy Eights. Rosa holds up her empty hands showing that she's out, meaning she won, and the others moan and call her a cheater the way they do every game no matter who wins. I really don't see the point of it all.

"You seen that chick up there?" Jackie asks, nodding to the strip of balcony outside Henry's apartment. "It's the wife, yeah?"

"It must be," I say. I saw the email from the owner today, saying his wife was continuing the lease for now and planned to move in, which I find desperately sad. If that were me, I'd want to be as far away from the place as possible. I guess she has her reasons, though. I don't plan to share this information with the pool girls, of course.

"That's rough," Rosa says, reshuffling the cards.

"Hard to believe he's…like, dead. He was so nice, ya know?" Crystal says.

"And hot," Jackie adds, flicking a cigarette butt into the air.

"Inappropriate!" Crystal snaps.

The butt lands in the pool, and one of the kids starts wailing and splashing water at it as if it will attack him.

"For Christ's sake, Kevin. Just toss it out…just… God, take a pill!" Crystal stomps over and fishes the butt out of the water, flicking it onto the wet concrete. "Happy!?" Kevin stops crying, and she returns to the table, picking up the hand Rosa's dealt her.

"Ya want us to deal ya in?" Jackie asks me as the toddler on her knee pushes a melted Junior Mint into her ear. She swipes at it with a napkin and sets the child on the ground. The constant chaos of misbehaving and screaming children seems only a minor annoyance to these women—something that just exists in the background that they're forced to address now and then in order to keep the children alive, but requiring no effort beyond that basic instinct of not letting them starve or drown.

"Nah, I gotta patch a hole in the drywall in 102."

"How the hell do you know how to fix drywall?" Rosa asks.

"It's just a small hole. Putty and some paint," I say.

"But still. It's weird," Crystal adds. "You're like a normal chick. Pretty, even. I guess. You know any other chicks who fix dishwasher pumps and patch drywall? You should get a man for that."

"Yeah," Jackie agrees. "You could be on *The Bachelor*. You look like one of them chicks."

"Like Ashley B," Crystal adds. "With the glossy hair."

"No. She looks like Ashley K, stupid. Ashley B isn't there for the right reasons. She don't look like Ashley B."

"Anyway," Crystal continues. "You won't get no man with those overalls and dirty nails. Jackie could give you a manicure."

"How you know how to fix pipes and stuff?" Rosa asks softly.

"I went to jobs with my dad. I was gonna go into business with him after school—handyman services," I say and then see their looks soften and their eyes flick back to their cards.

I had a few gin fizzes one night by the pool and shared with the pool girls that I didn't really have my parents anymore. It was just me and my dad growing up for most of my life. My mother died when I was still young, so when he lost the house and shifted between rehab and homeless shelters around my senior year of high school, I was on my own and the dream of a father/daughter company—Abbott Family Repair—died along with his sobriety. But he himself? Not actually dead... for the most part. Technically. I received pitying looks when I joked about how he didn't even know who I was the last time I went to visit—that he just sat, slumped in his armchair in urine-soaked pants, calling me Roxy and asking if I wanted a stack of pancakes.

They don't ask me questions about my family anymore. It's unrelatable for them, I suppose; their lives revolve around their kids. Family is all they have, Crystal always says—it's everything, so I seem extra pathetic to them with no kids of my own and no parents to speak of, I'm quite sure—like the loneliest person in the world.

The silence is awkward, so I just get up, unnoticed, and head to the front office for my supplies and wonder for the thousandth time today how I got here. Maybe that's my answer—that it's weird I can patch drywall. That's what Reid always said in a roundabout way. When I think about how and when my life started to spiral out of control, I make lists in my mind of things I did wrong.

I went to trade school instead of real college. I wanted to be a mechanic, since my dad was clearly in no shape to start a business with me. I thought, who ever heard of an all-girl auto shop? No one. I could hire only female mechanics, and we'd be the best, and every woman in the state would want to bring their car to us because they knew they could trust us and not get hit on or ripped off. I thought it was genius. I thought I'd get funded on *Shark Tank* even...but when I met Reid, I slowly started to give up on the idea. He thought it was weird. Oddly masculine and not practical.

Then I thought we could flip houses together since he was a real estate agent and I could fix anything. We'd make a fortune, get our own HGTV show even, 'cause how many couples have the wife be the contractor? But I wasn't a wife, was I? And I embarrassed him or emasculated him, like it was my fault he doesn't know how to use a circular saw. So, that's the first bullet point on the mental list of ways I fucked up my life. I let Reid decide I should pursue something more normal—something where I wouldn't be called a lesbian or would make him look bad. Court reporting, he tried to convince me, would be good. But I hated typing and gave up on it.

The bullet points on my mental list pile up. What an idiot I was for living with a man shortly after meeting him and acting like not getting married or having anything in my name was okay with me. I know deep down that how badly I wanted kids—a family—was the major bone of contention. It was fine he thought marriage was stupid, but he wanted kids, too, and after two failed pregnancies, things changed between us. I think we both gave up a little, but on happiness.

But really, my biggest fault was aging. Maybe if I'd stayed under thirty years old, I'd still have my old life. Pitiful. I'm not proud of having these thoughts, but I can't seem to control them when they ride in on waves of regret and resentment.

Another thing I know is that I can't goddamn stay in this dump. The compensation is mostly the crap apartment I get for free, plus a pittance for necessities. I need to find a part-time job I can take, then I can save a little and get away from this hellhole. I've tried over the months I've been here to find something. Trying to get a job at an auto shop is almost always the same general experience. They never actually call after I apply, so I show up there and ask to talk to the boss, who is always male, and who looks me up and down and *sometimes* suppresses his laughter, but more often can't help himself and smirks the whole time I'm explaining my skills.

Then, when he realizes I actually do know what I'm talking about and that I'm qualified, I'll see a sort of embarrassed flush bloom on his face, and then he'll get me on a technicality—that I never actually finished my certificate program—although I will guarantee you none of the coverall-clad men in the back of the shop giving me sideways glances from the underside of a Chevy sedan have any certificate or formal training of any kind themselves. I'm a chick. That's it.

I applied at Milly's B&B as a housekeeper and a couple bartending gigs that no one called me back about, either. So I feel like I have no choice, I have do it again. The thing I said I wouldn't do. I have to try to lure a guy in. Just this one more time…and maybe get five hundred bucks or so to get me through until I find something. I won't get greedy. Just enough to get by for now.

So after dark, I get a drink at the Lamplighter across the street. The place is exactly what you'd imagine a dive bar across the street from The Sycamores to be: dimly lit to cover all its filth, deep red carpet stained with decades of spilled beer and cigarette burns, the palpable smell of stale smoke and the bleach that tries to cover it up. The vinyl bar stools are held together by duct tape, and a pool table with purple felt and warped cues is in the corner where a few men argue over the legality of a bank shot.

"Don't Stop Believin'" blasts from the jukebox and a few couples in the corner booth sing along in the obligatory exaggerated way one must when the song plays. The busty blonde uses a spoon as a makeshift microphone, and the guys laugh insecurely at themselves.

I belly up to the bar and order a Hamm's beer. It's not everywhere you can get this shit on tap. My dad says it tastes like pears, and you know what? It sure does, so it's my favorite. I can tell I'm probably the only one who orders it because it's stale and flat, but that's okay. I'm not here for the drinks. It's just a prop.

"Some will win, some will lose. Some are born to sing the blues…" the man next to me sings, leaning in too close.

"Christ, ya want an Altoid or somethin'?" I ask him, but he just leans to the couple on the other side of him, unperturbed, and continues his song, eyes closed, fist clenched. I see another guy squeeze in beside me to order a drink. I notice the pale circle of skin around his ring finger. Bingo. Perfect target. I could start with the drunk guys because it'd be faster, but a married guy who doesn't want you to know he's married is exactly what I'm looking for, so I'll be patient.

He nods a hello at me—since we're squeezed in so close it would be more awkward not to—and then looks at the drunk guy belting out the Journey lyrics. We raise our eyebrows at one another.

"Song's overrated," he says.

"Oh, yeah?"

"Yeah, 'Open Arms' is a better song. It was their number one chart hit, too," he says, and I already hate him. I can't really explain why—maybe just the fact that he has any opinion on something so stupid at all. I suppress the urge to roll my eyes, so I blink a few times instead and bite the inside of my cheek.

"Good point, good point," I mutter.

He asks what I'm drinking and laughs when I tell him, and then he orders the same, and it begins. Some Steely Dan, some Eagles, and three or four Hamm's beers later, and he's asking if I wanna get out of here. This is when I start to nervous sweat. It could all go terribly, terribly wrong, but I do it anyway.

"I live just across the street," I say.

"No way." He stumbles ever so slightly as he gets up from his bar stool.

"Yep. You could come over for a nightcap if you want to," I say, and he smirks.

"Well," he says, clearly surprised at this offer and not expecting me to have gone anywhere with him. "Sounds great."

We walk out of the door and into the hot, still night air. He places his hand on my ass as we walk across the street, and I almost instinctively elbow him in the gut and then quickly remember that I can't do that, so I pretend not to notice. I break into a brief jog to clear the busy road. He follows, and when we get to my front door, he kisses me and pushes me up against the wall as if we're reenacting a scene from a romantic movie.

I want to gag from the sour taste of beer on his thick tongue and, God, the scratching from his goatee. It's like he's giving my face an exfoliation treatment. But I'm forced to giggle at this so I don't scare him off, and I shift out from under his arm and unlock my door.

"Hold your horses, cowboy." God, did I just say that?

When we get inside, he doesn't seem put off by the repulsive interior. He doesn't seem to notice what a dump it is at all. He's here for one thing, of course.

"That nightcap," I say. "Make yourself at home, I'll grab the drinks. Maybe find some music or something."

He flops down on the green sofa and turns on the TV. I hear the opening music to a *Law & Order* episode as I pull two beers out of the fridge, then short sound bites from commercials and sitcoms play as he scrolls through channels. My hands shake as I open the capsule of Rohypnol into his beer and swirl the bottle a few times to mix it in.

It wasn't hard to get the roofies. The guy that hangs around outside Misty's Cabaret on Ninth practically advertises he's selling, so I asked him and he delivered for five bucks a pill, if you can believe it. So I'll do this as quickly and practically as possible. He'll pass out, I'll take off his shirt, take off mine, but keep the bra on because I'm not a pervert, and take a handful of photos that make it look, undeniably, that we are in bed together. Then dress and wait.

And this is exactly what I do, but he doesn't wake up. The last guy was only out a few hours, but this guy had more to drink, maybe. He's not dead; I checked his pulse. I kicked him a couple times—not hard, just to see—and he twitched. He's fine, he just won't get the hell up and out of my apartment. I can't have people see him leave in broad daylight.

I make a cup of peppermint tea and change into sweats, then I watch the last half of *The Fugitive* on TV and desperately want to go to sleep, but I wait some more until about 4:30 in the morning when the guy wakes, horrified. He swallows and looks around. He grabs for his T-shirt on the floor next to him and pulls it on, then weakly gets to his feet.

Showtime.

"Oh, hey, I...I'm sorry. I guess we... I must have... I must have passed out. I didn't realize I had that much to drink." He looks at his phone, and his eyes widen. "Shit, I gotta go. I'm sorry. It was—"

"Your wife's been calling. Jenna? I assume it's your wife anyway. Yeah, you should probably go."

"Sorry?" he says, stuffing his phone in his pocket and moving toward the door. "How do you...?"

"Here's the thing. I don't enjoy doing this, but I need five hundred bucks. I'm going through a rough patch."

"Uh...are you asking... I don't even know you," he stutters.

"Right, but I know you would be upset if this got back to Jenna." I turn the phone and swipe the handful of photos I took of us. I know he doesn't remember if we had sex or not. The panic in his eyes is really not something I like to see, even though he deserves it.

"You're blackmailing me?"

"Yeah. Sorry."

"Are you fucking kidding me? What's wrong with you?"

"What's wrong with *you*? Jenna's photo pops up when she calls. She's nice-looking. Probably a catch. She's worried about you. You probably have kids worried about you, too, so who's the psycho in this situation, really?"

He stares silently for a moment, taking it in. "Still you," he says, and he pats around his pants and pulls out a small gun.

I can't believe I didn't think to look for that. I'm not cut out for this sort of thing. My heart leaps to my throat, but I try to act calmer than I feel.

"You're gonna delete that, and… I don't want to have to do anything here, so just…just delete it, and I was never here. Seriously. Do it."

I can see his hands shaking. "Dude, you might be a cheating asshole, but you're not gonna turn into a murderer over five hundred bucks. Don't you think that would be a little nuts?" I ask, and his face flushes red.

"This whole thing is nuts! What the fuck? I…"

But I know he knows he's screwed. "Listen, just go get five hundred bucks, bring it back, and you can watch me delete the photos. I'll show you I didn't back it up or send it out. You can look through my whole phone. I'd have no reason to. I don't even know you. I just need the money. Like I said, I'm not proud of this, but you shouldn't be proud of what you did, either. I feel sorry for poor Jenna. Jeez." And with this I can tell he wants to lunge at me or pull the trigger or anything to lash out, but what can he do? Ruin his life over a relatively small amount of money? Lose his wife, go to jail? No way.

He does what I ask. He storms out and slams the door, and I can't stop trembling from having a gun in my face. I sit down and take a couple of deep breaths to calm down the light floaty feeling in my head, and I worry that he won't come back.

But he does come back. Twenty minutes later, he gives me an ATM envelope with five hundred in twenties, and I let him watch me delete the photos. Before he leaves, he turns back one more time, looks me up and down, and spits in my hair. And calls me a cunt.

When I lean over the sink in the darkness of my apartment with the canned laughter from an *I Love Lucy* episode echoing in the background, white light from the black-and-white TV screen flickering across the walls, I let myself cry. I promise myself again a promise I know I won't keep—that I will never do this again. That I got lucky, but just barely.

5

ANNA

The heat in the apartment is suffocating. I spent the night cross-legged on the floor with a bottle of wine and an egg foo yong, just sifting through boxes of Henry's things. Between the piles of notebooks, art supplies, and miscellaneous crap he already had here, and all his things I brought from the house, including countless boxes from school that sat unopened since he was let go, it will take me an eternity to get through it all. But there must be clues in here—some sign—an indication of what the hell happened to him and why he'd do this. I don't know what that would even look like, but maybe I'd know it if I saw it.

But it's midmorning now, and last night's wine is pounding in my temples and sitting sour and acidic in my gut. My shirt is clinging to my skin, and I feel like I can't breathe in this room. I tinker with the air-conditioning unit in the window again. It just made a rattling noise and dripped yellow water onto the battered wood floors last night so I gave up on it, but now I have to call someone named Cassidy Abbott to fix it, I guess. It's on the lease paperwork to call the caretaker, but a chick handyman seems unusual, so maybe I have it wrong.

I dial the number, and it goes to voicemail. Of course it does. I leave a message and step out onto the balcony for air.

It's generous to call it a balcony, because, of course, it's really a shared walkway. Most units have a camping chair or lawn chair next to their door. The person next door to my unit has a Radio Flyer filled with half-dead plants and a coffee can overflowing with cigarette butts. There are a few pink tricycles with handlebar streamers and flowered baskets in front of 202, and across and down a floor an exceptionally hairy man sits in a folding chair, in checkered boxer shorts, reading the paper.

I fan myself with an old *People* magazine and watch the women playing cards by the pool. I wonder if it's one of them who left me that note. The one flicking ice chips from her drink at a ten-year-old in the pool, telling her to stop splashing her brother, or the quiet one wearing bedroom slippers, sucking on a blue Popsicle stick. But why would they? Maybe hairy guy? Maybe…ugh. I mean, it must be one of these people.

I watch as an impossibly thin woman with ghostly blond hair and strangely short bangs steps out next to him and lights a cigarette. She's practically swimming in a pair of pink shorts and a tank top. She's giving him a hard time about leaving his dishes all over the place. She tries snatching his paper to get his attention, but he pulls it away before she can, so she smacks at the paper and calls him an idiot, then disappears back inside.

I'm startled by a voice behind me.

"You Anna Hartley?"

I turn to see a woman in denim overalls and long, wavy dark hair piled in a heap on top of her head. She's striking, even sweaty with no makeup, and I don't put together right away that she's the handyman or caretaker or whatever they called it in the lease.

"Uh, yeah. Why?"

"You called me."

"Oh, you're Cassidy…"

"Cass," she corrects, in a swift, practiced way.

I nod and open the door to the apartment. I begin giving her the rundown on the noise the air conditioner is making and how I really need it to work, and she stops me quickly.

"Yeah, that's not my jurisdiction," she says.

"I'm sorry?"

"The air conditioner isn't part of the building. A tenant bought it and stuck it in the window. If it don't belong to the building, I don't fix it. You're on your own." She starts to go.

"Wait. Henry wouldn't have bought this."

"Okay?"

"So it's not my problem. It's part of the rental."

"You the wife?" she asks, her eyes softening slightly as she stands backlit by the sun in the doorframe, practically blinding me. I shield my eyes with my hand.

"Yeah."

"I'm sorry about what happened," she says, picking up her tool bag from the ground. I want to ask her about him, but I don't know where to start yet. It's not the time.

"Look, Home Depot is totally out of ACs with this heat-wave. Amazon will take a week. I'm fucking dying in here, okay. You can't just look at it?"

"It's a liability thing. Sorry."

"Wait," I say to her back before she makes it to the stairs. I follow after her and show her the note left under my door. The words *GET OUT* stare back at me as I hand it to her.

"Someone left this for me. Do you know who would do something like that? I mean, since, I guess you probably know everyone here?"

She looks at it and doesn't seem at all disturbed or surprised even. "Huh."

"What do you mean, huh?" I snap. "It's a threat."

"I mean, not really."

"I could call the police."

"Go for it," she says, and I find myself prickling with annoyance.

"Just… Are there any… Do you know why someone would leave this for me?"

"I mean, everyone here is a quack if you haven't figured that out yet. Yesterday I had to pull four Reese's Pieces out of a kid's nose with pliers in 107, and last week I had to drain the whole pool 'cause someone took a shit in it. Could be anyone. Probably a kid—a prank."

"Yeah," I agree, a bit defeated.

"Ask the 'pool girls,' they see everything," she says, nodding toward the women who are permanent fixtures at the table by the pool. "And bat your eyes at one of the guys around the place. You'll get your AC fixed," she says as she descends the concrete stairs.

I sleep most of the day away in front of a box fan with a melted ice pack on my chest on a bare mattress. The days and nights run together, and I have no working body clock anymore. Maybe I'm still in shock. Everybody mourns differently, they say. It would be easy to let myself sob into his pillow and try to capture that last remaining scent of him, but instead I stripped the bed and washed everything because allowing myself to fall into the darkness threatening to pull me under is something I know I'd never return from. So I try to be just strong enough not to follow in Henry's footsteps, although somedays I imagine myself going to sleep on the train tracks at Willow's Crossing, only a few blocks away behind the liquor store, and then it would all be done. But finding answers is what keeps me here, in this utter shit pile of an apartment building.

The horizon begins to look like a watercolor with blazing orange streaks and purple clouds, and the air is cooling ever so slightly outside, so I pull a High Life out of the mini fridge and sit in the terribly uncomfortable metal chair that's propped outside the front door. I never knew Henry to drink High Life, and I can't imagine him acquiring a chair like this, but I guess there's a lot I don't know about him, isn't there?

The loudest of the pool girls is swimming with an infant in her arms, cooing at him and swooshing his little legs through the water, side to side. He smiles and flexes his fingers in delight.

I see face-tattoo guy from 119 watching the woman, her giant breasts floating above the water's surface. I almost call him a perv, but I don't. The old me would have, but this version of myself can't quite muster up the emotional energy to care.

Then I see Callum in the small adjacent parking lot next to the building; he steps out of a beat-up Volkswagen and beeps the door locked. When he crosses the concrete patio surrounding the pool to get to his door, he looks so incredibly out of place here in his shirt and tie, pants that are a little too baggy and a messenger bag strapped across his chest that takes me aback a little. He must have come from work. Henry's school, I think, and I take a deep breath and push the thought of our life before it all crumbled to bits out of my mind. Maybe Callum is the place to start. He knew Henry. I have to start somewhere.

I wait a couple of hours until dusk fully sets in. Everyone is inside their units, and the pool is glossy and actually looks almost pretty in the dark with its blue light and calm surface. Smells of curry and onions and hamburger grease spill out of open apartment windows. No wonder the pool girls are always outside; it seems other folks don't have AC, either, and their lives and conversations are on display for anyone walking past. A soundtrack of crickets chirping, meat sizzling, the clanging of forks scraping across dinner plates, a baby crying, and a couple arguing plays all around me.

Before the sun fully sets, I make a decision. I'll try to talk to Callum. It's a place to start. My hands shake as I pull out two more High Lifes from the fridge and walk down the concrete slab to 114 and knock.

His face is a mix of confusion and surprise when he sees me standing there.

"Uhhh. Anna, right?" he asks, trying to rearrange his expression into something pleasant. I'm surprised he remembers my name.

"Yeah, yes. I'm…sorry to just show up. Am I interrupting you?"

"I, um… I guess not," he says, but I get the distinct feeling that he doesn't want me here, just showing up unannounced while he's trying to relax. "What can I do for you?"

"I just…I wanted to ask a little bit about Henry, if you have time. Or I mean not even right now if you're busy, but I just… I know you worked with him and knew him, so I just…had a few questions."

"I mean, I don't know what I can offer, really. We weren't very close or anything, but yeah. Of course. You can come in if you want," he says.

I nod and hand him the two beers in my hand.

"Oh, okay. Thanks," he says, and he must think I'm an idiot. High Life for God's sake. Why am I even bringing alcohol to a strange man's apartment? What must this guy think?

Inside, Hamburger Helper sits half-eaten in a skillet on the stove and the place smells like…childhood. Ground beef and onions mixed with dewy summer air coming through the window screen. The TV plays a ball game and bathes the room in a flickery blue. He turns the volume down and apologizes for the mess.

It's not actually that messy. I can still see the feminine touches his wife must have added to the place. Throw pillows on the sofa, an accent wall, and wispy curtains. The rest is covered with man stuff—an Xbox console, a mountain bike leaning against the wall, a beanbag chair, and empty Pepsi and beer cans cluttering the coffee table.

I sit on the edge of an armchair—definitely the wife's choice—

and he picks up a few cans and throws them away as if they were an annoyance, left there by someone else, before he sits across from me on the sofa and hands me one of the High Lifes he's opened. He's wearing cargo shorts and a tight T-shirt, and I find myself noticing the way the sleeves hug his biceps, and how big his six-foot-three-inch frame looks in the tiny apartment. Sad and out of place—a giant in a cage sort of vibe. He has a short tapered haircut and sad, dark eyes that avoid mine when he speaks. I don't quite know what to make of him besides that he's clearly a broken man, so maybe he does fit in here better than I thought.

"I'm so sorry about Henry," he says, picking at the label on his beer. Then he makes eye contact. "He was an amazing guy. The kids loved him."

"Thanks," I say, forcing myself to hold back tears at the sound of his name. "I guess I...I just wanted to ask about when he got laid off from the school. I feel like... I don't know... He told me it was budget cuts, but that's when I feel like things sort of changed with him, and so I always wondered if he was being... I don't know, being honest with me about that. If there was anything else going on...happening, that was...off?"

Callum takes a deep breath and blows it out through pursed lips. "I mean, besides the silly rumors about Mira, you mean? I don't know, not that I noticed. But I don't think that had to do with his getting let go. The arts are always getting cut. A music teacher was laid off last week, too, so I mean, I don't really know."

"Rumors?" I stop midsip and look at him.

"Yeah, the... Oh, God," Callum says, his face reddening. "He said he mentioned it to you, or I wouldn't have..."

"What rumors? What are you talking about?"

"The whole thing with... I mean...teenagers are, you know, sort of terrible by definition..."

"Says the high school teacher," I interrupt.

"Well, that is why I'm uniquely qualified to say that. They

sometimes can be *slightly* dramatic, and their mushy brains are not fully developed quite yet, so all the significance of consequences for their actions—not always thought through. There was just a rumor about a *senior*, Mira Medford. People whispered about it a bit—that there was something between her and Henry."

"What?" I say, feeling a fist of pain pushing on my chest. Could this be the reason for his complete change of personality?

"Anna, I'm sorry. Let me back up. I'm not close with Henry, right? We've had drinks a few times, talked in the teacher's lounge. All the residents here were really pretty amazing at taking turns helping to take care of Lily, so I saw him in passing a few times when it was his turn to bring her a casserole by or something, but I know enough to know he's not that guy. We have mice in the science lab, and one went missing, and all the freshman girls decided it was because I stay late and put mice up my butt for sexual pleasure. There are still drawings on the whiteboard when I come in some days of 'sexy mice' with boobs. I'm telling you, since I can't take back ever putting that information about the rumor stuff into your brain, that's how high school is."

"Okay, point taken, but what exactly was said about him?"

"It's not so much what was said—something about them having sex in the locker room after hours—it was that she transferred schools the next term, and he was laid off. It was the timing, not so much the dime-a-dozen rumor," he says, and a high-pitched ringing fills my ears.

I swallow hard. The soft mumble of a baseball commentator emanates from the TV. A yippy dog's bark can be heard from another unit, and everything feels dull and surreal suddenly.

"I mean, if you're asking what was different or changed, I'm just saying that's the only thing I heard, but I don't think it's anything to… It's likely nothing."

"Lily, that's your wife?" I ask, because although I met her, the name's not ringing a bell.

He gives a curt nod, and his face falls as he looks to the floor. "Yes."

"So the residents organized ways to help take care her, do you feel like he was pretty close to a lot of the people here? I just... I guess that's hard to picture, so..."

"Yeah, he seemed like...a very popular guy around here," he speaks pensively and softly. "I mean, maybe he was just try-ing to stay distracted. I know the layoff hit him hard, but once he was around The Sycamores full-time during the day, I'd see him hanging out with everyone. He gave painting lessons to the pool ladies, manned the grill for the Friday night bar-becues, threw the ball with the kids. He was that kind of guy. Well, you already know that."

"I never knew any of that," I mumble, astounded that he lit-erally had another life here he never told me about.

"We had a health aide for a while," he continues, "but we couldn't really afford her, and Lily swore her jewelry was going missing, so when everyone started to chip in to take care of her, it was really something. Rosa brought tamales, David brought a kitten, which wasn't actually helpful at all, but it's the thought, I guess. Jackie painted her nails. Henry did that—started a rota-tion, I guess you could say, of the residents visiting, helping. It was really something," he says, and his eyes gloss over as if re-membering it might make him break down this very moment.

I nod as if this all makes sense to me, although none of it does. Henry's character—the natural teacher and caretaker in him, the kindness—that part does, just not this apparent mul-tifaceted existence he kept hidden from me.

After a few moments of silence, Callum places his beer on the coffee table, his shoulders drooping as if the weight of speak-ing about his late wife has exhausted him.

I feel like I should go, and I don't really know what else to ask him because I'm still absorbing what he has said. "Well," I say, standing and moving toward the door.

I don't have an end to the sentence, and the silence hangs in the air until he echoes, "Well," and follows me to the door.

"Thank you, for talking to me, I..."

"Yeah, anytime."

"Can I give you my number, in case... I don't know, you think of anything else that might help?"

"'Course." He scribbles it on the back of a Chinese take-out menu, and I leave.

Outside, the crickets chatter in the heavy air, and I walk across the pool concrete toward my unit, thinking of Henry and how little I really knew him in the last months. I'm not the kind of person who blames myself about things outside of my control, but I do wonder if my obsession with wanting more than our life together was what changed us and sent him over the edge.

A conversation we had a few months ago comes in a flash of memory. It was a Saturday morning, and I went out for strawberry scones from Dicky's. I picked up the mail on the way in and found him sitting on the floor in a beam of sunshine streaming through the window. He was playing with Sticky, the neighbor's cat who found its way through our sliding glass doors every other day because he wouldn't stop feeding it frozen fish sticks. He had a cup of coffee in hand and seemed happy.

But when I opened another rejection letter from a journal I submitted a story to, I soured the morning like I always seemed to do—obsessed with proving myself, with getting published— making something of myself above all else, even though he was happy just to be together and be a middle-class artist, getting by. He was doing what he loved every day, and we did okay, so what was there to complain about?

My chest tightens when I think about his contentment—his happiness that I had a knack for spoiling.

"I'm fucking done," I yelled when I opened the envelope.

"Oh, honey, I'm sorry."

"I'm a complete loser."

"Don't say that." He sat next to me on the couch.

"You want me to show you the box?"

"Not the box," he said, but, of course, I pulled a shoebox from the bookshelf anyway and tossed the rejection letter on top of the growing pile.

"Why do you even keep those?" he asked, but I ignored him and pulled one out theatrically.

"Dear Ms. Hartley, you're the worst. Please never send us anything again." I threw the paper over my shoulder and took another out.

"It doesn't say that."

"Dear Ms. Hartley, suck a bag of dicks."

"Okay, come on," he said, exasperated.

"I even tried poetry again, Hen. You know? I mean…"

"I do know," he said patiently, accustomed to my rants.

"And did I even get into the *Midwest Review*? No. Let's see who did!" I pull out the journal and open it. "Olivia Hackerman, age six." I clear my throat for dramatic effect before reading her poem:

"'We went to the pond. There were fish in the water. Why are fish ugly?' A literary masterpiece."

"It's a haiku," he says.

"I know that."

"And it was cute they chose a kid for the slot, Anna, come on that's—"

"It is cute. It's adorable! But… I just… I quit. Like for real this time. Maybe it's time to accept that and just. Go."

"Go where?"

"Ibiza. Get jobs on the beach, whatever. Something different and far away because fuck this. No one wants me, and I reek of failure. Smell me." I offer the sleeve of my dress, and he pulls me down to sit beside him.

"Hey, no, you don't," he said. The hurt in his eyes is something he couldn't hide. He thought I was disappointed in him—our life together, like it wasn't enough. And it wasn't that, not really. Now I ache with the memory.

I'm jolted out of my thoughts and stop cold as I approach my apartment door, and I see a small package. Who would have sent a package? I haven't even had time to change my forwarding address yet. Was this there earlier when I was distracted on my way to Callum's and I just missed it? Or was someone looking for me while I was gone? It's unsettling either way.

When I kneel down to pick it up, I see my name written across the brown paper it's wrapped in. My heart speeds up. I hesitate to open it. I look around, down the long stretch of balcony on either side of my door, I peer down over the railing, but the poolside is empty. Then I look at the box in my hands again and decide to open it. I slowly pull the string that's tied into a bow at the top and peel back the paper.

When I pluck open the cardboard top, I scream when I see the box is overflowing with wriggling white maggots. Some fall out onto my wrist as I gag and try to seal it back up as quickly as I can. I throw up in my mouth and swallow it down as I run the length of the concrete walkway around the side and toss the box into the thicket of locust trees behind the building.

Tears prick my eyes as I hold my hand to my heart and catch my breath. Someone wants to get rid of me. It's not a prank. It's a threat. I walk back over to my unit and stare down at the property, the pool, the warm light behind each apartment window. Something is very wrong here.

6

CASS

I snake a wet clump of black hair and gray slime the size of a golf ball out of the bathtub drain in 107. I toss it onto the tile floor with a smack and try not to gag.

"It's fixed," I holler out to Crystal who is on the sofa with a Twinkie, caressing her very pregnant belly and watching an episode of *Maury* on the TV. She tries to make her six- and seven-year-old girls rub her feet, but they run around the room, squealing in mock disgust. Then when the TV studio audience roars and cheers on the Maury show, I hear Amber or Tiffany, I can't tell which kid it is from here, ask what a paternity test means, and Crystal tells them to shush up, go out and play.

"Those lions are gay," I hear an unfamiliar voice say from the doorframe. I look up to see a kid about ten years old who I don't recognize.

"Pardon?" I say, and he nods to one of a half dozen picture books on a rack near the toilet. The one on top is called *Noah and the Flood*.

"The lions marching into the ark. They both have manes, which means they're both male. That's inaccurate, or else we wouldn't still have lions today," he says.

"Uh, yeah. I guess you have a point," I respond, and then the littlest kid, Kevin, runs into the bathroom where I stand once again hovered over the drain, giving it a final snake, and he picks up the wet hair clump before I can stop him and runs at his sisters with it. By the time I'm in the living room, they are already screaming and flailing out the door and chasing each other around the pool deck, and the strange Biblical expert child has run outside with them.

"I owe ya one," Crystal says, then screams after them, "Close the door, Tiffany, goddammit!"

I go and close the door and sit on a plaid recliner, wiping my hands with a soiled kitchen rag.

Crystal pushes a bag of White Castle burgers across the coffee table. "Want a slider? There's chicken-ring ones in there."

"I'm good," I say as she lights a cigarette and laughs at an audience member on the show who stands at the mic, hand on hip, saying something about someone's "baby mama" and something about a "broke-ass bitch."

"Who's the kid?" I ask.

"Oh, that's Frank. Mary's grandson. He's visiting for a while. But between us, I think his mom took off with some meth head and moved to Tampa, so he might be around awhile."

And then the kids explode back into the apartment; the oldest girl is sobbing. She has the clump of hair stuck to her neck where Kevin apparently threw it.

"Now that *is it*," Crystal says, trying to maneuver her way to her feet. The other girl starts crying for no apparent reason. "That's what you get for giving Jasmine a haircut in the tub, I told ya!"

When she finally does get to her feet, Kevin starts to run, but she grabs him by the arm and swats him on the butt. "And if you can't behave yourself…" she begins, but Kevin is just laughing at her. He wriggles away, running to his room before she can say anything else. She gives up easily and crashes her weight back down into the sofa with a sigh.

I wonder for a minute who Jasmine is and why a six-year-old would be giving someone a haircut, and then I see the poor bald *Aladdin* doll on the coffee table—the Disney princess is surrounded by LEGO and sports specks of orange Cheeto dust in her buzz cut.

Crystal is wiping Amber's neck like she's expertly wiped a thousand hair clumps off a child before this one and consoles her with a SpongeBob Pez dispenser. The girl sits and shakes out colorful candies into her sticky little hands; her nails are pink and chipped, and she looks up at me with pouty lips as though I'm to blame for all of this because I unleashed the hair clump.

I ache for Reid and our home and the babies we planned to have and the life that was stolen from me, and it's all I can do in this moment not to burst out crying, and I'm not sure why. It's no worse than any other wretched moment on any other demoralizing day in this pit.

So I pick up my tools and leave, unnoticed. The girls and their mother have already moved on from the situation and are talking about fairy glitter lip gloss colors. Video game noises rumble from somewhere back in Kevin's room as I exit.

I sit in the front office and swirl around in the desk chair, fanning myself with an old *Better Homes & Gardens*, thinking about what to say at my job interview this afternoon. The Egg Platter left a message and said I could come in and talk to the assistant manager about some night shifts, and even though the tips are better for cocktails than for huevos rancheros and corned beef hash, I'm gonna take it if they offer.

I watched a late-night show once where some guest talked about meditation and how it can change your whole life because it's all about your mindset, and I tried it. I really gave it a shot one night. I sat on the beanbag someone left in a storage unit in the basement, and I put on some music I found on

YouTube with flutes and chimes and shit, and I tried to think about nothing.

But they don't tell you that it's impossible to think about nothing at all. Like, unless you're dead, your brain has thoughts, and so when you try to make it all still and quiet, that's when the real dark thoughts poke through. It reminded me of a church we went to when I was little.

We had a sleepover one night, and they called it a lock-in, which sounded kind of scary to me, but we laid our sleeping bags out on the church floor and had pizza and fruit punch that they called "refreshments," which I thought was fancy-sounding, and we got to watch *The Sandlot* projected onto a wall from an old-timey projector, and then we whispered to each other after lights-out until we fell asleep. And in the middle of the night, it was inky black in the big room except way, way up high where there were rows of tiny windows that looked like flashlights in the darkness. They pierced the room in creepy beams of moonlight, and I remember being really scared and peeing in my new Rugrats pajamas... That's exactly what meditating is like.

It's the laser beams of sharp, horrifying thoughts slicing through the stillness in your mind and taking you to all of the places you're not supposed to be thinking about.

It usually starts at the beginning, for me, with a mental list of things I did wrong. I never got the associate's degree I started 'cause Reid talked me out of the "masculine trade" even though I loved it. But it's not really his fault, is it? It's mine for being a dumb sheep. I had choices. And then, of course, I think about all of my choices and how most of them were bad, and then I think about how I worked at a Pick 'n Save. Why? Because I didn't get the damn associate's degree. And then what did I do? Stupid idiot me, I moved in with a guy who never wanted to get married, and I ignored all the red flags. No matter how unsupportive or distant or hot and cold he acted, he was Reid

Chapman. He was the real estate god with his photo on the side of a bus—with the floppy hair and poppy biceps who all the single chicks from far and wide seemed to giggle over and gawk at no matter where we went.

Out of all the girls in fur boots and titty shirts and expensive highlights who sipped green apple martinis at the bars we went to and wrote their numbers on cocktail napkins, he chose me. Sure, it sounds pathetic when you say it out loud, but I felt really special when it was happening.

It started with a few after-bar, drunk kinda deals, but then, somehow, we made each other laugh a lot. I never thought I was funny, but he thought I was and said nice things about me. Then drunk nights turned into weeks and actual daytime dates, not just 2:00 a.m. stuff...and we morphed into a couple.

And then he bought one of the houses he was showing because he just couldn't pass it up—it was a mid-century with potential, and a good investment. When he wanted me to move in, I felt like I was in a fairy tale. It's different than keeping a toothbrush at his place and sleeping in the bed he had sex with a buncha other girls in over the years—this was our new start. I thought we were really something together. I even went to special trouble to never tell him when I had to fix his bad drywall work or retile something behind his back after he left for work. It was a labor of love. If I'm honest, I rebuilt half the damn house from the ground up practically, in my almost five years there. I thought I was literally building our life together.

So maybe Kimmy is the young waitress he's been banging in the walk-in cooler for at least a year at the Bulldog where she works, but she can't be the first. I was one of those women I hate. I just didn't want to see it.

I pick up my phone from the desk and start to scroll to Kimmy's Instagram to cyberstalk her one more time today. I have a fake name on Insta—Brandy Alexander. My theory was that she's too stupid to know it's the name of a cocktail, and she's too desperate for attention to deny a follower, so I get to see all the intimate details Cass Abbot cannot. I remember the other waitress at the Bulldog who stood there in awe—Jessie was her name—the day I showed up and screamed at Kimmy, who was beet red, holding a giant tray of steak dinners next to a family seated in a corner booth. I flush with shame at the memory of this—how unhinged I was when I found out about the betrayal, but that doesn't stop me from commenting on Kimmy's photo right now. Her Insta post says golfing with my baby, and she's holding a golf club laughably wrong in her white shorts and sports bra outfit. *You don't like golf, you stupid bitch, you're just clinging to Reid on his day off. But guess what? If he can do it to me, he can do it to you.*

He's fucking Jessie at the Bulldog, I type and send. It's childish and terrible, but I smile a satisfied smile, and then I see Callum at the block of mailboxes outside the office door. He pulls out a handful of junk ads from his box and tosses them in the bin. Before he can get away, I yell to him from the open window.

"Hey!"

He jumps a little.

"Sorry, hey, hold up a sec," I say and pop out the front door.

"Oh, hey, Cass. You scared me."

"Sorry, hey. Yeah. I was just wondering if you could do me a teensy favor?"

"Sure, what's up?" he asks, tugging his messenger bag back up on his shoulder.

"That new chick in 203, you met her? Anna?"

"Uh, yeah. I did."

"Oh, good. Well, I need someone to help her with her AC."

"Someone, meaning me?" he asks.

"It's a thousand degrees. I feel bad for her. You know the owners made a big deal when Leonard's microwave blew up and started the fire in 111, so I mean I wasn't here then, but still, there's a rule—no electrical and no more HVAC. I guess they think I'm gonna start snorting the Freon or something, but it's a liability thing."

"That's not true, I saw you rewiring someone's outlet a couple days ago," he says.

Damn. I thought that would work. "Right, right," I say, chewing my lip and giving up on finding another excuse. "It creeps me out, okay. Being in there. His widow. It's all…"

"You want me to do it," he interrupts.

"You teach science, right? You can probably sort it out."

"Look, I would, but the last thing I would think she needs right now is some guy showing up with a tool belt to— No, that's creepy. Just call the owner."

"I did. You know how they are. It'll take forever. You own a tool belt?" I ask, trying not to smirk.

"No, that was just… I mean…"

"I'll take a hundred bucks off your rent if you fix it."

He pauses and considers. "Do you have the authority to do that?" he asks.

"I mean, if you fell from the balcony 'cause the railing was loose or got your balls stuck in the pool suction valve—you know, something you'd sue for—then I would, yeah. So I can bend the truth a bit here."

"Wait, if I fell from a balcony, and it was the apartment management's fault, I'd only be offered a hundred bucks in credit?" he asks.

"Christ, Callum. I don't know. It's all I got, give me a break here. Just forget it."

"No, sorry," he says before I'm all the way back through the office door. "I'm happy to help, of course. Sorry."

"Thank you," I say and slam the door, then I grab my keys and exit the back to my car so I can get to the Egg Platter by 4:30.

I wait in a red vinyl booth and watch a line cook press the life out of a sad grayish burger patty with a spatula. A middle-aged waitress with saggy eyes places a runny plate of eggs in front of a man so lonely-looking it could take your breath away. He wears a baggy suit, and his hair is greasy, and it makes my stomach hurt to look at him. The pimply teenaged cash register kid sticks his face under the soft-serve machine and squeezes vanilla-chocolate swirl into his mouth until the waitress flicks him in the back of the head. Then, two teen girls appear and sit on the opposite side of the booth from me.

I'm startled for a moment until I see their respective name tags: Ashley and Ashleigh. They introduce themselves as the assistant manager and the second shift supervisor.

Ashleigh—with the *eigh*—looks my résumé up and down and then asks, "What makes you want to join the Egg Platter family?"

Oh, god. I have to make my face remain in an appropriate expression while I try to impress two children for a job I don't want. Here goes.

"Um," I begin, then I see a sign behind the counter that says "Free range chickens. Organic."

"Your high standards. Organic chickens. That's…important," I say, nodding too many times.

"That's good. Good answer," Ashley with an *ey* says.

"Yeah," the other agrees. "Do you know Bob's Pancake House and Cozy Waffle get their eggs from Gleeson's where they debeak their chickens?"

"Pardon?" I say, not sure if I'm supposed to have a response to this.

"Oh, my gosh, they do, they crack off the end of the chicken's beaks so they can't fight, but the only reason they fight is cause they stack 'em up like Velveeta slices in these little cages. Oh. It was on a TikTok clip from an *Oprah* show I saw. Oprah cried. The cameraman had to come up and bring her a Kleenex. Her mascara ran a little. Sad."

"So sad," the other Ashley echoes. Then she makes a pouty face and a heart shape with her hands.

They ask me where I see myself in five years and if I have customer service experience and a bunch of other mindless questions they read from an interview form the owner supplied, and by the end of it, I'm so utterly demoralized that two high school girls have my fate in their hands that I think I'll start screaming. I feel like I could actually just leap on the table and screech out a primal howl and start throwing breakfast burritos at everyone's face at the utter injustice of the position I'm in, but then, Ashleigh with an *eigh* asks me if I can start next weekend—the graveyard shift—to see how I handle the 3:00 a.m. drunks.

"Really?" I say, my eyes welling and my expression softening and my hatred for myself growing with every moment I sit here in gratitude for a barfly shift at the goddamn Egg Platter. I actually think she expected me to refuse the Saturday graveyard offer, but I can't, can I? "Yes, that works," I say, standing up and trying to rush the ending of this meeting before anything changes or they change their mind.

When I leave, I feel lighter. The sun is beginning to set, and the air is dewy. The smell of the deep fat fryer wafting from the back of the building reminds me of the county fair as a kid, and I smile. I actually smile. It feels like the very humble start of something.

I drive around a while and feel like I want to call someone to tell them the good news, and I'm struck hard, maybe for the first time really, that I have no one to call. I mean, the shift from having girls' brunch and cocktail parties and real estate dinners and organizing charity events to living at The Sycamores and being broke happened so fast I couldn't process it all, and nobody calls me. My book club and Sunday brunch friends don't answer my posts or messages, not really. A few curt, noncommittal responses when I've asked to get together. I guess our friends were really his friends. Whoever he's with is the new Sunday brunch "wife," and I've vanished.

There were a few neighbors and yoga girls who were small-talk friends, but when your life crumbles, you really see it all for what it is, and there is no one to call.

I don't cry. Of course, I could never call them anyway to tell them such pathetic news. That I have the first thing of my own in years and it's a diner job. They'd laugh me right off the phone, wouldn't they?

I drive to Gunther's Pub because it's only a few blocks from the apartments and I can walk home if I need to. I usually wouldn't spend the money on drinks, but I have something to celebrate, finally. A small step in the right direction. So I play Van Halen on the jukebox, and I make out with some guy with cowboy boots on the tiny dance floor and drink too many whiskey sours and stay too late.

And then, when it's almost last call, I decide to stumble the few blocks home with my sandals in my hand so I don't roll an ankle. When I enter the iron gate to the pool area to cross to my unit, I hear something. The pool water is still, and the night is quiet, all the residents long asleep except for a sound—like a low rumbling voice, then a cry, it sounds like.

I drop my shoes and tiptoe quietly down the concrete walk, keeping close against the building, so I'm not seen. Then I hear crying.

"What the fuck is wrong with you!?" a male voice seethes.

I see Rosa now. Holy shit. She's standing around the corner from her apartment door and her husband, Eddie, has her by the hair. He's in her face. She doesn't respond to him. Then he picks up a brick and slams it with enormous force into the wall next to her head—inches from her face.

I gasp and cover my mouth with both hands, then quickly duck behind the corner of the building. I don't know what to do. Should I call the cops or will it be too late if I don't try to help her now?

The crash of the brick must have startled the chick in 203. Anna. Because I see lights come on, and her door crack open. Most people are used to chaos around here and wouldn't bat an eye at a loud noise, but she's new.

"You wanna end up like him!?" he yells, then he smacks her head into the wall with a crack, and she falls to the ground.

I lose my breath. The shock of it paralyzes me for a moment. Then he storms off, and I can hear his pickup start up in the parking lot. I run to Rosa on the ground, and she is quietly crying, holding her hand over the gash on the back of her head.

"Hey, hey, it's okay," I stutter, still shocked. "I'm gonna get some… I…have a first aid kit. We can…"

"No. I'm fine," she says, holding the wall behind her and unsteadily pushing herself to her feet.

"Rosa, you're not fine. I can wait with you till the cops come. We can get you…"

"No cops," she says, and then she squeezes my arm hard. "You don't know what you're getting yourself into, so please. Stay away." Then she holds the side of her purse up to her bleeding head, stopping the trail of small dots of blood pooling on the concrete, and walks away from me until she disappears behind her apartment door, and then the lights go dark.

I look up to Anna on the balcony, her hand cupping her mouth. She looks back at me, our eyes lock, and a helpless, vacant stare is exchanged, suspended in the heavy air for a few moments, and then she rushes back inside. Probably to pack her things and get the hell out of here as fast as she can, if she has any sense.

7

ANNA

Maggots. It's all I can see when I close my eyes. Wriggling, wet maggots. I have to shake out my hands and take deep breaths to get the image out of my mind—the feel of them falling onto my skin. My stomach lurches as I try to unsee it and focus on the road.

I drive around searching for a Starbucks in this godforsaken neighborhood and think about the threats, and then the woman from 103 being struck by her husband. Do I tell someone? Are any of these surreal events connected to Henry?

I was asked to stop back at the police station later today for some more questions. They still have Henry's laptop and don't have the phone records back yet, so I think maybe it's about that. Maybe they found something new. If I tell the police about any of this when I go in, is an unsigned note and a box of insects enough for them to give a shit about? No, because I can already hear them telling me there is nothing they can do about passive pranks with no suspect or actual threat—probably kids having some fun. They'll make a report and put it in a file cabinet, is what they'll do. But Rosa from 103—do I get involved?

When I finally reach a Starbucks six miles from The Sycamores, I realize I really need to stop and buy a Keurig because I can't do this every day. How do these people live so far away from good coffee? It's incredible. I order two iced mochas, so I can put one in the freezer for tomorrow until I can find a department store. I mean, where is the nearest Macy's even? It's like I've been dropped on another planet at The Sycamores. Why did Henry want his studio here is the real question. It's the question I keep coming back to the more time I spend at this place. If he really wanted space, he could have cleaned out the garage or drywalled the basement and made a studio. I just supported him having a studio—it was more affordable than converting the basement, he liked the way the light came in in the morning, he'd made some friends. I figured they were other artist friends. In my wildest dreams I wouldn't have imagined this. What the hell was he really doing here?

When I park in my spot outside the apartment, I get out and toss my empty mocha in the dumpster and take the other coffee and a bag of cheese Danish with me, and then I see Eddie's truck parked two spots down. I saw him washing and waxing it this morning. I don't think I've ever seen anyone actually wax a vehicle before that in real life. And I was keeping an eye out for Rosa—to see if she was okay. I saw her by the pool midmorning, thank god, spreading out a beach towel patterned with Elmo wearing a snorkel, and sitting her son down on it with a Ziploc of goldfish crackers. I felt a flood of relief at the sight of her even though I heard her say she was okay last night. That is not a woman who is okay in any way whatsoever.

I scan the parking lot to make sure nobody else is around. I glance to the pool to make sure nobody notices me, and then I dump the mocha in the bed of Eddie's waxed truck. It's immature—a stupid and minor act of retaliation in reaction to the massive weight of the terrible way he behaved, but it still felt good, and if I'm lucky, I'll be on the balcony watching the moment he comes out and discovers it. Psychopath.

I take out a bag of Whole Foods groceries from my trunk and begin to walk to the apartment like nothing happened, when I'm startled by a man appearing on the walkway in front of me out of thin air.

"Oh, let me help you with that," he says, taking my groceries from my arm before I have time to protest.

"Um, thank you, but... I don't..."

"You're in 203, right? I'm just a couple down from you in 206. It's no trouble. I'm going up," he says and begins walking, so I just follow since he doesn't leave me a choice.

"And you are?"

"Oh!" He stops and turns around, offering out a hand to shake. "Barry. You're Anna, and you live in Henry's old place, I hear." He doesn't wait for me to answer, he just turns and continues walking up to my unit, chatting away about how the heatwave is upsetting his tomato plants and how I'll just love it here when I get to know everyone and that they grill out by the pool most Friday nights—just dogs and burgers. Beer, of course, and that everyone brings something to share. When we arrive at my door, he's out of breath.

"Well, thanks for the help," I say, reaching to take my grocery bag, but he doesn't offer it up, which is a little creepster.

"I can help you in," he says, and I reach for my bag and take it.

"That's okay, but thanks." I open my door as he lingers.

"My pleasure, Anna from 203. I'm happy to help. Anytime. Whatever you need."

And with that I nod as politely as I can muster and slip inside, closing the door behind me. I barely put down my groceries when there is a knock at the door. What the hell does this guy want from me? What did Henry see in this place, seriously? I'm more creeped out with each passing day here. I try to think of a polite way to tell him to get lost, but when I open the door, I see Callum holding an AC window unit, precariously balancing it on a bent knee.

"Whoa." I swing the door open to let him in so he can set it down since he looks like he'll drop it.

His face is red and veiny from the strain. He sets it on the table, takes out a cloth, and wipes the sweat from his forehead. "Hey," he finally says.

"What are you doing, exactly?" I laugh.

He stands in front of the box fan, catching his breath. It's strange to have a man in here—in Henry's private space. "God, it's like the surface of the sun in here," he says.

"Yep," I agree.

"I heard you needed your AC fixed, but I don't know how to fix an AC, so I just popped this out of 115. Nobody's lived there for months, so...if it gets rented, we can figure it out then. For now..." He pats the top of the AC unit.

"Oh, my God, I could kiss you!" I say, and then immediately want to take it back as his face grows even redder, if that's possible. I quickly shift gears. "You're a lifesaver. Thank you," I say, and he smiles, adjusts his ball cap and gets to work unscrewing things from the old unit in the window.

I pour some powdered iced tea mix into a plastic pitcher while he pokes and pounds at the ancient behemoth of an AC, and when I return, he's yanked it from the window frame. He is struggling to carry it to the table when I see something odd.

On the windowsill is a key. I recognize the faded blue metal star attached to the key ring. It's old. He had it for years until I gave him the duck-wearing-a-scarf key chain a few years ago as a gag gift, but he loved it. This faded star ring has been sitting in a glass bowl by the front door for ages, and now it's here. Hidden out of sight. My heart speeds up, and I grab the key and turn it over in my hand. There is a small yellow tag attached that says "storage." It's in Henry's blocky handwriting.

Why would he have hidden this? Why was it shoved under the AC unit like that? I slip it in my pocket.

After Callum finishes installing the new AC, his shirt is soaked through with sweat, and I feel bad he's gone to so much effort for me—taken up his morning for me, but I'm grateful. He takes the cup of iced tea I offer him, and then he leans over and clicks the power on the new unit, and it rumbles to life. I clap, and he bows, and then we tap our cups together in celebratory cheers. He sits on a folding chair in front of it and takes in the cool air for a moment.

"Glorious," I say, and he smiles at me. He's a quiet guy, and I find I don't really know what to say to him, either. The brief silence is broken when an ice-cream truck can be heard pulling into the parking lot piping out the organ rendition of *London Bridge Is Falling Down*, making the song sound somehow creepier than it already is. I stand next to him, and we look down at the pool deck and watch the kids hold out begging hands to the pool moms and run barefoot out the iron gate into the lot.

"Diabetes truck," he says, and I almost spit my sip of iced tea on him.

"Pardon?" I ask.

"That's what my parents called it." He smiles. "I guess that was meant to be a deterrent."

"You're still bitter." I smile back.

He stands and puts his drink down. "I'll get this dud out of your way," he says and goes to the old broken AC unit to pick it up.

"Wait, that means you've never had a Choco Taco?"

"Negative."

"Well, I have to buy you one for all your hard work," I say, and he doesn't protest, just sort of smirks as he lifts the AC, and I open the door for him and follow him out.

We sit on a rotting picnic table on the edge of the property watching the ice-cream chaos unfold. A Chipwich and a

Dreamsicle have already hit the hot pavement and the sound of crying toddlers rivals the organ music coming from the truck. One of the moms fishes for more change and argues with the driver when she's a couple dimes short. An older boy in swim trunks is going around snapping people in the legs with his wet towel with one hand and eating the bubblegum eyes of a Pink Panther Popsicle with the other.

"What do ya think?" I ask Callum after he takes a bite.

"Hmm," he says, catching the dripping ice cream with a tiny napkin.

"Stale?" I ask, and he laughs.

"Little bit," he says.

"They're always stale. I forgot that part. Childhood nostalgia must have clouded my memory." I toss mine in a metal trash bin, and he follows suit.

"It was the thought that counts," he says, then stands. "I better get back."

"Hey," I say before he can go. "Is there, by any chance, a storage unit here somewhere?"

"Kind of. There's basement access over there." He nods to concrete stairs near the front office. "Some of the residents rent them to store extra stuff, but if you need storage, I wouldn't use them if I were you."

"Oh, why's that?"

"Well, they're damp and full of mice, or so I hear. I don't have one, but that's the word," he says, and I don't tell him I'm looking for Henry's unit—to see if the key really is to storage or just some strange decoy, because what the hell do I even know anymore about what he was hiding? I should ask Callum more. He might know, but ever since I got those threats, I don't want to give anything away to anybody until I know what's going on.

"Gotcha, thanks. And thanks again for your help, really."

"Sure thing," he says, and tips his ball cap with a shy smile before he walks away.

I decide to wait until dusk—after the residents are mostly inside their apartments—before going down to the basement. I don't want anyone asking questions or gossiping about me because from what I overhear from my perch on the balcony, everyone's dirty laundry is fair game around here—it's not just the pool ladies spreading it about.

There were seven or eight residents down there on deck chairs yesterday, drinking Colt 45s and talking about why Mary's grandson is staying with her. At the beginning of the conversation, it was because the mother took off with some guy, but by the middle, it was because she's doing life without parole in a maximum security prison for killing the father of the boy. By the end, it was settled on that she definitely stabbed him in the shower two dozen times, "Jodi Arias–style," but that he deserved it. It's incredible, really. I can't tell if it's a bit of fun or if the pool whispers could cause any real damage.

The more private I can keep my business, the better, I can already see that.

In the late afternoon, I drive to the police station to meet with Detective Harrison. I'm irritated that they won't divulge more over the phone when I talk to them. Did they find something new? Do they know he said he killed someone? They can't because of course he didn't. I'm the only one who heard that, I know, but still…my heart pounds as I get closer to the now-familiar building, and a sixth sense washes over me that something is different this time. Something is wrong.

I wait in a small room with a folding table and two plastic chairs that looks like an interrogation room I've seen on *Snapped* or a *20/20* episode. When Harrison finally comes in, I instinctively start to stand, but he gestures me to sit again, and he has a hard look about him—lips pursed into a thin line and a crease in his forehead. He sits opposite of me.

"Thanks for coming in, Ms. Hartley. Can I get you anything?" he asks, fiddling with his tie.

"Did something happen? Did you find anything on his computer—a note or something? Why am I here?" It felt routine when they said they had more questions, but I am starting to feel panicked now that I'm here.

"I just want to go over some of the basic information again with you...if that's okay?" His face is purposefully neutral, and he leans back in his chair and brushes the small stack of paper in his hand with the edge of his thumb.

"Again? I feel like I've told you everything I know a dozen times."

"I know. You have been very helpful, but I just want to ask again about that final phone call," he says, and I don't know if I can bear retelling it. It's bad enough the hollow echo of his voice uttering his final words haunts me every single day and keeps me up at night. Don't make me say it out loud again. My heart aches. I feel tears forming behind my eyes already. *I fucked up our whole lives*, he said, *and I'm so sorry, but I just can't— I can't do it anymore.* How many times do I need to tell them the same thing?

"You don't have to tell us about the conversation. You have been very consistent with your statement..." he says.

Consistent? Why would he use that word? Of course I have. It's what happened. I feel pricks of heat form under my shirt. What does he want from me?

"But at the end of the conversation," he continues, "when you say you heard the loud bang and the call dropped, can you tell me what that bang sounded like? Can you remember?"

"I've already told you this. Like maybe when he jumped, his phone smacked on a rock below or something—not a gun I think, just a...crack. I said this already."

"You have, and we appreciate it. It's just a bit more important now—the exact timing. In light of some new information—"

"What information?" I cut him off.

He puts the papers on the table with his hand placed on top. "I know this will come as a shock, Ms. Hartley, but the autopsy report came in, and... Well, it's become evident that this was not, in fact, self-inflicted." He pushes the report across the table, but I can't pick it up; I just stare at him, my mind spinning. I look down at the cover page of the report, and it blurs. My head is light, and a wave of nausea washes over me.

"That's... No, that's wrong, that's not possible. I was talking to him. He said that he can't do it anymore—and then, and then... wait. *You* said he jumped. And I mean, he must have because he was severely depressed, and he said he couldn't... I don't understand what you're saying." I stand and pluck my T-shirt away from my chest to try to cool down and not pass out.

"Of course that's what everything pointed to because of your report of the phone call and his documented history of depression."

"I don't understand."

"He wore a Fitbit," Detective Harrison says, seemingly searching me for something—some reaction—and I don't know what he could possibly be getting at.

"Yeah, I got it for him last year," I say, not sure if my words are even audible. My mind is clouded with memories of that day—he wanted to get into running and intermittent fasting for whatever godforsaken reason—because he read some article, I guess, so I got it for him just because. And of course, he lost interest in running and fasting two weeks later, but he still liked it because it tracked his sleep. He'd tell me how many times he woke up in the night, according to his Fitbit, nearly every morning. He was like a kid about how cool the information was. "What does that have to do with anything?" I ask.

"These gadgets track a lot of things...like heart rate, but they also tell us when a heart stops. And according to the watch, his time of death was hours after that phone call. The assumption was that the bang you heard was his phone hitting a rock, or…" He stops, and I know he doesn't want to say the sound could have been Henry hitting rock.

He continues, "If he jumped and his head hit the rock, he would have likely been rendered unconscious and then drowned in the water below." He sees the tears running down my face and pauses. "I'm sorry. I know this is hard. It's just that that was the initial assumption from the information we had," he says, waiting for me to put something together, I guess, but I'm not. He was found right below where his car was parked—right below where he jumped from the cliff. So what is Harrison saying?

"Neither of those things happened—the head injury or the drowning—not the way it initially looked. The Fitbit information was the first clue that something was off, but then the exam found that the wound on his head was not consistent with hitting the rock on a tumble down, and there was no water in his lungs."

"What does that mean? I don't know what that means," I say, but I think I do know, and I can feel my heart pounding against my rib cage, and my hands begin to tremble.

"It means he was placed in the water after he died. And it means the wound to the head was caused by something other than rock. He couldn't have caused that blunt force trauma to the back of his head himself," he says as gently as he can, I suppose, but the words still thunder in my ears and steal my breath.

"You're saying someone murdered him. That's what you're telling me."

"At this time, we are documenting it as foul play and opening a full investigation, yes."

"No. That's not… Who could have… It's just not possible," I'm mumbling, and my mind is reeling. Then the door opens, and another detective I've seen a few times before comes in. He greets me and then sets a small device in the center of the table.

"We have additional questions now that the circumstances have changed, so we'd like to record our conversation if that's okay with you. You do have the right to have a lawyer present, but this shouldn't take long—just some basic questions," he says.

Oh, my god. A lawyer.

The bile pushes up into my throat. I have to steady my breath and angrily brush away the tears that keep falling when I suddenly realize that this is, in fact, an interrogation room, and I'm a suspect.

8

CASS

A few days later, I sit in front of a box fan in the front office and peek out the blinds to watch the pool girls play Texas Hold'em at their plastic table. Rosa is with them, and she seems as if nothing at all happened last night. I wonder if they know. Crystal and Jackie told me to take the afternoon off and come celebrate my new job with a couple of High Lifes, and I said I would, but I'm not especially good at pretending nothing is wrong, and something is very wrong with Rosa's situation.

After almost an hour of indecision, the sweltering heat makes the decision for me, and I pull a T-shirt over my swimsuit and join the ladies at the poolside.

"Hey! Look who it is," Jackie says overenthusiastically, pumping her fist in the air. She's obviously been pouring some Seagram's into her Mountain Dew this afternoon. Rosa smiles at me and pulls out a chair for me to sit. Crystal pulls a High Life from the Igloo cooler by her side and hands it to me.

"Egg Platter, huh?" Rosa asks, as easy as can be. I guess if she wants to pretend everything is normal, that's what I do, too.

"Yeah, I guess so," I say and crack open my beer can.

Jackie lifts her plastic Dora the Explorer cup, chock-full of Capri Sun and vodka, and says, "Cheers."

"Yeah, thanks," I say, meeting her cup with a tap.

All the kids are out. Jackie's boys, Gordy and Earl Jr., doing cannonballs with Kevin and making the girls scream and squirt them with their Princess Jasmine squirt guns. The new kid sits on a deck chair reading a book. That's not something you see around here very often. When he sees me, he mindfully book-marks his page and comes over.

"Hello. My grandmother tells me your name is Cass, and I thought she said ass, but then she corrected me, but I guess that *would* be your name without the C at the front," he says, and Jackie spits out her drink, laughing.

"Have you met Mary's guest yet, Ass?" Jackie asks, smirking.

"Uh, kinda."

"I'm Frank," he says. "Like Old Blue Eyes. I was named after him and his old-world charm."

"Sinatra, huh?" I say. "That's cool."

"Well, I'm glad you caught the reference, most people around here don't."

"What the hell is that supposed to mean?" Crystal snaps.

"He's ten," Jackie says. "Take a pill."

"Well, it's very nice to meet you, Sinatra."

"Likewise," he says, holding out a hand for me to shake, and I do. "I was just wondering if you were going to be fix-ing anything else today. Like if you needed any help?" he says.

"You like fixing things?"

"Yes, I like to know how things work. It's my hobby. Well, sort of. I don't have tools, but I could help you. Hand you stuff or something."

Rosa, Crystal, and Jackie watch our conversation, back and forth like they're watching a tennis match. They look to me for my response.

"I'd love that," I say. "I don't have anything else today, but I have to turn over 105 in the morning if you wanna help."

"What does turn over mean?"

"When someone moves out, I clean it, paint. In 105, I gotta get the built-in microwave working again 'cause someone... someone who won't be getting their security deposit back— exploded a tuna casserole in it...so there's a smell. Sound fun?"

"Yeah!" He beams from ear to ear.

"I start bright and early. You have to bring the coffee." I smile, knowing that Mary makes great coffee and will be thrilled to have someone to make it for.

He gives me a salute and says he'll be there. Then he goes back to his book. Before the girls have a chance to giggle at me about it, my phone pings, and I assume it's a service call because those are the only sort of pings I get these days.

When I look at it, I freeze a moment. I cannot believe it. It's an invitation to the Summer Blitz—a charity ball that I helped organize every year for the last six years, but since the scene I caused when I discovered Reid and Kimmy together, I've been ostracized from everything. The Sunday brunches with the girls especially—there have been twenty-nine of them since I moved to The Sycamores and not one invite. Not that I'm counting. Camille Garcia called once to see how I was, but I could hear in her voice she was uncomfortable. Reid filed for a restraining order he didn't get after I punched him in the back of the head, and all the husbands rallied around him—all my "friends" were their wives. But Reid has known the guys since college and was in a couple of their weddings, and I was just an extension of him. So when I was replaced, their loyalties shifted to Kimmy.

All of the weekend trips to Cabo, shopping and prosecco afternoons, game nights, dinner parties, barbecues, all of it was just robbed from me in one horrific moment. I didn't even suspect he was cheating. I just happened to be on my way out to pick up ribs to-go when Jenny Winters stopped by unexpect-edly, and we decided to make it a rosé-on-the-back-deck sort of evening. Barney's doesn't deliver, so I told her to catch up on the episode of *90 Day Fiancé* I'd already seen, and I'd run out, and we'd watch the next together.

Reid had said he was gonna stay late at the office and do a late showing that came up. *Shocked* isn't a strong enough word to describe what I felt when I saw them in a corner booth with a couple dry martinis and his hands up her skirt. The white-hot white rage just overcame me. I'm not proud to admit I hit him, but it felt like a reflex. I had never struck anyone before in my life. I walked up behind him and stood there a moment, my mouth agape, and he didn't even notice me—didn't feel my presence—just so absorbed in Kimmy's vagina that I didn't even exist. I'd even ordered him his favorite baby backs and mashed potatoes for later, that son of a bitch. And somehow, after all that betrayal, he's the good guy. He kept the friends and Cabo and game night, and fine, yes, the house, because I was just a guest there, as it turns out.

This invite must be a mistake; the party is tomorrow, after all. Someone must have forgotten to take me off a list, but I got it anyway. A happy accident…and I know they don't want me there, and if I showed up, it would cause a huge scene. The most pathetic part of it all—I know, I am fully aware of how truly disgusting I sound—but I want to see him. I want my life back. I want him to change his mind and come to his senses and realize he made a huge mistake. I want to go.

I'm jolted back into reality by the thwack of a curly fry to the head. I pull it out of my hair and look to see Crystal, ready to toss another one.

"What's the matter with you? You gonna throw up, chica? You look green."

And then, for some reason, I decide it's a good idea to tell the girls about how my ex and how his new trophy girlfriend will be at this party, and I was invited and deciding if I should go. It just spills out for some reason before I can think.

"Oh, shit," Jackie says. "You gotta go, dude."

"Yeah," Crystal says. "You can't let that bitch win."

"Well," I say, "I mean, it's not exactly a competition, but if it were, I'm gonna say she won."

"I don't know," Rosa pipes in, to my surprise. "How old is the guy—your ex?" She's clipping the top of a Go-Gurt tube and handing it to her kid, George, who runs off across the pool deck in Crocs that are too big for him.

"Thirty-nine, why?" I say.

"And you're what, thirty-six?"

"Five," I correct her.

"And you said the new chick is twenty-two. It's probably a midlife crisis thing. It's not over. He'll get tired of a girl that age. Stick it out."

"What the hell is wrong with you?" Crystal says.

"What?"

"Is it the 1950s? Did I miss something? You don't want him back, do you?" Crystal turns to me, and I guess my frozen look answers her question. "Oh, Jesus."

"You're one to talk, you got three and a half babies and zero baby daddies," Jackie says.

"That's 'cause I don't take shit like that from no dude. Listen. You gotta go and show this new chick she don't bother you—that you ain't afraid of her."

"We'll go with you!" Jackie says, suddenly delighted by her own epiphany. She yells across to Gordy to shut up and stop hitting Amber with a pool noodle, and then sits at the edge of her chair to explain how great of an idea it is. "We can take Crystal's minivan. It'll be like a party bus!"

"It's not really an open-to-the-public sort of thing," I say, but she stabs a finger into my phone.

"I saw that shit. It says Cassidy Abbott and family. We're your family. How are they gonna say we ain't?"

I think about my Oscar de La Renta—the strapless, silky black one he always loved me in, sitting in a box in storage and how it would feel to put it on again and walk in there—an invited guest—like I belonged—like I don't care anymore. None of those people have seen me in months. They don't know I live here. Maybe Barry from 206 could come as my date. He's a weird guy, don't get me wrong. He collects Samurai swords and enters hot dog eating contests, but they don't know that. He's tall and pretty good-looking, as long as he doesn't talk.

I could look like I moved on—with a new man and friends to boot. Like I don't need them anymore. I could get closure—have them all think I'm successful in my new life. Maybe Reid would even talk to me. Congratulate me.

"It's formal," I say, hoping that they actually have formal attire but without actually wanting to ask that.

"We won't embarrass you, Cass," Jackie says.

"Oooh, we'll go shopping," Crystal says.

"And get our nails done at Luxx. They give you free wine even though you can't drink it 'cause your hands are stuck in little plastic dryers," Rosa says.

Jackie shakes my shoulder and jumps up and down. "Yeah! We're going to a fancy ball! Woot!"

I pause. This might be a terrible idea, but in this moment, it feels like all I've been waiting for—an opportunity to get my old life back. If they see me as one of them, there would be more invites, and I'd be a peer again. Maybe there'd be brunches and dinner parties again. I have a better shot, at least, than rotting here with no in at all.

"Okay," I say quickly, and they all cheer.

Crystal stands and does a little dance, then clicks her cup into everyone's one by one and starts singing to herself, "We're going to a party, hey-hey—fancy ball, yeah!"

Three High Lifes later, the sky turns purple with ribbons of pinks and oranges burning on the horizon, and the katydids and cicadas buzz in the treetops. The girls have taken their kids inside for dinner, and the property is quiet except for the humming box fans and the low rumble of TVs behind apartment doors. I can smell the skirt steak Leonard in 111 is grilling, and maybe it's the slight buzz from the beer or the satisfaction that I have a job and a master plan to see Reid finally, but it feels something close to what happiness used to feel like.

The moment is short-lived because as I walk back to my apartment, I hear voices coming from the laundry room. The door to the laundry room is next to the office and is always propped open with the lights on. There are four quarter-pay washers and five dryers, but two are broken.

I see Rosa inside under the flickering fluorescent light, holding a basket full of folded clothes. In front of her is the back of a man in a sweaty white T-shirt. He's raising his voice, but he's speaking Spanish, so I don't know what's being said.

When he slams his fist on the top of the washer, the clang of metal makes her cringe and back up. That's when I duck behind the garbage bin next to the laundry door and hold my phone on top of the lid, aimed inside, and start recording. If this fucker thinks he can get away with what I saw last night, he's sorely mistaken. I'm not gonna let this happen.

Now she's speaking really quickly and crying. It sounds like pleading, but I still can't understand it. Then he strikes her. I cannot believe I'm seeing this. How has no one else here done anything to help her? I'm peeking with one eye around the side of the bin, and I see her on the ground, the back of her hand dabbing at the cut on the side of her lip. He hisses out some final words, and then he's gone.

I want to help her, but I can't imagine how she'd respond to seeing me witness this. A second time. Lord help me, if it's twice in as many days and in a common area, what the hell goes on behind their closed door? I mean, how the hell often does this happen? I don't want to upset her, but I have to help. I watch as she pushes herself to standing and hunches over the washer, steadying herself with both hands, and just breathes for a moment, trying to collect herself. I don't go to her this time. Because I have a better idea.

It's worked before, so I can make it work again, only this time, I don't need to roofie his drink or take sexy photos next to him. I just need to let him know he crossed the wrong person—someone who has no tolerance for lowlife men, and I'll show him the video and tell him I'll take it to the cops, get him arrested and evicted, even—that I'll testify for a restraining order or whatever she needs if he ever hurts her again. I'll put a stop to this, and he won't know what hit him.

What's he gonna do?

9

ANNA

I can't be here anymore. I stand in the middle of Henry's studio-turned-my-temporary-apartment. Flecks of dust dance in beams of sunlight streaming through the cracks in the curtains, canvases are piled against the walls, boxes stacked to the ceiling, and everything feels cluttered and like it's closing in. I can't be here. I can't absorb what the police detective told me. Who would ever hurt him? He didn't have enemies. He was just a normal person—but normal people don't get murdered, right?

I think of going back to our house. They said it would sell quickly which is why I put everything in storage and thought it would make sense to just stay here while I sort his things and look for a place to move—maybe Costa Rica or Ibiza or one of the places we always talked about, but now I'm more lost than ever. I could move a bed back into the master and just get out of this hellhole until it sells maybe. I called my parents, and they thought that was a good idea. But there's something keeping me here. Like, whatever terrible thing happened to him happened here, and people know more than they are saying.

I hear some shouting down at the pool, so I abandon my

thoughts and open the apartment door. I lean over the railing and squint against the morning sun glare to see what's going on.

I catch a flash of something in the pool—a kid I think—he's flailing, sinking under the surface, and then I see Callum crossing the pool deck from the mailboxes, running, tearing off his messenger bag from his shoulder and jumping in, pulling the kid out.

My hand flies to my mouth. It all happened so fast, I take a moment to register what actually just occurred—that the kid was drowning. When he's sitting safely on a deck chair, with Callum knelt down in front of him, I see something even more shocking. The father—that Eddie guy—yells across the pool at him.

"What the fuck is wrong with you, bro?" He starts making his way over to Callum and the kid, marching across the deck with a scowl. A handful of residents are at the pool, but I didn't see anyone else try to help. Maybe it just happened too quickly. People are muttering and watching what's unfolding but not moving to see if the kid's okay. It all seems so strange.

Eddie stomps up to Callum, and I see he's actually angry, looking for a fight. Not at all grateful Callum just saved the kid's life. He elbows Callum out of the way and yanks the kid up by one arm.

"Go inside, George," he says, and although tears are running down the little boy's cheeks, he doesn't make a sound. He wraps the towel around his shoulders and runs, barefoot and shaking, toward unit 103 and disappears inside the door.

"Excuse me?" Callum stands. "Your son just about drowned. You're asking me what the fuck is wrong with me? What the fuck is wrong with *you*?"

"He was learning to swim. That's how we do it. It's not your place to interfere like that!"

"Are you out of your mind? He was under the water," Callum says, but he's backing up ever so slightly. He picks up his bag and holds it in front of himself. It's subtle, but it looks like he's trying to shield himself, and I don't blame him. This guy looks deranged.

He pushes Callum's shoulder. "I'm the parent. He learns to swim the way I decide he does. So you touch him again, it will be the last thing you do. Got it?"

"How about, instead, I call child services and report you for neglect and child abuse? Psycho." Callum's words are shaky as he says them, but he says them, and I cringe. You can tell he's scared but trying to do the right thing.

"Yeah, try it. That will definitely be the last thing you do. And I mean that. Sincerely," Eddie says, and everyone around the pool shrinks, probably wishing they were anywhere else—not knowing what to say or do.

"Oh, you're threatening me? You hurt that kid again, and it's the last thing *you* do, sir! Two can play this game, and only one of us needs a serious psychiatric evaluation, so try me, nut job!" Callum yells, but there is self-doubt in his bravado that I can hear all the way from here. The sort of ease and confidence with which Eddie confronts him is clearly not in Callum's nature. I can even see his cheeks redden as he awkwardly tries to stand his ground.

Then I see Rosa come out the front door of her apartment, and Eddie must see her, too, because he immediately backs away as if nothing happened. He walks over to his truck and lights a cigarette. Rosa looks around a moment and doesn't see him, then goes back in. Callum looks around, too, but much more insecurely, and then nods as if he's won the argument and heads for his apartment door.

"He shouldn't have done that," a voice from behind me says, and I leap, hand to heart.

"Shit!" I say, turning around to see a tiny woman sitting in a torn deck chair next to her door, smoking a Camel Light and shaking her head as she peers down toward the pool.

"You scared me," I say.

"Uncle Fester," she says, holding out her hand. "I scare a lot of people, but I don't take it personally. Boo," she says, laughing.

"No, I mean. You startled me. I'm sorry. What was your name?" I ask, shaking her hand out of obligation because she hasn't put it down yet.

"Babs, but they call me Uncle Fester, and…he shouldn't have done that."

I can see exactly why they call her that, although it's awful. Her head is shiny bald, and the bags under her eyes are remarkable. I'm not sure if she's sick, and of course, I don't ask. I have no idea what to make of this strange woman who is apparently my next-door neighbor.

"Shouldn't have thrown his own kid in the pool, you mean?"

"No. Callum. I think that's his name. He shouldn't have interfered. No bueno." She chokes on a puff of her cigarette and coughs, waving the smoke away.

"What? He just saved that poor kid's life. No one else was even paying attention, and his father just…"

"Be that as it may, he just embarrassed Eddie Bacco. He's on Bacco's shitlist now. You know him? Callum?"

"Kinda," I say.

"You should tell him to watch his back."

"Why? That guy seems like a nut, but you don't think he's actually dangerous."

"Oh, honey. Ya see a lotta shit when you're invisible. I went out late one night to the Shamrock over on Eighth for some smokes—like over a year ago now—and I see Eddie and some other guys behind the building. There's a guy on the ground. A bloody guy, and they dump him right in the dumpster, no shit. Couldn't believe my eyes. I wasn't supposed to be there, but they didn't see me."

"What?" I say, my heart speeding up, my chest pounding, thinking about Henry and if this unhinged man could be con-

nected. The sky darkens, I notice, as if on cue. A few fat drops
of rain fall, and I see some of the moms gathering up Ziploc
bags of snacks and baby floaties and starting to shout at the kids
to get out of the pool before lightning strikes it.

"Yeah, and they were saying some shit back and forth, but
mostly in Spanish and my Spanish kinda stinks, but I got the gist
that the guy owed them like five hundred bucks for some meth
or somethin'. Can you believe that? Poor fucker in a Shamrock
dumpster for five hundies. What a world we live in," she says,
and I just stare at her a moment, not knowing how seriously
to take her. She could be a quack for all I know. The story is
outrageous, and this place is full of nutters.

"Seems like being humiliated in front of the whole apartment community is worse than owing him five hundred bucks.
I think he just pissed off the wrong guy, just sayin'."

Rolling thunder rumbles behind the dark clouds, and the few
older kids left on the pool deck cover their heads with towels
and squeal as they scurry indoors. Her words feel like a punch
to the head. Drugs. Is that what Henry's death is about? Did
he get into something like that? I can't imagine it, but at least
it's a thread to pull on.

"Wait, so you actually saw this? And you never told anyone
what you saw?"

"No one ever asked me," she says matter-of-factly and then
picks up a martini from the floor next to her chair that I just
now noticed, never mind that it's midmorning. She eats an
olive and blinks at me.

"What do you mean?"

"I mean, nobody ever asked me anything about seein' a dead
guy, so no. It never came up."

"You saw someone get murdered," I say, trying to keep the
judgment out of my voice so she doesn't shut down or something.

"Well, not really, I heard a guy get murdered. I only saw a guy get dumped, technically."

"Don't you think you should report it?" I say, trying to hide my disgust and utter shock.

"Not my problem. Why would I want to get myself in the middle of that? I think he's like…not just part of a cartel, but like a drug lord," she says, and now I am having a hard time taking her seriously, but I don't know what to think.

"So nobody knows this guy is…cartel? Nobody around here knows? Did Henry know? Did you know Henry?" I add desperately at the end because it just dawns on me that she lived next door to him, and he never mentioned her.

"What a gem that guy was. So sad about what happened. You're the wife?" she says, and I nod. "Yeah, you look like you don't fit in here, so I figured. What is that, Gucci?" she asks, rubbing the hem of my dress between her fingers.

I pull it away. "So you knew him," I say, sitting on Henry's metal chair opposite her.

"He painted me once," she says, beaming.

"Really?" I hold back tears thinking of Henry here, in his studio, everyone's friend—making everyone feel so important the way he always did. I imagine him at dusk, a brandy and ice sweating in a lowball glass on his wood table covered in brushes, all the windows open with a breeze spilling through, his subjects sitting on the chaise longue, posing for him as he paints them into life on canvas. It was when he was at his happiest. Mostly gritty portraits, photorealism, rarely nudes, and never elegant, glossy images. Just real people—with every line on their face and fold of fat raw and present in his work. My heart soars with joy for just a brief moment thinking of him this way—happy and peaceful.

"Yeah," she says. "We chatted about how you guys were gonna visit Roswell for the weekend, and I told him to get alien abduction insurance, and he didn't believe there was such a thing, so we looked it up on his phone, and no shit, lots of people have insurance in case of alien abduction, and he thought that was really funny. I said he has a better chance of running into a 'foot!"

"What?" I ask, numbly.

"A bigfoot. Anyway, besides that time, it was just a wave here and there when he came and went. Small talk once or twice when he drank a beer on the balcony. I didn't know him well, but still… I would have never thought he'd…you know. End his life. He always seemed happy to me."

I think of that trip we took to Roswell, just like she said, months ago, and how he bought little green alien salt-and-pepper shakers for my parents because my mom would get a kick out of them. My hands tremble at the memory, so I try to change the subject to get as much information out of this woman as I can.

"People must know this guy is dangerous. I mean, don't you think? Does his wife know what he does?" I ask.

"I don't think so. Did you meet Rosa? She almost passed out when Jackie ripped off a toenail runnin' across the pavers next to the building. White as a sheet. A drug lord husband who kills people for sport. Gonna have to say she doesn't know. She knows he went to prison, of course, for drugs, but the rest?" She shakes her head and slurps down another olive from her martini. "He puts on the changed-man act—a man who has a good job as a trucker—a family guy now."

"Prison?" I gasp and then lower my voice. Maybe she's not crazy, and this guy is really as big a threat as she says, but nothing makes sense anymore. It's all so surreal. "Then how is that possible the wife doesn't know?"

"Well, I thought—I guess everyone still does think—that Eddie's a trucker. Over the road, you know. Gone for weeks at a time. It's been that way a long time—since he got out. Now, I think that he's probably not a trucker."

"Ya think!" I say, again too loudly.

But she just smiles as if having a revelation. "Hey, it's nice to have someone to talk about this to finally." She lights a new cigarette off the one in her mouth and then offers the package out to me. I decline. "Well," she continues, "who the fuck knows where he goes, but it's nowhere good. Ohhh. I wonder if he has another family somewhere, and someday they'll catch him and make a Lifetime movie about it, and we get to play ourselves in it. What a hoot that would be! It'd be fun to be in a movie, don't ya think?"

"Look," I say, trying to refocus the conversation. "I know you didn't know him very well, but Henry—he didn't know this guy, right? He didn't get involved with… I don't know, drugs, or…"

"Oh, gosh, I don't think so. Henry was a good guy. Great guy. I can't imagine him getting involved with that," she says, and I feel grateful to hear it come from someone else. He *was* a great guy like everyone keeps saying. But none of this adds up.

"You don't think you should tell the police about this—about what you know?" I ask.

"I'm old. I wanna watch *Gunsmoke* with a gin martini and be left in peace. Not interested in getting my throat slit in my La-Z-Boy one night because I poked my nose into Eddie Bacco's pile of shit. Stay far away from that guy is all. Tell Callum, too." Then Babs picks up her half-empty martini and stands. She points at me, a sort of *you got that?* gesture, and then disappears inside her apartment door, mumbling that it's "hot as shit out here" as she goes.

I numbly walk into my own unit and stand staring at the wall, my mind reeling with the words *cartel, murder, meth*. I have to be living in a parallel universe right now. I'm baffled. Absolutely mystified. Did Henry get wrapped up in this? I mean, what other explanation is there?

I do tell Callum. I text him and tell him everything Babs just told me, so he knows it all immediately. I can't really bear to repeat it all in person, although it probably deserves an in-person conversation. I need to figure what the hell is really happening here. I need to dig into this storage unit and see if Henry is hiding something.

First, though, I start to hunt through every junk drawer and keepsake box and backpack—any crack or crevice where he might be hiding drugs. God, I can't believe I'm even saying that, but what if that's why his demeanor started to change over the last months? It would make sense.

His toxicology report was clean, but just because he wasn't on something that day doesn't mean anything. He hid it from me, though… I mean, if he was doing these drugs, he was an expert at deceit. But I guess addicts can be. Shit. What if he was selling it, not using? God, what if he wanted to make extra money or something? I thought we were doing pretty well. Not great, but comfortable enough. I take a breath and stop my rambling thoughts and focus.

After I dump all of the kitchen drawers and search under the mattress and in the pillowcases, I start to pull out linens from under the bathroom cabinet, and nothing. It's a small place. There are boxes I haven't gotten to yet, but nothing on the surface. Then I open the medicine cabinet, and it's empty.

I mean there's a face lotion, a comb, and some razor cartridges, but I know he keeps painkillers close. The Oxy for his knee surgery and some pain meds for when his rheumatoid arthritis flares. He can't work without them when he gets a flare-up, so the fact that there are no drugs at all in the place seems even more strange than finding additional illicit ones. I could maybe see a scenario where he bought some seemingly benign drug from this guy, not knowing who this maniac, Eddie Bacco, really was because he wanted something stronger for pain. That actually seems possible. But what the hell does it mean that *all* his meds are gone? Was he going somewhere? Did he take them with him on purpose?

I truly cannot wrap my head around what could have possibly happened to him, and all of it is more unsettling the more I learn. I grab an umbrella from its hook next to the front door. A pang of longing for Henry washes over me when I see it's his favorite—the one with the blue sky and cloud pattern on the underside of it—a sunny surprise when you open it up.

The thunderstorm has moved everyone inside, so it's a perfect time to go down to the storage units without anyone's questions. The smell of wet earth and summer rain feels like a slight comfort until I open the door to the small detached building where the storage is, and the rain thunders deafeningly hard on the tin roof, sending shivers up my arms and stealing my breath for a moment. I continue anyway and look around to see a makeshift storage area—five-by-ten-foot rooms with cement walls and chicken wire doors, which seems prisonlike and out of place.

I can see through the wire into each unit, so I don't have to try my key in each one. I can quickly rule out the units packed with tricycles and a Barbie Dreamhouse or the ones with potting soil and terra-cotta pots stacked up in piles. I try numbers six, ten, and fourteen, which only have sealed cardboard boxes, but nothing. Then, when I see numbers one through five behind me against the wall, I can immediately see which is Henry's.

It's piled with canvases, some portraits, many blank still. I recognize his bike that I hadn't even noticed was missing from our garage in all the numb shock of clearing out the house. I try the key in the lock, and it clicks open. I push in the wire door and look at it all for a moment. I set my phone down on a pile of books and try to decide where to start digging in.

There are at least a dozen boxes, which I'm afraid to open if I'm honest, but before I can even peel the tape off one of them, I hear something. The scrape of a steel door. The door I came in—the one I propped open, is swinging closed, and I see a sleeve. Someone's arm is closing it.

"Wait!" I scream, and as I run toward the main door, the wire door to the unit starts to slam shut as I let go of it. Before I can stop either door from closing, it's black. It's utterly black, and as the rain continues to beat on the tin roof, my screams vanish in the air. The wire unit door locked when it slammed closed, and my phone and the key are inside. I begin to panic.

I feel my way to the front door and try to open it, but it's locked. Someone has locked me in. I beat on it and scream until my voice is raw and my fists are bruised, but no one comes.

10

CASS

By late morning, all the tuna casserole has been successfully scraped out of the microwave and the living room has been sloppily painted a ghastly off-white color, so Sinatra and I sit on a couple of five-gallon paint buckets in front of the open front door of 105, eating grape Popsicles and watching the rain sizzle off the steamy concrete sidewalk.

"And what's that one?" I ask, continuing a game we've been playing all morning where he shows off his knowledge of all the tools in my bag.

"An angle grinder," he says, with a hint of *duh* in his tone.

"Okay then, smarty pants. What is this called and why?"

"It's a Phillips head. It's named after the inventor," he responds, which is something I didn't know, but of course he does.

"My mom used to have me open her wine bottles with one of those," he adds, and I give him a blank stare trying to imagine how one would do such a thing. "She didn't have an opener sometimes, so I'd just push the cork down into the bottle." He says this like that's a normal thing kids do for their alcoholic jailbird mothers.

"Ah," is all I can think to say.

I see Eddie cross the pool deck, pulling his ball cap down to shield himself from the rain and then picking up a slow jog until he reaches the tin awning his truck is parked beneath. The guy always seems to be fixing his pickup, yet it never seems to be fixed. He just pokes at it and spends a bunch of time on his phone between constant visits from a few of his sketchy-looking friends. Maybe nobody else notices how odd it is, but he parks in view of the front office, so I see it—I see the friends with their backpacks and sunglasses, who never stay too long and shake hands with each other a freakish amount. I wonder if he's selling pot or something? Handing off dime bags to these guys. Man, if he is up to no good, maybe he'll be even more scared when I show him the video I have. Maybe he has more to lose than I thought. I need to make my move today. For Rosa.

"Hey, Sinatra. How about if you finish up sweeping and mopping and take this garbage to the dumpster, I buy you McDonalds for dinner?" I say, and his eyes light up as he gets to his feet.

"Really?" he says, and I am starting to get the feeling that crappy McNuggets are the best thing to happen to this kid in a long time, and it sort of breaks my heart.

"I'll do a good job," he says, collecting the Popsicle wrappers and dragging the trash bag outside the front door.

"I know you will. What's your favorite at Micky Dee's?" I ask him.

"Whatever you like...whatever you think," he says eagerly, and my heart swells a little. I resist the urge to hug him. Resist the draw to try to erase whatever it is he went through that made scraping tuna casserole out of a microwave the highlight of his week. Instead, I say...

"See, you gotta watch out there, Sinatra. What if I got the Filet-O-Fish? Let me tell ya...they put cheese on it. Fish and cheese don't go together. It's sick and wrong."

"That's okay," he says. "If you like it."

"How about a Happy Meal and one of those lava hot apple pies that destroy the roof of your mouth?" I ask, and he nods vigorously.

"Cool. I gotta go do some stuff, so just come by the office around dinnertime?" I say, and he's already starting to sweep the patch of linoleum in the depressingly tiny scrap of galley kitchen in the apartment.

"Grandma Mary says dinnertime is when *Murder She Wrote* comes on and she can start to defrost her Lean Cuisine, but I don't know what time that is?"

"Anytime you want, how about that?" I say, hoisting my tool bag over my shoulder and walking out into the rain.

"I have to help Grandma Mary with her pills at dinnertime," he says.

"Oh, well then, lunch. Late lunch. Just stop in in a couple hours."

"Okay!" Frank beams and waves as I leave and then gets to work sweeping, and I feel my chest tighten upon leaving him, and I don't know why. But I keep my eyes on Eddie Bacco leaning on his truck, and I try to think of how to lure him into the front office without anyone really noticing.

By noon, the rain has dissipated, and the humidity is suffocating, and I spin back and forth in the office chair, keeping an eye on Eddie outside but not knowing exactly what to do—what I'll say. I figure if it's technically afternoon, maybe offering him a beer will seem…normal. It's Friday, after all. The residents always get together and grill by the pool on Friday evenings. I can tell him I bought a bunch of beer for the Friday potluck and does he want one 'cause he looks hot? That's not creepy. I think he'd bite.

But just then, one of his weird friends shows up and they talk in whispers, and I can't hear what they're saying, so I decide to walk outside the front door to the mailbox block and act like I'm inserting notices into a couple mailboxes, but they stop talking when they see me. I notice a few packages for a couple residents that are too big to fit in the mailbox, so I walk one package over to 207 and drop it off. The other is Callum's, and since I know he's teaching summer school today, I pull it into the office and text him to pick it up.

The friend is finally gone, and it's now or never. I think I'm doing the right thing. Vigilante justice. Guys like him can't get away with this shit, so he needs to know someone is watching. At least this is what I tell myself, but my hands tremble violently. I take in a deep breath and try to steady them as I pick up two Bud Lights and walk outside.

"Oh, hey, Eddie," I say, and I can hear my voice shake, so I clear my throat. "It's hot as hell out here, eh?"

He nods and wipes the sweat from his forehead with a cloth that he shoves back into his jeans pocket.

"Ya want a beer? I bought a bunch for later, but it's that time of day." I look at my wrist, at a watch that's not there, and say, "Beer o'clock." God, I sound like a moron. "If you wanna cool off a minute."

He looks around like someone might be pulling a prank on him, and then shrugs and walks toward me. "Yeah, okay," he says, and I nod back and slip in the office door.

I made sure all the blinds were closed, so nobody would see me threaten him. I mean, I have done this many times before with more dangerous people than him, and it always worked out. I'm not even exploiting him for money this time. Of course, doing this in the middle of the night would be ideal, just like I did with the others, but I don't have access to him then. I just need to do it. I remind myself that I have the upper hand and I'm doing the right thing and to stay calm.

The office is dim with the blinds closed, and it feels icy cold after stepping in from the sweltering heat. It's awkwardly quiet—just the hum of the air conditioner and a low rumble of thunder in the distance. He looks uncomfortable and like he's regretting his decision as he takes the beer from my outstretched hand. He drops his bag on the dusty coffee table covered in *People* magazines from God knows how many years ago. It's just about then that he registers how awkward this is.

"Well, thanks. But I better go, I got a trip," he says, moving toward his bag.

"Oh, you're a truck driver, right? Big rig?" I ask, but he doesn't answer. "That must be hard. How long ya gone?"

He gives me the oddest look and then says, "Couple of weeks. I better get going."

"I thought your car was broken down," I say, nodding in the general direction of his perpetually broken pickup in the parking lot. "How do you get to the lot? Is that where you pick it up? There's probably a warehouse or a truck lot, right?" God, I can't stop rambling.

He picks up his bag and moves to the door. "I have a ride."

Most days, the door to the office is propped open, and Barry is sitting on the worn leather sofa chatting away about swords or some mundane thing or another, or Crystal, who refuses to pay for internet, is at my desk checking her social media and smoking, or Babs is shaking up martinis for everyone. It really does feel like I live in a college dormitory half the time and I'm the RA with a revolving door, but today it's quiet and empty and not what he was expecting when he walked in here. I can tell that he feels the energy shift and again thanks me for the drink and he hoists his bag onto his shoulder.

"Wait," I say quickly. He stops and turns to me. "I have something to show you," I say, and I guess he thinks it's sexual maybe, because the look on his face is one of surprise mixed with intrigue. He drops his bag again and walks over to me.

"Oh, yeah, what's that?" he asks with a smirk on his face.

I turn my phone to him and play the video of him and Rosa in the laundry room—the yelling, his raised voice. I watch him look at the phone, his head cocked, shock spreading across his face. The phone is facing away from me as I show him, so I don't see him strike her, but I hear it and study his reaction as she falls to the ground. Fury. I think that's what I see. Red blotches dot his chest and face, and his eyes narrow, but he's silent.

The video stops. He just stares at me with a look that frightens the shit out of me—like he could attack at any second.

"I just want you to leave her alone," I say, and the words sound confident, but I'm backing up and shakily shoving my phone into my pocket.

"Or?" is all he says, a terrifying coldness behind his eyes.

"Or I show this to the cops—get you kicked out of here or arrested. I'm watching you is all I'm saying, so be a man and don't hit women. That's all," I say, feeling my courage returning with these words, because I'm right, and he's the one who's wrong here. I fold my arms in front of me to emphasize my point. "I backed up the video," I add quickly, in case he thinks of trying to take my phone.

So really, what's he gonna do? It's broad daylight, and I have a security camera in the corner, pointed right at him, although he doesn't know I switched it off to ensure nobody ever sees this. People come in and out of here all the time. He's not gonna freak out or try to take my phone if he knows what's good for him.

"I'm sorry," he says, so calmly the hair on the back of my neck stands up and chills tap across my shoulders and down my back. "Who the fuck do you think you are exactly?"

"Someone who isn't gonna let guys like you get away with that shit," I respond, and then it happens.

He rushes me in a white-hot rage—with blind hatred in his eyes, so quickly I can't even move or react—and slams me up against the wall so hard it knocks the wind out of me, and I gasp for breath, but I can't get any air in because he's squeezing my neck with both hands. I can feel a drop of blood slither from the back of my head onto my shoulder, and I see an explosion of stars behind my eyes.

I know everything is about to go black if I don't inhale in a matter of seconds. My arms flail, and I claw and grab at anything on the desk next to me that's within reach. I can't see anything, so I just blindly feel and pray for something there that I can defend myself with—anything I can hit him with and escape his grasp.

"You thought you could blackmail me?" He laughs and I try to kick at him, but I don't have enough oxygen. My body feels numb.

The room spins. I am going to lose consciousness. I clutch something from the desk next to me—I hook the handle with the ends of my fingertips, just barely. It's a pair of scissors. I can't see him, everything is a blur, so I just blindly grab them with the little strength I have left and stab at him to get him off me. I feel his grip loosen, and I fall to the floor. I still can't see. Everything is swirls and stars, and I'm so lightheaded I can barely push myself to stand, to run, and then finally my breath starts to steady, and I look up to see him standing there with wide eyes and an open mouth.

I scurry backward across the floor to move away, and I stand and lean against the wall, still steadying my dizzy head with my hands, and then I see it—I realize why he's stopped choking me and is standing impossibly still.

The scissors are plunged into the side of his neck, and blood is seeping out of the corners of his mouth. I think a sound like a scream escapes my lips, but I can't be sure. The shock paralyzes me for a few moments as I grip the wall behind me and try to catch my breath.

I watch him pull the scissors from his neck and hold the wound, but the blood spills over the top of his hand, and then he stiffens. His eyes bulge, and his gaze is fixed straight ahead. His mouth falls open, and he collapses to the polished concrete floor with a crack so loud, bones must have snapped as he smacked the surface. He goes completely limp. Dark blood slowly pools around his head, and his body twitches before it goes still again.

I cup both my hands over my mouth so I don't scream, but the sobs can't be suppressed. *What have I done? Fuck! Fuck, fuck. What have I done?*

I rush to him and stand over his body, trying not to hyper-ventilate. I rest my hands on my knees and drop my head. *Holy shit.* The blood travels in tiny rivers across the concrete floor and pools against the braided area rug under the coffee table, creating a horrifying blaze of red against the white wool. Oh, God. What did I do?

Just then, I hear a tap-tap at the office door, and a voice calls. "Cass? You there?"

Shit. It's Callum. I told him to come and get his package. I snap up to standing and look to the door, thinking I can run and lock it before he comes in. I need time. I need... But before I can even take one step toward it, the doorknob turns, and Callum pokes his head in.

"Hello? You told me I had a..." He steps inside and sees me hunched over a bleeding body, and he freezes. I hear a sharp intake of breath as he holds his hand to his heart and looks to me, then to Eddie lying lifeless beneath me, then back to me, and we lock eyes.

"I didn't mean to!" I cry. I rush past him to the door and slam it shut behind Callum, locking it and standing in front of it with tears streaming down my face. "It was an accident. Oh, God. What have I done?"

11

ANNA

In the blackness, I sit near the entrance door where a slit of daylight cuts through the dark, and after a few hours of slamming my fist against it and calling for help, exhaustion takes over, and I give up. All I can do now is cry quietly and pray that someone finds me.

The rain has stopped now, and it's quiet. The earthy damp smell in this dungeon of a room makes me want to wretch, and my hatred for this place boils inside of me. My phone rings from inside Henry's unit and I can't see the screen, but the light illuminates the darkness. I quickly look around to see if there is anything in sight I can use to climb up to the egress window or tools I can break the handle off the door with, but the ringing stops, and it's dark again.

A few moments later I hear footsteps coming down the sidewalk. This storage unit is tucked away behind the main buildings, so nobody comes back here, it seems, unless they are actually coming to the storage area. I feel the wall and rise to my feet. I beat on the door again. "Hello! Is someone there!?"

And the door swings open. A figure is backlit by blinding sunlight, and for a moment, I wonder if it's someone who's come to hurt me. If I've actually been kidnapped or taken captive or something. It's this thought that makes me cower and back up instead of throwing my arms around the person and thanking them.

"Anna?" the man says. It's Barry. The annoying guy from 206. He sounds more surprised than someone who's come to kill me would, I think, but I can't be certain yet.

"Did you…lock me in here?" I ask shakily. Then he steps in, and I can see him clearly without the sun in my eyes.

"Oh, my God. You were locked in here? No, God. I sold a sword."

"What?" I ask, thinking for a moment he's messing with me—trying to confuse me, because he doesn't make sense.

"I keep my collection in my storage unit. Sometimes I sell them on eBay. God, I'm so sorry. How in the world did you get stuck down here?"

"Someone locked me in," I say, blinking back tears that are partly relief but still terror and confusion.

"No, nobody would do that—the wind was really going there for a while. I'm sure it just…"

"I saw someone do it," I say firmly.

He doesn't seem to know how to respond. He runs his hands through his hair and gestures to the door. "Well, gosh. Let's get you out of here," he says, and I don't know if I should trust him. Is he a psychopath who is going to strangle me and stuff my body in a plastic storage bin if I get close? I feel like a trapped animal. I keep looking at the triangle of light from the door behind him and wonder if I should try to make a run for it. What has this place done to me? Maybe he's just getting his whatever from his storage unit, and I've lost it.

"I have to get my phone…and I need to bring these boxes up to my apartment," I say, hoping he moves away from the door.

"Oh, gosh, let me help you," he says, and then he goes right to Henry's unit. There is a flood of relief that he's moved from the doorframe and his defenses are down and I could run out and lock him in if I had to. A question pops into my mind: How does he know which unit is Henry's? *Why* would he?

I stand outside the door and gulp in the fresh air. I should tell him he doesn't have to help, but I'm not going back in there if I don't have to, and now that I'm out and safe, I let him. He tells me we'll have to clip the wire door open in order to reach in and get the key, but that'll take some tools. My impatience boils as I wait for him to call Cass about some sort of industrial clippers or whatever he's talking about...

"No answer," he says, "but she won't mind if we break it open. You need your keys. The thing's on its last leg anyway." He goes to his unit where a dozen swords hang on display in a very off-putting way. He plucks one of the curved swords with an emerald green handle from its place on a shelf and swipes at the rusty square that the lock attaches to on the unit door; it easily comes loose from the screw and falls to the floor.

All the while I'm watching this from outside the main door, still shaky and ready to run if he suddenly decides to try to dismember me with one of his swords, which I haven't ruled out as a possibility quite yet. But then he smiles, and does some weird court jester bow with a hand flourish as if he's mastered a great feat, leans his sword against a wooden beam, and begins helping me pull out boxes.

"Thank you," I say as he hoists a couple of boxes up on his shoulder. He hands me my phone as he passes me, then continues on to bring them up to my apartment door. Although I finally feel like I'm safe from being murdered, I don't offer to help. Maybe I am overreacting, and someone did just close the door so the room didn't flood and ruin people's things— they didn't hear me because the thundering rain was so loud. That's possible. And Barry is probably actually just trying to help. Occam's razor, I can hear my dad saying, is the philosophy that the simplest explanation is usually correct, or something like that. Still…

I rush up to my apartment and pull the boxes inside as Barry sets them down on my doormat, keeping my distance. I look at my phone, but there's just a text from my mother checking in and two missed calls from my friend Monica. Nothing from Callum telling me he got my message and will be careful.

I watch Barry labor up the stairs with a heavy box of books, and I'm grateful, but I also can't shake the feeling that there's something off about him. He's an attractive guy, and if you just saw him, you'd lump him in as a popular guy in school and someone with a few special lady friends who works in a cubicle and plays golf on the weekend, but when he talks he's… I don't know. Almost childlike. Too eager to help, missing that chip most people have that should tell him when he's talking too close or overstaying his welcome. He's just oddly clueless, I guess, is the best way to describe it. Maybe harmless. Maybe not.

When he's brought up the last box, I offer to pay him for his time because I have to offer him something, and I'm not inviting him in.

"Oh, gosh, no way. I'm so sorry for what you went through. I'm just here to help."

Before I can respond, I hear a voice say, "Girl!" and Barry and I both turn and look down to see a woman with white capri pants and heels with a silk blouse and a single string of pearls around a very delicate neck. It's Monica. She's shielding her eyes from the sun with one hand and the other is on her hip.

"I've been calling for ages. I was going to Paradiso's for brunch and wanted you to come. You don't answer your phone anymore?" she asks as she navigates the wet pool deck in heels and makes her way to the staircase to come up.

Barry pats my arm and tells me to call if I need anything else before he leaves.

"Hi," I say, hugging her tightly when she enters the door to the apartment. "Sorry, I…" and then I stop and decide not to tell her that I was locked in a dungeon for hours, probably by a psychopath who's out to get me, and that I feel like I'm losing my mind here. I'm glad to see my oldest friend, but all I want right now is to shower off the last few hours and then bawl into my pillow for a good while before I can absorb one more thing today.

"Wow, Anna. Yikes. This was his studio? God, I imagined some Joanna Gaines shit going on—it sounded romantic, like a loft with exposed brick and soaring twenty-foot vaulted ceilings with beams. God, is that a popcorn ceiling? What the hell?"

"I don't know," I say. "I thought the same thing when he showed it to me last year, but if this is how he got his inspiration, who am I to judge?"

It shouldn't be that shocking. I mean, it sort of is. He probably could have rented the kind of artist loft with a cityscape view she's describing, but he's known for gritty portraits—real people, unfiltered. This place meant something to him for reasons I can't understand but for reasons that were his own; that I can at least accept. I feel protective of him when someone doubts him like this, and she should know that.

"Sorry," she says, pulling a bottle of champagne from her oversize Coach tote. "Just—" she looks around with raised brows "—not what I expected. But, hey, I brought brunch to you. Thought you could use it."

She smooths her sleek black hair with her hand nervously and looks around like every surface is too disgusting to place her bag down. She can come off a bit… I don't know, crass? Direct maybe. Is that the word? But I know her enough to know that acting like things are normal and we can drink through any problem is key. Talking aimlessly about the everyday mundane and ignoring the impossible, traumatizing reality is the way you get through hard times, and sometimes that's just the kind of friend you need—one who won't ask you how you feel. Not because she doesn't care, but as a very purposeful strategy to keep you in good spirits and distracted.

It might not be what I need right now, but a mimosa and idle conversation about her new hair stylist "who does stellar lowlights but who's sadly moving to Lake Havasu" and "what is she going to do" is going to keep me from losing it right now, so we pull out a wooden chair from the small kitchen nook and set it up next to the ugly metal chair on the balcony and sit, drinking warm bubbly and SunnyD out of Dixie cups.

Below us, some of the pool girls are already bringing out a folding table and taping a dollar store plastic cover over it where they place sleeves of Solo cups and hot dog buns and other prep for the Friday evening barbecue.

Monica must be stunned into silence by the place because her lips are pursed and her eyes are darting around. She swats away a fly as if even that is a product of this filthy place and would never have bothered her somewhere more posh. "So you…live here now?" she asks.

"No. I mean, I'm just going through all his stuff, and it was paid up for the next month, so why not take my time while the house sells?"

"Then where? You know you can stay with me and Steven, right? I mean, his mother is there now, ugh, but just for another week, thank Christ. She told Katie her Barbies were dressed like whores and then ordered colonial prairie dresses for them. Can you believe they even make those? Now Katie's playing Amish village or *Little House on the Prairie* or whatever the hell she's doing out there, because her dolls 'rough it' in the backyard now and she wants to sell Barbie's Dreamhouse for a decent profit, Christ. So I mean, if you need Realtor referrals or anything," she says, and I smirk at this.

"But really," she continues. "If you don't wanna go back to

your house, we have the pool house. It's private. You can stay as long as you want."

"Well, thanks. I'm still figuring out what I wanna do." I don't tell her I still dream of just leaving and wandering the world and not buying another suburban house and not begging for a mid-level, soul-stealing journalism job I'll get turned down for anyway. "I just need to sort through everything here and... I just need to figure out what happened," I say, willing my voice not to break.

"Tell me you know, like really, really know that what he did was not about you. He was depressed. I mean, I just hope you don't blame yourself or..."

"No. I know," I say, cutting her off. And actually forgetting for just a moment that nobody else knows it was foul play. I can't tell her. I can't even say the words out loud. I just need to know more before I start to publicize this and then subsequently drown in the pity and questions and unsolicited advice. I need to stay clear and focused. For Henry.

The whoosh and sputter of a match being lit behind Monica's head makes her whip around in her chair and spill a splash of mimosa onto her blouse. "The fuck!" she yelps.

"Oh, hey, ladies." It's Babs. She wears a pink housecoat and yellow flip-flops. She inhales deeply on her cigarette and smiles at us.

"Jesus," Monica says, likely out of shock at the woman's appearance. She looks to me for an explanation, then back to Babs.

"Smoke?" Babs asks.

Monica shakes her head and looks to me again with raised eyebrows.

Babs leans over the railing, releasing a hearty cough that somehow turns into a laugh. She gestures with her cigarette. "Little Kevin pooped in the pool again." We look down to see very pregnant Crystal crying as she tries to fish it out with a tiny butterfly net and simultaneously screaming at Tiffany and

Amber to get out of the pool, but they are both gleefully try-ing to cannonball themselves on top of it.

"They're gonna get the pink eye," Babs says.

Monica stands wide-eyed, with her heart to her chest.

"You new here?" Babs asks. "I'm Uncle Fester. Welcome." She holds her hand out for Monica to shake, but Monica mum-bles "excuse me" and backs up until she bumps into my apart-ment door, then slips inside.

"No," I say, "she's not a tenant, just a friend who stopped by."

Before I can go inside behind Monica, Babs asks, "You warn Callum about Eddie? Haven't seen either of 'em today. Just sayin'."

"I did, yeah," I say and then start toward my door.

"You ain't gonna drink this?" she asks, picking up my half-empty mimosa cup.

"All yours. Gotta run."

In the short time I've been here, the strangeness of the place has almost begun to feel normal somehow, and then I see how Monica looks at it with fresh eyes, and question again if I should just go. Just give all his things away. Donate the paintings, call the Salvation Army to do a pickup for the rest, and get on the next plane to a beach. Fucking anywhere, really.

It's very tempting, but when I stand looking at the tower-ing boxes of his whole life, I can't do that. I'd always regret not trying to figure it out—understand what happened to my sweet Henry. Then a terrifying thought hits me. What if I can't leave town? It seems like they think I'm a suspect. What if this goes on for years, and my life is destroyed even more than it is already?

I'm gonna find the truth, goddammit. There have to be answers in between all these pages of books and photos and scribblings.

"What are you doing?" I ask Monica as she opens and closes cupboards in the kitchenette.

"Looking for booze. This place requires vodka, not champagne. What the actual fuck?" There are only four cupboards, so she finds Henry's minibar pretty quickly. She washes a martini glass caked in dust that I can't imagine Henry even having, let alone using, and pours Seagram's and expired Cran-Apple juice into it. She perches on a stool, sipping her drink, and takes the place in.

"Does Henry still have Lorazepam stashed away? I could use one. How are you staying here?" she asks, and I stop rifling through the box I've picked up and look at her a moment. How would she know Henry had Lorazepam? It strikes me as odd, but there's probably an easy explanation.

"I can help, ya know," she says.

"Help?"

"I can go through the boxes with you. We'll order delivery from Giovanni's, and there's enough booze, so yeah. I just need some sweats. These are Dior." She brushes her hands across her white pants.

I think about this a minute. She doesn't know what we're looking for. Hell, *I* don't know what we're looking for. Certainly not a confession note from the murderer, signed and notarized in one of the boxes. I'll know it when I see it if it's important, but there's no harm in having her help. She thinks I'm just sorting it out for keep and donation piles. It would be nice, actually. Who wants to do this alone?

We order a cheese lover's and mix martinis, and Monica is smart enough to play some neutral television show in the background—a PBS detective show, nothing that could cause me to spontaneously bawl like most songs will do these days. And we sit on the floor and start to pull off crinkly tape and rifle through endless kitsch and clutter. Mostly old textbooks, art supplies, and unframed canvases stored in neat piles with sheets of Bubble Wrap in between. I pack the mundane items back into the boxes they came from, give them a Sharpie *X* on top and move those in front of the kitchen counter to stay organized. After a couple hours of this, Monica is lying on the floor scrolling with her phone over her face, and I'm already tiring of this myself. What the hell am I even looking for?

Across the room, a handful of paintings catch my eye, so I cross to them and pluck out the one he painted of Monica.

"Aw, I always loved this one," I say, touching its rough surface, remembering Henry painting Monica at a cookout we had by the lake with a few couples from church.

"Oh, God. Look how fat I was. I look like I swallowed a Christmas ham."

"You were pregnant," I say.

"Still," she says.

I smile at the portrait of her in a blue sundress with her hand on her belly, looking out at the sparkling water.

"I love it," I say, then I perch on the edge of the couch and cut open a few bigger boxes; nothing but drop cloths and brushes.

"Well, you have to keep these, they were his favorite," Monica says, handing me a stack of old LP records.

I take them and flip through Nat King Cole, Dean Martin, Glenn Miller. I feel my cheeks go hot and red when she says this. If these were his favorites, I would know that. How does she know that? He only played them for dinner-party night because it made him seem sophisticated. What is happening right now?

"Dean Martin especially, right? Cooking bad pasta and singing 'You're Nobody Till Somebody Loves You' into a wooden spoon." She laughs, sort of singing along with the melody a moment, then stops cold. "Sorry. God, I can't imagine how hard this must be. Shit. Sorry," she says, but it's not that.

It's just, where is she getting this from? I've seen Henry sing Dean Martin into a wooden spoon cooking dinner, but when has she? It doesn't make sense to me. But I'm probably just

losing it in general with everything going on and not recalling. There could have been a dozen times he did this when I
was pouring drinks for guests on the patio for all I know. I'm
being ridiculous. And I'm becoming delusional. I really need
to keep it together.

"It's… I'm okay, yeah, we'll keep these." I tuck them into a
keep pile behind the sofa and take a sip of my martini. I need
a break from this.

She's mindlessly shaking out an old leather-bound book on
the floor—the way we've been doing all afternoon—looking
for any tucked-away photos we might miss, and then she turns
it back over and flips through a few of the pages. Suddenly, I
see her face fall. She closes the book and stares at the cover, then
opens it again, then quickly shoves it into a box next to her.

"What?" I snap.

"What?" She makes a terrible attempt at pretending she didn't
see something upsetting. "Shit," is all she says.

"What." I walk over, and she stands as if to stop me. "Monica. Seriously. What the hell?"

"It's…a journal I think. Unless he writes fiction. Does he…
write fiction at all? Maybe? Probably?"

"He wrote some poetry. We met in a poetry class in college,
you know that. Not… Why? What?"

"Oh, God, yes. That's probably what it is then. That makes
sense. Forget about it. Old bad poetry…" She tries to force a
laugh, but I snatch the book and carry it to the couch.

I open it, perched on my knees, and search for what she saw
that made that look fall across her face, and it only takes seconds to see. It's written in one form or another on every page.

"Oh, God." My hand flies to my mouth.

"Honey, maybe there's an explanation…like…"

"This is not poetry, this is…" I stand. I can't catch my breath.
My face feels numb, my hands are shaking. "I gotta go," I blurt,

grabbing my keys. "Sorry, I just...I gotta get out of here right now."

"Okay," she says. "I get it. I..." She quickly grabs her bag, leaves her heels and mimosa supplies, and follows me out. Then I lock the door and just run.

"I'm sorry," I say again, as I bolt to my car, and I have no idea where I'm going. For a brief moment, I want to run to Callum, and I don't understand why. His car is here, but all of his lights in his apartment are off, so I don't bother him.

I just drive. I just let the tears fall and beat the steering wheel with my fists and speed through the winding desert roads until I can figure out where to go.

How could you leave me with this? What have you done, Henry?

12

CASS

"What the hell happened!?" Callum says breathlessly as he runs to Eddie's side and kneels down. I stumble backward in shock because at first it looks like he's embracing the man or something, but it's not the reaction I expected. Then I see he's gone into autopilot and is performing CPR.

I've never seen anyone do this in real life, and it's actually really violent, the forced breathing, the pumps on Eddie's chest with his full body weight. There's a pile of pool towels for the kids stacked up on a shelf, and he's grabbed one to try to stop the bleeding.

I don't say that there's no point to all this. Words won't come at all. I sit on the sofa and bury my head in my hands, and I want to cover my ears so I don't hear the sounds he's making, and I want to scream. Instead, I sob quietly into my palms. After a few minutes, it's still, and I look up to see Callum slumped against the wall next to the body.

"Jesus," he whispers. He's covered in Eddie's blood. It's around his mouth, the side of his face, streaked down his white polo shirt. "He's gone."

I continue to cry, quietly at first, then in uncontrollable hiccuped sobs. I try to explain what happened, but have trouble catching my breath. "He tried to kill me."

"What?" he says, and I watch him take in the room, the scissors on the floor next to the desk, the marks on my neck.

"It's my fault, I know, but I just… It was an accident. He was choking me, Callum. You have to believe me. I was defending myself. He…" I trail off, not knowing what to say, the trauma of it all still making my head swim.

"Oh, my God—wha…why?" Callum says, pushing himself up from the floor and sitting across from me. He stares, fear and confusion in his eyes. He picks up a cloth from the table and wipes the blood from his face, shaking his head in disbelief and looking down at himself where Eddie's blood has soaked through his shirt. He looks like he's in shock. "Were you mixed up with him?" he asks me.

"Mixed up with him? No. What does that mean? I don't… I don't even…"

"Drugs. Did you buy from him? Why was he after you?"

"Drugs?" I say, pulling up the hem of my tank top to wipe my wet cheeks.

"So you don't know who he is then?"

"God, Callum. You're not making any sense!" I stand now, pacing. "I know who he is. It's fucking Eddie. You know Eddie. The idiot from 103. I found out he was hitting Rosa—like abusing her, so I recorded it. On my phone one night—so I showed him. Just now, I…said I'd turn him in if he didn't leave her alone. That's it."

"Oh, Jesus," he says. Now he's the one cradling his head in his hands.

"What? I'll tell the police the truth—that it was… I can explain that he had me by the throat." I try to keep talking but I lose my breath, and my cries are mixed with shrieks for air as I panic again when it all starts to settle in. "Oh, my God."

"Does anyone else have keys to the office?" he asks, and I

shake my head, but I don't know why he's asking. "And both doors are locked," he says, walking around and checking the locks, smoothing down the closed blinds. Then he stops cold and points to the security camera above the desk with wide eyes.

"Besides the owners who live in Phoenix? No. No residents. Why?"

"And both doors are locked," he says, walking around and checking the locks, smoothing down the closed blinds. Then he stops cold and points to the security camera above the desk with wide eyes.

"Off," I say. "Why? Everyone's gonna know anyway when I call it in. We have to call them now, or they'll think I'm hiding something—lying—they can tell that shit, you know. How long someone's been... Oh, my God. I'm a murderer," I say and before I can break down again, he stops me.

He puts his finger to his lips for me to keep it down. He sits on the couch and looks at Eddie's pack. I sit opposite him, rocking, keeping my cries hushed, shaking my head over and over in disbelief.

"Listen, I need you to stay calm, okay. But we're fucked. So just try to stay quiet, and I'm gonna explain something to you," he says, and he's beginning to terrify me almost more than the weight of what I've just done.

"This guy...isn't just dangerous, not just connected to a dozen people who could have us both decapitated and left in a Mexican desert tomorrow, he's cartel. And if I'm right about all this, we're beyond fucked if anyone connects us to this."

"You're not making sense. You're freaking me out, and you're not even making any goddamn sense. First, how the hell would you know that, and...you didn't even do anything! You just tried to help, so you're fine. I'm the one who's fucked."

"Everyone watched me threaten him by the pool, his blood is all over me. Literally! And shit... I searched him. I was tipped off he might be...that I should be careful, so I looked him up.

Online, you know? It was a half day at school, and when the students left, I learned all about the guy on a public school computer. Fuck. Fuuuuuck."

"So what? So fucking what? What the hell are you talking about? If he's that dangerous, then he's dead, and the cops will see who he was—believe it was an accident—that I was threatened. Good. That's good, right?"

"It's not the cops we need to worry about," he says, and I stand and begin to pace the floor with my hands over my eyes and my head tilted to the ceiling and try to calm down—try to take in what he's telling me.

"I don't know what that means. See…" I finally say, grabbing Eddie's bag. I start to dump out Eddie's things all over the dusty coffee table. "He's a long-haul trucker, it's all maps and porn and Red Bulls…" I start to rant manically but stop.

We both freeze when we see what actually falls out on the table—a gallon bag with many smaller, taped-up bags full of white powder and three stacks of hundred dollar bills bound in rubber bands.

"Oh, God, oh God, oh God…" I start to panic. I stand, then sit, then stand again and go to the office chair and try to breathe. "We gotta call the cops. Like right now."

"Shit," Callum says. "This guy doesn't work alone, you know. When your face is on the news, then what? I want to call the cops and get the fuck out of here as much as you do, trust me, but we have to think a minute."

I blow out a hard breath and go pick up the beer I was drinking and gulp it down. "Shit, shit, shit." I try to get a hold of myself. "How did you find out who he was? How would you know that?" I ask.

"Anna."

"Anna? The wife in 203?"

"Someone told her they saw him…like, *off* someone."

"Off someone? Like they saw Eddie actually kill a person?"

"Yeah, and she said that it was for a lesser offense than humiliating him in front of everyone at the pool the way I did and to watch my back."

"But you looked him up. The internet isn't gonna tell you he's cartel. So what did you find out that makes you think he's so dangerous? Just that? Could be a rumor."

Before he can answer me, I hear a small tap-tap at the office door. His face goes ghostly white, and neither of us move.

"Cass?" a small voice calls. "It's Sinatra. I'm here for my Happy Meal."

My hand clasps my heart, and I sit in front of the door and stare across the floor at the back of Eddie's head. A thread of blood trickles down the back of his pale neck. I imagine little Frank walking in and seeing this, and I feel bile push up into my throat.

"Fuck," I whisper.

"Who's Sinatra?" Callum mouths to me, but I just shake my head. He stays ducked down by the couch in the dim light, and we both stay perfectly still.

"Um, Cass? I'll take a Filet-O-Fish or whatever you think. It's okay if you forgot," he says, and now tears stream down my face, and I squeeze my chest with my hand and will myself to stay silent.

"Okay, sorry. Bye," his little voice says, and then I hear his footsteps down the concrete path until they disappear, and I collapse into my knees. Somehow my crying has morphed into numbness, then white-hot anger.

"He's dead," Callum whispers.

"What?"

"Eddie Bacco," he says.

"Really? Fuck you," I say and leap up. I don't care about maybe potential danger, because this is real danger. Maybe he is tied to bad guys who could behead me. That's a *maybe*. But I go to prison for sure if I don't call this in right now.

Then Callum hands me Eddie's wallet from his pile of things on the coffee table. "I mean, Eddie Bacco died two years ago— murdered. So who the hell is this?"

13

ANNA

I can't breathe, I can't think. I just drive the two-lane desert highway until it's almost dusk, stopping at a dive bar in the next town. I thought about going to my parents' house, but I just spent the two weeks after Henry died in their guest room in the fetal position, and I can't bring myself to go back or even talk about this. The only person I want—the only person I need— is Henry. He's who I would talk to about this, but even if he were here, I couldn't, because he's the one who betrayed me.

I sit in a back corner booth inside the Junkyard Tavern. It smells like stale beer and urine. A few drunk guys in cowboy boots are slumped over their drinks along the bar, the jukebox pipes George Strait and competes with the baseball game on the TV; it's all white noise and loneliness. I order a beer and stare down at the journal on the chipped vinyl tabletop. I open it again with trembling hands.

There are entries almost daily for a while, and then they slow down to a couple of times a week. They go back a year— before he moved his studio to The Sycamores even. I read one of the first entries:

I'm such a monster. How can I feel these things so strongly for someone besides my wife—my incredible wife? I know I should walk away from her and be a better man...especially for Anna. But I've never felt love like this before, and I didn't even know it was possible. That sounds so awful.

He was a poet and a painter and always said that keeping a journal means taking time for yourself and manifesting what you want in life, so it doesn't really surprise me to find such detail. Although I always assumed he was outlining ideas and goals and travel destinations. He did that sometimes, scribbled about the things we'd see in such-and-such a country when we went on a trip. He'd tell me I should journal—at least just list things I'm grateful for, because it's scientifically proven to support better health and happiness and all of that.

In all of my wildest dreams, this is never what I expected to find. We deeply trusted one another. We were best friends. I know it was a rocky couple years, and we started to change and grow apart, but I was certain it was a phase.

I read on:

People would never expect the two of us together. They wouldn't understand. It's wrong, I know, I know, I know. No matter how many times I've painted her, over and over—maybe a hundred times—I can't get enough. I cover my studio in brushstrokes of her body, and the longing for her is euphoric and painful at the same time, and then the shame rushes in. I have no right to be doing this.

I close the book and order a double Maker's Mark. I think for a moment I might begin to scream and wail and tear the pages out, but I don't do that. I find that I'm numb. It's too much all at once, and the shock of it brings a surge of adrenaline and waves of nausea. And then all variety of complicated questions.

Was I stupid for not knowing? Was my life a lie? Was this good man—and he was good—someone living another life altogether or just going through something? A crisis, a short-lived meltdown that I would have forgiven? Was he trying to claw his way out of the grips of his depression by any means that made him feel good—feel alive—or was he really in love?

A few men with weatherworn faces and muddy work boots shuffle in the front door. The workday is over. An REO Speed-wagon song blasts from the jukebox… "And I can't fight this feeling anymore." It makes me lurch. I push the whiskey away from me. I suddenly decide I need to stay sharp. I can drown myself in alcohol and pity, which I fully deserve to do, later. But right now, I need to think.

And the question I need to know the answer to is: What's with the fucking Sycamores? The only explanation he gave for choosing it was that it was a cheap place for a studio—something different for a while. He didn't need cheap, not really. I mean, not like *this*. He'd sold a couple pieces recently, and yeah, a teacher's salary is crap, and I was between jobs, but I had good savings, and he had a good gallery show. His painting "A Long Winter" was a portrait of an elderly homeless man with a deeply pockmarked face and longing eyes. Someone paid twenty-five thousand for it at the show, and afterward, Henry went to find the subject and gave him a few grand.

So did he really just hear the place was cheap? Or maybe he liked the grit the place seems to embody, and then as an added bonus, he happened to have a private studio to see this woman and paint her and sleep with her. Or did he choose this studio *because* of her? Did Callum even tell him about a vacancy like Henry said, or did he meet the woman that time he went to the pool barbecue Callum invited him to after school, and then he made it happen?

I remember vaguely; it was Memorial Day weekend, and I was supposed to come here with him. Some of the teachers were gonna swim in the pool and grill. I don't remember why I couldn't go. I think I had a work trip, but a few weeks later Henry mentioned the studio. So which came first?

I need to find out two things right now. Does anyone know of a woman who doesn't live at The Sycamores but hangs around a lot? The pool girls like to gossip. That shouldn't be too hard to find out.

And then I am going to find this Mira Medford, the high school girl Callum told me there were rumors about. *I know it's wrong*, he says in his journal. *People would never expect us together*, he says. Would he really do this to us—to her, to *himself*—with a student?

I pull my phone from my pocket and poke at it with my finger. Mira Medford Vadnais High School. It's a unique enough name, and I know her school and town, so images pop right up. The first is of a redheaded girl with pale skin and a smattering of freckles across her nose. She's thin-framed and delicately pretty. She's wearing a racing swimsuit and holding up a silver medal. A few more photos show her diving off a swimmer's block, her body expertly curved to plunge into the water with the least amount of splash and race the breaststroke. That's her stroke, it looks like. She has other group photos with the swim team who are going to state this year. Mira, the redheaded swimmer. I have a face now. Could this be his obsession?

I leave a twenty on the booth and walk out of the bar, ignoring two gross men saying something like "sweetheart" or "where ya goin', baby?" before I reach the door and get in my car. I need to go back to The Sycamores and find Callum. Getting him to give me more information about this girl, or an address perhaps, won't be easy, but I have to try.

When I arrive in the parking lot, the pool area is buzzing with residents setting up for their Friday barbecue. Rosa is waving flies from the potato salad, Babs is pouring vodka into the punch bowl. The kids are running wild and stealing cookies off the food table, avoiding swats on their hands from distracted mothers.

Before I cross to my unit, I see Callum's mailbox sitting open next to the front office. I go over to see the messenger bag he always has slung over his shoulder, resting on the ground underneath his mailbox. I close the box door and look around. It's as if he was checking his mail before he got abducted by aliens, or at least that's the creepy energy I'm picking up on.

I text him first and ask if we can talk. No reply. Maybe he just laid it down there a minute and went into the office for something. I move to the office door and turn the handle. Locked. It's never locked. In fact, it's usually wide open and filled with oddball residents hanging around.

"Hello?" I knock a couple of times. "Callum? Cass? You in there?"

I know I hear movement inside. I think I hear a whisper, but nobody answers. There's a back door, I remember, so I walk to the back of the small building. Something's going on in there. I can feel it.

14

CASS

After Callum has Eddie's many driver's licenses spread out on the office desk and we are searching the names of each one on the office computer, I hear it. A knock on the door. It's Anna. She calls for both of us, but then after a few moments, I hear her footsteps disappear down the path, and I exhale.

When the back door starts to open, my heart drops to my stomach so quickly that my knees almost buckle and my head buzzes, bursts of lights flash behind my eyes, and I think I'll faint right there on the floor. And even though I know it's locked, it's only a chain, so it smashes open the three inches the chain allows before it catches.

"Hello?" she calls again.

Callum has leaped to his feet but is now frozen in place, his hands cupped over his mouth, his body hovering above the office chair. He looks like a mannequin he's so still. I'm hiding behind the wall that separates the front area with the couch and coffee table from the small back hall where the back door is. Neither of us move or breathe. How did she even know there was a back door? The back of the building only has a spread of rocks and dirt where I park. You wouldn't even notice it unless you were lurking around. She doesn't seem the type.

"Okay then," Anna says. "Whatever."

I hear her shuffling around a few more moments. The light of a cell phone turns the crack of light through the door blue, then it goes dark, and her footsteps retreat once more.

Callum's phone pings, and we still don't move, but he looks down at the desk as it lights up. I shoot him a *what the hell* look. Is she texting him? Why? After a couple more minutes pass, I tiptoe over to the desk, and he sits back down in front of the computer and picks up his phone.

"She says, 'I have your bag and I need to talk to you,'" he whispers, and shrugs.

"Goddammit, Callum, you're not..." I don't need to finish the sentence for him to know I'm asking if there's something between them, and then I instantly feel a stab of regret, remembering how recently he lost his wife.

"Are you kidding?" he asks.

"Sorry. Well, don't respond to her. Shit. Let's just... Did you find anything yet?" I ask, focusing back on the search for the names on the IDs.

Callum exhales. He looks at them again. The first name is Randall Mont, age 33, from Bozeman, Montana. Callum types in the name, and it comes right up. The same face on the ID pops up in some news articles from a couple years ago. Deceased. Murdered. My eyes scan the paragraphs in disbelief. Body burned alive in a car out in the desert. Remains identified with dental records.

We don't speak. I see his hands shake as he types the next name in the pile of IDs.

Kurt Walters, 46, from New Port. The face comes up again. Dead. Foul play. Shot execution-style in his own driveway.

"Jesus, fuck. What? What does this mean?" I hiss, because I can't scream it.

Callum picks up the next ID and shows it to me. I think my heart stops. I gasp and cover my mouth. It's a photo of Eddie Bacco. It's his face, but his name is really...Victor Becerra?

I grab Eddie's wallet and look at the ID he actually uses, the one that says Eduardo Bacco, and then sit next to Callum, holding it next to the Victor Becerra ID.

"Shit," he says.

"Eddie's ID is a guy who kind of looks like him—he could pass for this guy if nobody knew any better. But Eduardo Bacco from Alberta, Canada, is dead. And Victor Becerra is the real Eddie."

"So he..." Callum says, then stops. Maybe not wanting to say it out loud—that the body on the office floor is really named Victor, and he kept the identities of his victims, and all the talk about danger and cartel is now a very real thing.

Callum types in the rest of the names on the remaining IDs. Ronald Hardin, Jimmy Diaz, Albert Bashir... All dead. All attached to lengthy stories about unsolved murder, drug-related crimes, known ties to cartel, or low-level dealers.

A sharp bark of shocked laughter escapes my lips. We most certainly fucked with the wrong guy. "So we're basically dead then," I say, leaning my hands on the desk and hanging my head, trying to breathe.

We both leap at the sound of the dead man's phone ringing. I look down at the glowing screen buzzing across the coffee table. "Blocked number," I say, and we both just stare at it until it stops.

A car horn honks outside on the street. I hold my chest, feeling like I might literally have a heart attack from the stress of it all. I peek through the front curtains and see a black car with tinted windows parked across the street, then the phone rings again.

"Don't touch it," Callum whispers.

"Why the fuck would I touch it?" I spit back.

The phone stops. We don't move. It rings one last time, and when it finally stops, the car screeches away from the curb and disappears.

I collapse onto the couch. "We're dead."

"I mean..." Callum says. "Eddie, Victor—whatever his name is, he doesn't do this alone. I guess, yeah. If the news shows you—*us*...attached to...whatever it might be, self-defense, an accident, manslaughter, it doesn't really matter. We killed what looks to be one of their head honchos. This is...fucking bad. But I mean what choice do we have? I don't know. I guess we do call the police. What the fuck else can we do?"

"How do we explain the massive gap between the time of death and calling the cops? They can figure that shit out, ya know," I say, and then I feel a tap at my heel and see a stream of blood that has made its way across the floor, pooling around my flip-flop. "Oh, God," I whimper. I hop up and sit on the desk, kicking off both of my shoes. "Oooh God."

"Okay, calm down," Callum says. "We need to stay level-headed here. I'm telling you. The police will learn who he is and believe you when you say you panicked and saw his IDs and didn't know what to do—I'm not really worried about getting arrested. I'm worried about..."

"Retaliation," I finish his sentence.

"A thousand percent worse than jail," he says.

I imagine myself asleep in bed one night while a figure in black silently picks the window lock and slips into my room, slitting my throat in one sweeping motion, ear to ear, before dropping my body into a storage container full of sodium hydroxide...and in a matter of hours, I'm liquefied into the consistency of mineral oil and dumped into the Rio Grande. *What have I done, what have I done?*

"Okay," I say. "What if we don't call the police?"

I can hear more people arriving at the pool deck outside as dusk sets in—kids are shouting to one another, the distinct throaty laugh of Babs floats over the hum of chatter, the dog in 119 barks. The aroma of grilled onions is heavy in the air. We're both expected to be out there.

"God, I mean... I know. I know what you're saying, but I just don't think we can do that. We're not...we don't have the slightest idea how to...do something like that. Shit. No. It's too... I don't even know anymore. I thought of that, too, for a second, but now I don't know."

"He's an absolute fucking monster, right?" I say, and Callum nods. "So maybe we're not doing such a terrible thing if we just...don't tell anyone." Even as I say it, I want to take it back and call the police and reverse time and never have seen him hurt his wife and never have interfered and never have agreed to move to this shit-fuck hellhole to begin with.

"His wife has to be in on it. Rosa. She must be a part of this," he says, sitting up straight and looking again at the ID of Eduardo Bacco. He types the name into the computer again and scrolls some stories.

"Eduardo Bacco was murdered just over five years ago, so if Victor has been using his identity since then, and he married Rosa around four years ago...what are the odds that she knows who he is? What he does? Does she think he's Eddie—totally oblivious, or should we be worried about her, too?" he asks, then pushes the chair away from the desk and leans his head back and runs his hands over his face. For a moment, I think he might cry again, but then he stands abruptly and faces the window. He peeks out the blinds on the poolside of the room and looks at the party forming on the deck.

"I don't think she knows. She has a kid to protect. I don't think she's in on it," I start to say, then shift gears. "It doesn't matter because she'll never know."

"It might matter," he says. "Does she know he was coming in here? Does she know what you were going to do?"

"No. No. He was leaving—he was heading out for two

weeks. He was about to leave. Oh, my God. Right. He was leaving…on the road. Nobody will miss him for a while. We have time, I mean not two weeks, but a couple days before it will start to be questioned, right?" I say, but I don't even really know what I'm saying.

Neither of us speak for several minutes. Our minds both reeling, rationalizing, playing the tape forward.

"This is fucking crazy," Callum finally mutters.

"We can't just sit here like this. We're expected out there, and…people will start to notice the blinds closed and door locked. It will look suspicious. We have to do something," I say. I feel the panic rising again like a wave in my chest.

"We call the police, Cass," he says and then he adds, "Right?" with doubt in his voice. "Shit. I don't know. Shit." He lets out a growl of frustration.

I just start talking without knowing really what I'm doing. "We wipe off his phone and put it in his truck. It won't be odd that his phone records show it pinging here, of course, and he was getting a ride, so it won't be odd that his truck stays here while he's gone."

"A ride." Callum barks a humorless laugh. "The shady car full of other drug lords and murderer-types out front was his ride to his regular-guy job as a trucker. Wow. I mean. How is this even happening? This shit doesn't happen to normal people. This is…" He cradles his head in his hands and trails off.

"My car is right outside that back door. What if we…we wrap him up? There's a closet full of linens by the back door. We can leave him in there till it gets dark and then put him in my car."

"Jesus," Callum says, but his eyes are darting back and forth, contemplating this, I can tell.

What choice do we have? He is a monster. He is a terrible person, and it's a civic duty to have gotten him off the streets. I repeat these thoughts to myself.

"Why should we be punished—no…very likely *killed*—for

happening across the wrong sociopath? He's dead either way. So we either risk our lives, and by risk I mean probably get slaughtered in our sleep, or we just don't tell anyone. It was self-defense. We didn't do anything wrong. It's his fucking fault we're in this mess."

"Okay," Callum blurts.

"What?" I say, unsure I even wanted him to agree, confused and dizzy and nauseous with all of this.

But when we look at one another, the decision is made. The threat is too great. I think about all of the alias names we searched on the office computer and how it implicates us, but I have to believe we will be so far from suspects of any kind that it will never be discovered. Even so, I sit back down in front of the screen and tell Callum to get Eddie to the utility room, and I'll get the cleaning supplies and sheets.

"We'll take turns at the party," I say. "I'll clean, and you tell them I got a call from management about a leak in one of the vacants, but I'll be there. Then you slip away once you're seen at the party for a while, and I'll stop in for a bit—make it look normal because if anyone looks back on this night and says we were gone or acting weird… If the shit hits the fan with all this, we can't be remembered being fucking weird."

He nods, silently agreeing.

I try not to throw up when he grabs under Eddie's armpits and pulls him across the concrete floor, leaving ribbons of red in his wake. Callum is ghostly white, and I see him trying to slow his breath and calm himself with every step.

Once Eddie's locked in the utility room, Callum takes off his blood-soaked shirt and cleans up in the laundry room sink. There are boxes of clothes and other crap people have left after they moved out lining the walls in the back closet, and I tell him he can find a T-shirt there. When he comes out, he's wearing a stranger's pale green shirt, and his eyes are glossy and fearful.

"God," he says.

"I know," I whisper. "Go."

Callum slips out the back door.

I tremble as I walk to the closet and fill the mop bucket with water and bleach. I pull all the hand towels I can find off the shelves and pour a bottle of floor cleaner over the blood until it turns pink and translucent. Then I kneel on the floor and start to scrub until the shaking becomes uncontrollable and my body convulses as I sob harder than I ever have before.

15

ANNA

I swear I heard something inside that front office. The blinds are closed, and it's locked which is unusual on its own, but there was movement. I know it. I toss Callum's bag onto Henry's small desk inside the front door and look around at this unknowable place that looks very different than it did a few hours ago. It's no longer filled with his scent and his work and his personal things I treasure, it's now filled with potential clues and suspicion.

If he painted her a hundred times, where the fuck are all these paintings? Not at our house that I cleared out, not in the garage or with his school things, or the storage unit we kept. I've been through every inch. There are countless stacks of unframed canvas and paper portraits stacked against the walls. I grab at the pile closest to me and start sifting through them. Most of them are faces of strangers—volunteers who sat for him, some homeless person who he paid in hot meals in exchange for painting them, some residents here. Babs's face smiles a toothy grin in an eight-by-ten oil on canvas. She holds a gin martini and has a red boa wrapped around her neck. A few paintings are snapshots in time. He painted the ladies playing cards by the pool with a streaky orange sunset on the horizon behind the building. There are no faces I see painted more than once, let alone a hundred goddamn times.

I push the stack aside and look through another—same thing. Most of these I've seen. Some are unfinished. None are faces painted again and again. I don't understand. What did he do with them all?

I lie flat on the floor and stare at the ceiling fan. I try to decide if I'm more angry at him for what he's done to us, or at myself for being so removed that I didn't even have an inkling something like this could happen. How did I make him feel that if he really loved someone else, he was still stuck with me? I can admit we were closer to best friends than red-hot lovers over the last few years. Would I have understood? Let him go? Forgiven him—told him to go have the family he wanted? He didn't believe I would, or he wouldn't have hidden it. If I'm honest with myself, I don't know how I would have reacted. I'd probably just hold on tighter until I suffocated our relationship. He's all I've ever known. No matter what he wanted, he'd never break my heart, and my body aches at the thought of this. I'm utterly exhausted.

I hear a muffled rendition of "Sweet Home Alabama" piping from someone's Bluetooth speaker on the pool deck. A sweet and rich smoky scent hangs heavy in the hot night air, and the din of conversations and barks of laughter rise and fall from the party outside. I slip out the door and sit on the ugly chair on the balcony. I see Rosa and Crystal playing cards, face-tattoo guy flips burgers on a charcoal grill, and Jackie tries to make Earl Jr. eat corn on the cob, but he throws it into the pool and makes all the little girls scream.

Mary from 109 tries to coax a sad-looking boy to play with the other kids, and Gwen, who I met the once, is dancing by herself in a bikini top and cutoffs, trying to attract some male attention and waving her blue Big Gulp over her head to the slow beat of the music. Then I see Barry, who sees me and waves his hands in the air. Shit.

"Anna!" He hurriedly pulls a Corona out of a cooler full of ice water and holds it up, half dancing to the song and gesturing me to come down. "You gotta come. You're part of the family now."

As much as this sentiment horrifies me, another part of me craves some distraction and cold beer and does not want to sit here alone right now. I make my way down the concrete stairs and take the beer from him.

Crystal pulls out a plastic chair for me to sit, and I join them at the card table, timidly perched at the edge of my seat and picking at the Corona label on my bottle. *Who is it?* I wonder. Is his lover one of these women? That's hard to imagine, but they must know something.

Rosa hands me a paper plate with a hot dog and lump of potato salad on it, and I smile and take it with no intention of actually eating it. Jackie asks if I want to be dealt into gin rummy, and I decline. Then Barry pulls up the drink cooler to sit next to me and adds himself to the conversation.

"Beat it, Barry," Crystal says, and it seems that she notices his hovering is making me uncomfortable, but I'm not sure if she actually picks up on that or they're just hardwired to beat up on Barry.

"Girls only," Jackie adds.

"Yeah, okay," Barry says, holding his plate of beans and skulking away to sit with a few people I don't recall the names of. I feel like I'm back in a middle school cafeteria for a moment. He laughs too loud at someone's joke and peers over his shoulder at us a few times.

"How are you settling in?" Rosa asks.

"Oh, uh…fine. Thanks."

"For fuck's sake, Gordy. Just eat it!" Jackie screams, shocking me, my hand flying to my heart, and then I realize she's talking to her six-year-old who's crying because the top of his bun fell off his hamburger. "Five second rule. Take a pill." She wipes the bun off on her leg and puts it back on Gordy's plate.

He seems satisfied with this and sits on the ground with a Peppa Pig towel draped over his shoulders and eats.

"We sure miss Henry around here," Crystal says. "I hope it's okay to say that." Then she stands suddenly and yells, "Uh-uh!" with a waggle of her index finger, and her girls stop running around the pool's edge and slow it down to a speed walk as they giggle and elbow one another.

"Of course," I say. "I was actually hoping to... I guess, ask a couple questions about him—his life here," I say.

The women all exchange a look that I can't interpret.

"Sure," Jackie says, kicking her feet up onto Barry's cooler and sipping her wine cooler. Of course, nobody here knows about foul play, they think it was suicide. And unless it was with one of them, I have to assume they don't know about the affair, so maybe if I lead with his state of mind they'll open up a bit, assuming I am trying to understand his depression or mental state...which I suppose I'm also trying to do.

"Did he have a lot of friends here? Was he close to anyone?" I say, already gathering that he was the life of the party around here somehow.

"Oh, Christ," Crystal says. "Everyone loved him, especially the ladies. I'm pretty sure everyone here had the hots for him."

"Crystal!" Rosa says with a look that tells her to have some respect.

"She asked!" Crystal says. "I mean, we need a fantasy life, and Bobby is... I don't know. He has a pair of tits tattooed on his neck, kinda hard to get excited about that." All the girls laugh. "And Barry...sheesh."

"He reads palms and collects swords," Rosa adds. "If you like goth, comic books, and *Dungeons & Dragons*, he might be your guy."

"And Callum," Jackie says. "He's hot."

"Hot," Crystal repeats.

"But he's grieving and just…off-limits," Jackie says. "Wait," she continues. "That sounds bad. Not that Henry was fair game. He was your… Of course, I just mean…he was fun to have a crush on. Innocent, for realz! But there aren't many non–losers around here, and he was so nice to everyone. So it's hard to say who he was close to. We all sort of doted on him."

"No," I say. "It's fine. It's kind of nice actually." And it is nice. Weird but nice that he found a sort of home here, in a strange way.

"He painted caricatures of the kids by the pool sometimes," Rosa says as she squirts a generous mound of mustard on a chicken wing.

I don't really know how to ask these people what I want to know. If he acted strange. Did he get involved with this Eddie guy—with drugs or something? Did the woman he loved meet him here and maybe they noticed a stranger in and out of his door? Did he have enemies?

"So you didn't notice him hanging around a lot with any- one in particular—acting, I don't know, different in any way?"

"I don't know. I didn't stalk him or anything," Crystal says. "But nothing stands out. Why?"

"God, Crystal. She wants to know if he was depressed! Read the room," Jackie barks. "He didn't have trouble with no one." She lights a cigarette, and her face becomes dark and somber.

"We were all surprised to hear about…what happened. I guess he was down and all. Depressed, whatever, but…nobody thought, like, suicidal," Rosa says. She pours a Coke into a plas- tic cup and hands it to her son, who tugs at her dress.

"So he painted most of you, I guess."

"Oh, yeah!" Crystal grins. "Remember when you sat for him, Jackie?" Rosa and Crystal start to shake with laughter.

"Fuck you, Crystal," Jackie says, tossing her hand of cards at the back of Crystal's head as she's bent over laughing into her knees.

"What?" I ask.

"She was so mad 'cause he painted all her fat rolls." Crystal is flush with tears rolling down her face. "She asked him to Photoshop them out! Photoshop!"

Rosa and Crystal are now in hysterics, and Jackie has her arms folded and her lips pursed.

"Who's the fat one, huh, huh?" Jackie leans over and pinches the flesh under Crystal's chin.

"I'm pregnant, you asshole," Crystal yells and swats at Jackie with a pool noodle she picked up from the ground. Rosa is snorting and slapping her knee.

Just then, I see Callum slip out the door of the front office and skirt around the side of the building, then waltz into the barbecue like nothing in the world is the matter. I knew he was in there. What the hell? He doesn't answer the door or my text and then sneaks out? Does he have a thing with Cass? Oh, my God, that has to be it. He was "busy" apparently.

Well, now that I know his little secret, maybe he'll be more inclined to help me and give me some more information about this Mira Medford… I watch him try to act casual as he inserts himself into a circle of people chatting. He's really bad at it, though. He seems obviously nervous and awkward. He pats Barry on the back, and someone hands him a beer. He looks around, side to side, and kind of rocks on his heels a bit.

Jesus, Callum. it's just sex. You didn't rob a bank. Calm down, I think as he notices me out of the corner of his eye and gives a funny little nod of recognition in my direction.

By this point, Crystal and Jackie are pinching each other's guts and hurling insults and one another, and Rosa is flicking playing cards at them, telling them to grow up. I write my number on a square of paper towel and hand it to Rosa.

"If you think of anything—like…just, anything you recall about Henry, especially the last few weeks, call me…if you don't mind."

Rosa stops flicking cards and takes my number. "Yeah. Of course," she says. "I really am so sorry."

"Thanks," I say, and head across the pool deck to where Callum stands. I stand next to him and butt into the conversation.

David, with all the cats, sits in a motorized scooter with a cat in the handlebar basket and picks at a paper plate of ribs balanced on his knee. Babs is telling an animated story about meeting Don Henley once at an airport, from what I can gather, but pauses to wink when she sees me.

"Oh, Anna!" Barry says, rushing to pick up a Styrofoam cup of punch from a foldout table next to the grill. "Here. Here ya go. Does everyone—has everyone met Anna?" he says eagerly.

"No, thanks," I say, holding my hand out to reject the punch. "I just wondered if you wanted your bag," I say to Callum, and I see his neck redden around the collar.

Barry and David look to Callum and then back to me like there might be a scandal about to be revealed.

"I think you left it by the mailbox, so I grabbed it for safekeeping," I say, and they all seem to accept this, and Babs continues her story.

"Oh, thank you," he says and excuses himself from the group.

"I'll get it," I say, and he starts to follow me to the stairs before we both notice a handful of people staring in our direction.

"I'll just wait here." He smiles bashfully.

When I retrieve his bag and hand it back, I say, "So, what's going on in that office?" and he looks, for a moment, like he'll pass out. I don't really care if he likes me, though. I just need to get the information I want from him without wasting any-more time.

"What?" is all he says, but his face betrays him as the blood drains from it.

"I saw you leave the office. I knocked earlier, texted. I mean it's none of my business about...whatever you got going on."

"Oh, God. No." He stops me quickly. "That's— No. Op-posite. It's the opposite of what you're thinking," he says, re-laxing a little.

"Opposite," I ask.

"Cass and... No. She was having...a meltdown, is all. She has this ex. He just walked out on her—I guess in a pretty epic breakup—like it could be a reality show bad. That's why she had to move here. After years together, he just—" He makes a *poof* gesture with his hands. "And she tends to sort of lose it every now and then. I was... I just stopped by to get a pack-age, and she was... I don't even know, like maybe suicidal, so I... Oh. God. I'm sorry." He cups his hand over his mouth, and his eyes flick back and forth. "I..."

"No, it's okay," I say. "I'm sorry. I didn't realize. I'm glad someone was there for her. You just seemed...nervous when you came out, so I assumed. Sorry."

"Oh. Well...yeah. It was just a lot to take in. Everything is...a lot lately," he says, and I nod in agreement. "I'm just...really tired," he says, and I have this fierce desire to hug him—hold him and tell him we'll both be okay just for the momentary comfort of it—to smell the trace of cologne on his skin and feel his arms around my back. I don't know why. I can't explain it. For a brief moment, I almost open my arms and pull him into me, but I don't. Of course I don't. What am I even thinking?

"So she had her heart broken," I say, knowing both of us can understand in a deep way—a more profound way than she'll ever know. He sighs, nods, and we look at each other. I decide in that moment not to ask him about the schoolgirl. I'll find her myself.

"Well, good night," I say, and I think he looks at me with a longing in his eyes, too, but I can't be sure. And it's probably disgusting that I could even feel this hunger for someone, but loneliness does funny things, and loss coupled with betrayal turns that into something hollow and desperate and… indescribable.

"'Night," he says, and walks away, back to the circle where Babs is still flailing her arms and talking away, and he sort of hugs himself and looks very small and impossibly sad, somehow.

At the top of the stairs, before I go inside, I see Cass come out of the office. She looks like a complete mess. Her face is red and swollen, and I can see that even from here. She walks with slumped shoulders over to the drinks cooler, pulls out a beer, and sits in a folding chair away from the group like a wounded animal. I guess Callum was telling the truth. I know what sorrow and fear mixed together look like, and that's exactly what her face reads.

Inside, I sit on the floor next to the messy piles of stretched canvas paintings and paper drawings. I close my eyes and absorb the sound of a few of the residents singing along to a Steely Dan song and the kids' laughter and the homey smells of food cooking, and I don't know whether to scream until my lungs are bruised and raw or if I'm comforted by it all for just a moment—for the life that goes on even though it feels like the world has truly ended.

I spread out a new stack of canvas paintings protected inside plastic sleeves, and just before I decide to let go for the night and go to sleep, one of the paintings stands out. My heart speeds up, and I pick up the image.

It's Cass. He's painted Cass. She's laughing. She has a strand of dyed pink hair falling across her eyes, and her elbows are leaning on her knees. She's looking away—to the side, her mouth wide in a belly laugh, her eyes sparkling. So, wait a second. Maybe there is only one painted image here and not one hundred, or maybe I just haven't found them yet, but this is not a depressed, suicidal, post-breakup woman. If she moved here because of a breakup, then she met Henry afterward. So why is she so happy? This is dated just weeks ago. She's mourning a loss. She had her heart broken. By who?

Henry, is this who you painted a hundred times and couldn't get enough of?

16

CASS

I didn't answer any maintenance calls today. I know what I said—don't act off. Don't give anyone a reason to think back on this time and recall strange behavior, but I can't do it. I cannot patch a leaky sink hose or replace the doorknob in 110. I can't go into the office for supplies or to answer emails—the office where Eddie is wrapped in bedsheets and lying on the utility closet floor with the AC cranked too high because neither of us want to Google how long it takes for a body to start to putrefy and smell.

I just sit on the floor of my apartment next to the bed and vacillate between certainty that we did the right thing and are national goddamn heroes for getting this man off the streets, and unparalleled terror and guilt—a feeling like I'll never be able to live with myself, and I'm going directly to hell.

Four days. I think it's longer than I assumed, even in this heat. I saw it in a movie once, and I think it can take four days before the smell starts to become noticeable. After everyone left the pool and were long asleep, and the air was still in the small hours of the morning, I turned off Eddie's phone and slipped it into the open slit of the passenger window of his truck. Then

I wished I would have used his phone to look it up because when they find it, they won't trace it back to me. I think we have time, though.

My phone pings with a message. I ignore it. It won't be Callum. We agreed no texts or calls between us. We'd meet in the office tonight, and we'd drive after dark and find a place to…leave him.

When it pings again, I grab for my phone off the nightstand and look at it. It's Rosa. Oh, God. Rosa. Why is she texting me? She never texts me.

I open it, my heart pounding. And then…it's just a photo of Crystal in a red spandex dress that barely covers her crotch. The text beneath it says, **ready to party**. I don't know why she's sending me this, so I just respond with a smiley face and try to steady my breath and not throw up.

I stay this way until late in the afternoon when I finally force myself to leave my bedroom and make a cup of coffee. I slip a T-shirt and shorts on and look out at the courtyard and pool deck. It's like nothing happened. It's just a sunny Saturday, like any other.

Sylvie waters her plants on her balcony, Letty in 102 paints her toenails on a lawn chair, and the pool girls are all playing cards with the kids running amok.

How does Rosa not wonder why Eddie hasn't contacted her since last night? He doesn't seem like the husband who checks in and offers I miss you's or I love you's every night, that's for sure, but it won't be long. A day or two, she might assume a lost phone or bad road signal, but not for long.

I think about Frank and how much I disappointed him in a world of people who do nothing but disappoint him, and I feel again like I could be sick. I draw the curtains and sit at the kitchen table in the cold dark of my small apartment until it's time to meet Callum.

A few hours later, I stand inside the back door of the frigidly cold office. The sharp smell of bleach and floor cleaner sting my eyes, and I'm afraid to move until Callum gets here, because somehow the irrational fear that Eddie could somehow not be dead and instead be lying in wait to murder me is a real, visceral feeling, no matter how ridiculous it is.

When Callum slips in the back door, pale and panicked-looking, I realize that he might be worse at this than me. I'm a wreck, but he increasingly does not seem like the kind of guy who can actually pull this off without giving us away. I don't have much of a choice now, though.

He takes a deep breath and then blows it out with puffed cheeks. "Okay," is all he says.

"I've been thinking about it, and I think maybe we just drive east into the desert. There's not much between here and Amarillo, so we just... I don't know... Just stop when it seems deserted enough," I say.

I have been thinking about this through the night and all day. I think about true crime shows and how they catch people, and I think about DNA and forensics and mortality and hell, and I think about my future and how we should have probably called the police. Maybe. I don't know. I don't know anything anymore, except that I want this to be over.

"And then what?" he asks, and it's confirmed that I truly do need to take the lead on this. I feel outside of my body and like a completely different person, saying the things I'm saying.

"Then we dig." It comes out in an uncertain whisper. But before he can even react, there is a hard rap at the front door of the office. We both leap and stifle a yelp.

"Who the fuck is that?" he mouths silently with a look of accusation in his expression, like I invited folks over for a cocktail party right now.

I respond with an exaggerated shrug, and then I hear them—the pool girls, giggling and hooting.

"Cass, come on! We're gonna be late, yo," Crystal says.

"What are they doing here?" Callum asks, and it hits me. The photo Rosa sent with Crystal in her booty dress. The party.

"Shit," I say back in a hushed voice. "We're all supposed to go into Santa Fe for the Summer Blitz."

"The what?"

"It's a big charity ball thing."

"Why are they going?" His whisper is sounding more like a hiss, and I can see the spit fly from the corners of his mouth.

"It's a long story. But I sent in a formal RSVP with all our names. Shit, shit. What do I tell them? I can say I'm sick. Shit." I hear them knock again.

"Get the lead out, Cass."

"You have to go," he says, shaking his head and squeezing the balls of his hands against his eyes for a moment. "You're the one who said the way we act right now is gonna be re-membered if this is traced back to The Sycamores. You already look...sort of terrible, and they're gonna wonder what's up with you," he says with a sigh.

"What about this?" I gesture wildly around the room in no particular direction.

"When you come back," he says, taking an exaggerated deep breath and shaking his head.

"My keys are there," I say, nodding to the desk. "To my car. My car is a few feet from the back door. When everyone is gone, and it's dark, you should..." I don't finish my sentence. I swallow hard and point my chin toward the closet Eddie is in. "You know." We'd already discussed using my car because of the trunk, not like his SUV hatch with windows on all sides, and there are already paint tarps in the trunk, so I don't say the rest of the words. He understands. Eddie isn't a huge guy, so Callum can move him on his own while it's quiet here.

"And when I'm back, I'll make it a point to pass your window. I'll pretend to check the sprinklers or something...so you know," I say, and I hear Crystal knocking again.

"For Christ's sake, Cass. Come on!"

"Fine. Go," Callum says, then he carefully opens the back door and disappears, and I open the front door where I'm first hit with Crystal's dress. It sparkles to a blinding level, and her pregnant belly stretches it to its limit. A long line of cleavage and bare thighs are all you see. Jackie is in an equally inappropriate getup. Her minidress is black leather and laced up the sides, like a goth Halloween costume she found at Hot Topic. And Rosa, bless her, wears a navy lace knee-length dress that looks like she's the mother of a bride at a wedding or headed to Mass.

Fuck me, I can't do this. What was I thinking? I got caught up in a moment wanting to go to this thing, not considering *this* is what I was bringing along and how it will make me look. There's gotta be a way out.

"What are you *wearing*?" Jackie asks in disgust, and I can't believe that she, of all people, is asking me that. Until I realize that I'm in shorts and a dirty T-shirt, with a nest of matted hair piled on my head and bags under my eyes.

"I…"

"Bitch, you forgot!" Jackie says. "Uh-uh! Well, we're going! I got a buncha minis and some Bloody Mary mix in my bra, and I'm ready to party. Come on. Let's get you dressed," she says, pulling me out the door.

Then I see Barry pull up in Crystal's minivan.

"We have a chauffeur," Rosa says with a giggle. He honks and nods. "We'll be a few minutes, Bare. Stay there."

By the time I've dressed and the girls have picked through my closet full of Versace and Dolce and Oscar de la Renta dresses and questioned again why the fuck I'm here and called me "rich bitch" seventy-five times, we're finally on the way. Barry has a playlist for the occasion and plays the role of chauffeur with enthusiasm, and Crystal has the back set up like a party bus with an ice-cream bucket of ice chilling peach wine coolers and some disco ball setting on her phone that's spinning red and pink lights across the roof. It reminds me of the roller rink I went to as a kid, and it's still as nauseating. Jackie starts yelling, "Shots, shots, shots-shots-sha-shots," and Barry gives a fist bump from the front seat. I look at Rosa, smiling in her church dress and shyly lifting her wine cooler to cheers Jackie, and I'm so filled with shame and regret I can barely keep a neutral face, let alone the smiling party face they all want from me.

My first mistake of the night is taking the tequila shot from Jackie. I decide I need to get through this without thinking about Eddie and what awaits me when I get back to The Sycamores. I need to make this night about an alibi—a happy-go-lucky Cass who would never hang out with the wife of the man she murdered, because she's not a psychopath. Everything is normal. Everything will be fine.

Inside the Eldorado Hotel ballroom, a crystal chandelier and oversize vases of white daffodils greet us at the entry. A long table full of tiny crème brûlées and cucumber sandwiches, caprese and bruschetta, and chocolate-covered strawberries are all arranged in neat rows on white linen tablecloths. There's an enormous tiered cake in the center and a rum punch station.

"Holy fucking shit," Crystal says with her mouth gaping open.

"There's a chocolate fountain." Rosa giggles, jabbing Jackie with one elbow.

"They have bacon-wrapped shrimp. I love bacon-wrapped shrimp," Jackie says, a look of bewilderment across her face.

"Don't worry. I brought my big purse," Crystal says, and I find that my reaction to this, my visceral *oh my God, what have I done? Kill me please* reaction to standing next to them in this environment, has become such a common feeling over the last seven months, I'm almost numb instead.

My eyes scan the room for Reid and Kimmy. I don't see them, but I do see Andrea and Becca. At one time they were my closest friends, but I became invisible once Reid moved on.

I don't know if it was actually loyalty to their husbands who were close with him, or just because I didn't have money any-more and was no longer valuable to them. I like to think they were just confused about the sudden break and that time would pass and we'd reconnect. I mean, that has to be it. They're still my friends.

I pull Barry over to me. He's the only one of the group who isn't a complete embarrassment, even though his pants are a little too short. I wave to Andrea, whose eyes widen in sur-prise at seeing me. She pauses before giving a little wave back and then turning around and whispering something to Becca, who turns to see me and then quickly turns back around her-self without acknowledging me at all.

Holy shit. Are you kidding me?

I see the girls at the food table filling their plates sky-high while Crystal shoves some shrimp into her purse.

"I want to introduce you to my friends," I say to Barry, who puts down the coffee cake he's eating and brushes his hands on his pants.

"Oh, great. Okay," he says.

When I walk over to them, I keep a close eye on their body language. Becca stiffens, and Andrea takes a gulp of wine. It's like they're afraid of me. I'm not the one who cheated and left. What the hell? Is it considered "taking sides" to simply be cor-dial to me? Are they that fragile? I just can't believe how every-one has turned into someone I don't know at all. But I suppose I have, too. I don't even know who I am anymore, either.

"Cassidy, my goodness," Becca says. She's perfectly polished with her long dark curls in a French twist with tiny flowers around the edges. Andrea's manicured nails clutch her wine-glass, and both women are shiny and glossy and perfect, with no bags under their eyes or grease under their nails.

"Who's this?" Becca adds, forcing a smile and shooting An-drea a look I can't interpret.

"Barry, this is Becca and Andrea."

"Oh, hey," he says, nodding too many times and holding his hand out to shake, which they are forced to meet with theirs. "Your nails are cool. They look like little Samurai swords," he says, and Andrea looks down at her ridiculously long curved nails and raises her eyebrows at him.

"Bare, can you get me a punch or something?" I ask, and he too eagerly agrees and makes his way to the food tables.

"Surprised to see you here," Becca says.

"I come every year," I say, standing my ground.

"Yeah. You know Reid will be here, right?"

"I haven't talked to him, so I wouldn't know."

She looks around in a way that makes me think she's hoping not to be seen with me. And it just now dawns on me that I can't be the pariah just for getting cheated on and dumped— he must be saying things about me for people to respond to me this way. Not just people; friends—or so I thought.

"How is Reid?" I ask, suddenly wanting them to be uncomfortable—to tell me something that will make sense of all this.

"As good as he can be, I guess, after, you know...everything that happened," Becca says.

"What...what happened?" I ask, genuinely completely confused.

"Really?" Andrea says, and then nudges Becca and points across the dance floor to someone.

"Oh, my God, it's Bethany Sorenson. Did you see her at Leah's wedding? God, it looked like someone stuffed a couple honey-baked hams into the back of her dress."

"And the worst part is she did that on purpose. That ain't too much buttercream—although did you see her shoveling it in at the cake table—she had those babies implanted."

"Ass implants. Ass-plants," Andrea says, and they burst into laughter.

"Who are we talking about?" I ask, but Becca ignores me, puts her glass on the bar, and tilts her chin across the room.

Andrea gives me a tight smile. "Well, it was nice to see you," she says, and they both turn and make their way to the other side of the bar where their husbands are in a circle of other husbands who probably wish they weren't here and linger in the bar area to watch a golf game on a mounted TV on the wall. I look in the direction she motioned toward, to see Reid and Kimmy moving through the crowd.

What am I doing here? This is the last thing I need to worry about. I order another shot of tequila and stand against the bar as they walk past, not seeing me, thank God.

It's like they're moving in slow motion as she flips her long blond waves and purses her lips, nodding to acquaintances as she moves through the sea of people like she's on the red carpet or something. She's all big boobs and skinny tan arms, and Reid...his short-cropped hair and clean-shaven face—the tux I know so well, the citrus cologne I can smell without even being near him.

An unfamiliar feeling surfaces—longing mixed with a hatred that feels uncontainable. I order one more shot. Then I stay out of their sight as I make a beeline to the table the pool girls have near the dessert buffet. Jackie has three fruity drinks in front of her, Rosa is dancing in her seat to the Bruno Mars song playing, which Barry is singing along to into a butter knife microphone, and Crystal is pounding miniature strawberry shortcakes.

I stare at Reid and Kimmy as they meet Becca, Andrea, and the group of husbands.

"Is that her?" Crystal asks with her mouthful of whipped cream. "Want me to go over there, scare her a little?"

"You ain't scary, bitch," Jackie says. "Look at ya." She flicks her belly.

"No," I say quickly. "Just... I think we should go."

"Go?" Jackie snaps. "There's an open bar. You're nuts. I'll take the bus home. I'm staying here."

Crystal digs into a plate of ribs and nods in agreement.

"Here." Jackie hands me a Long Island, and I take it. I wanted to take the edge off, but I don't drink often enough for three shots, a minivan wine cooler, and half of this drink to not have me feeling suddenly *very* drunk. It's like it all just hit me, and I want to take it back. I desperately want to go back in time and decline all of these drinks. I wanted to keep my wits about me, but that's not what's happened.

I feel like I'm swaying back and forth ever so slightly just sitting here, so I fear standing up, but I need to go throw up. I hear one of the girls call after me as I get up and rush to the bathroom.

I panic when I can't find it and then finally see a sign pointing down a flight of carpeted stairs. I run down, taking them two at a time, and vomit the sickly sweet tequila into the toilet just in time. The stall is spinning, and I want to die. I truly just want to lie down and not wake up in this moment. I'm so tired, so utterly miserable.

I sit on the bathroom floor having flashbacks of my early twenties, which is probably the last time I drank tequila, and try to breathe and force myself to sober up. Then I hear a loud thump and feel the bathroom stall door smack against my back and bounce off, slamming it shut. It opens again, and a frustrated Kimmy stands, hovering over me.

"Classy. I should have guessed you'd be puking." Her arms are folded, and she rolls her eyes.

I'm so shocked to see her I can't form words for a response. I just stare up at her and sort of scurry to my feet pathetically. I've only actually seen her twice before. Both times I was in a fit of rage, and this time I'm hammered, and she's a little blurry, but I can still make out how young and shiny she is. God, what must it be like to have skin like that? Or the glossy pouty lips and satiny golden hair.

"Fuck off," I say and slam the door in her face, but she stops it with her hand and jabs a finger into my chest.

"I know it was you. On Instagram, telling me Jessie from the Bulldog is fucking Reid. Nice try, but she's actually like my best friend, and I know it was bullshit—a pathetic attempt at breaking us up. You're seriously sad, and if you ever mess with my friends or fiancé again, you'd better watch your back," she says, and the word *fiancé* knocks the wind out of me. I feel my cheeks redden and a hot rage bubble up inside me.

She slams the stall door, and I hear the click of her heels on the tile floor, the flash of voices, and clinking glassware when she opens and closes the bathroom door, and I sit on the toilet seat and do my best not to hyperventilate. I have to put my head between my knees and stifle my cries to try to calm my breathing until I can pull myself together.

After a few minutes, I hear the bathroom door open again, and I freeze. I don't know why I'm cowering, afraid of a booby, blond twenty-whatever-year-old, but I'm so overwhelmed with the betrayal that I seem to be reliving it all over again; it's like it just happened, and I feel paralyzed. We were together for years, and he had a thousand reasons why he didn't believe in marriage—that I stupidly accepted—and he's engaged to the cocktail waitress from our favorite bar? It's too much and simultaneously the least of my problems right now, but the alcohol is buzzing between my ears and my anxiety is so out of control I don't know what I'm doing anymore.

"Cass?" a small voice says, and I hear a tap-tap on the stall door. "It's Rosa. Are you okay?" she asks.

Rosa. God. Please don't be nice to me. I can't do this.

"Girl!" a louder voice says, and I can tell it's Crystal barging in and whipping open the door. I almost fall out of the stall but catch myself. Crystal is holding a plate of macaroons and has a hand on one hip. "Are you pukin'? Is she pukin'? Naw-uh. It's too early for that shit. I saw the home-wrecker chick out there, all tacky dress and hanging on your man, lookin' like a Disney character. She's not worth all this."

"He ain't no prize, either." Jackie seems to materialize but has been leaning against the tile wall stirring her margarita. "He's not tall enough for you. And the fitted suit he's trying to pull off—he looks like Pee-wee Herman."

"Want me to spike her drink?" Crystal asks. "I always got a bunch of Benzos."

"No. Guys. Listen. I just need to go. I shouldn't have come. I'm sorry. I am, I know you're having fun…"

"It's okay," Rosa says sweetly.

"Yeah," Crystal agrees. "I already ate about ten thousand calories, and I got a buncha shrimp," she says, patting her bag, then looks to Jackie who slurps the last of her drink loudly through a cocktail straw. "And I think Jacks got her money's worth. Let's get you home." Crystal extends an arm for me to steady myself on, and I'm suddenly very moved by their support, even though I'm pretty sure Rosa talked them into this.

When we walk up the stairs together, back into the party, I'm not embarrassed to be with them. Rosa and Crystal keep me walking upright, and I'm proud to be with them right now. I don't mind what anyone thinks. These people actually care about me.

Then out of the corner of my eye I see her again. Kimmy is standing near the giant cake centerpiece with a couple of other women. She's touching her belly. I stop. The girls stop, too. They look to where I'm looking. One of Kimmy's friends squeals and also touches Kimmy's belly. I can hear small shrieks of "No way!" and "Congratulations!" and we all know what it means.

Even Jackie knows what it means, and she can barely walk.

She hollers to Barry, who's sort of dancing by himself to the music and slurping a diet Coke. "We're outta here, Barry!"

"Yep, okay," he says obediently, grabbing his keys and jogging over, and I'm in a daze as we start walking through the sea of people toward the main entrance when I see Reid right in front of me, a look of utter shock and dismay on his face upon finally noticing me.

I shake off the grips of Crystal and Rosa and try my hardest to appear sober. "Hey there. I guess congrats are in order," is all I say, but I see the look of panic in his eyes.

"What are you doing? What do you mean?" Reid asks.

And I am fully aware of how pitiful it is, but I blame the booze because for a moment, I smell his familiar scent, and I feel his arm bump up against mine, and I haven't been this close to him in so long that I just want to talk, want something so desperately from him that I am aware he can't give me, but I still try.

"Can I just talk to you for a minute?" I say, and I can hear the girls bristle behind me. I try touching his hand, but he pulls away. "What? I can't just talk to you?"

"Probably not a good idea," he says, cold and distant, and I need him so badly to give me anything right now—something to make me feel like I exist, like I ever mattered, like years of my life weren't a joke.

"Just talk to me," I almost plead, and hate myself so much as I say it.

Then Kimmy appears beside him, and I can feel the girls standing behind me like a little army. I know I should walk away, but I don't.

"Are you kidding me?" Kimmy says, smacking my hand away from Reid's.

"Don't touch me," I say, pushing Kimmy's shoulder with a hard poke.

"You're making a scene," Reid says with a dismissive, smug look across his face.

"You don't want a scene?" I say and then yell over the crowd, "Reid doesn't want a scene, everyone. But this isn't a scene. A scene is when you're miscarrying again, but that's okay because lover boy here is already working on getting someone else pregnant. *That's* a scene!"

"Santa Mierda, no," I hear Rosa say softly from somewhere behind me, but I don't care. I grab an oversize cluster of helium balloons, take a dinner fork from a table, and start stabbing at them, the deafening pops attracting everyone's attention.

"Heeey, everyone!" I yell.

"Oh, shit," Crystal says, and she tries to stop me and take my fork, but I'm too far gone to listen to reason. I see the faces of mostly strangers, but Becca and Andrea and a few others are familiar and staring at me like I've gone completely mad. Fair.

"Who wants to see a scene!?" I yell and pop one more balloon until I have most people's attention. "The home-wrecking bitch here doesn't want a scene, either. She only makes scenes behind people's backs! Not in public. God for-fucking-bid! Did everyone congratulate Reid on his engagement and their baby news?"

I see Reid give a group of friends a terrified look.

Then Becca comes over trying to be some sort of savior and touches my shoulder. "Okay, honey, come on."

"'Honey'? Really? Get the fuck outta here," I say, pushing her off me. "You knew. All of you knew!"

"You're embarrassing yourself. Stop," Reid says with a stern tone, grabbing my arm hard. His nostrils flare.

"No, YOU embarrass me! You embarrass yourself. Get your hands off me." I push him.

Kimmy tries to retaliate and protect him, but I turn around before she can reach me and push her so hard, she falls into the food table. It buckles, and Kimmy is lying on the ground with a five-tier coconut cream cake fallen on top of her, bawling and screaming that I'm a psycho, which I agree; right now, I sort of am.

Barry, of all people, hooks my arm in his and says let's go, that security is coming, and all of us rush toward the sliding glass doors.

"Take that, Barbie!" Jackie slurs as we exit, throwing a bacon-wrapped shrimp as one final blow, but it hits the glass and falls to the ground with an anticlimactic plop, and we all sprint to the minivan and tear out of the lot as fast as we can. The girls hoot and holler in triumph for a while, but then it's quiet.

The whole ride home is quiet, no music, just the hum of the highway. Crystal lays my head in her lap and strokes my hair as she and Jackie softly crunch on the purse-shrimp they stole. No one says much for a while, and then Jackie speaks.

"Let's egg his house."

"Oh, yeah," Crystal agrees. "The son of a bitch."

"It wouldn't be an unreasonable thing to do," Rosa adds to my surprise.

I sit up. "He lives a few miles up west on White Pine," I say.

And Crystal starts fist-bumping and chanting, "Hell yeah, egg his house, hell yeah."

"No, I mean I just want to go there. He still has stuff he never gave back to me. I want it. And I mean, I know he's not home."

"Fuck yeah you do. Let's go," Jackie says, and for the next few miles their enthusiastic support becomes a little much as they make up a variety of chants like "Fuck, yeah, get your shit. That guy sucks, sucks a dick," and other such masterpieces.

When we pull up, the sight of our house takes my breath away. I once thought about setting the place on fire. Well, to be fair, I dreamed about it. The sleeping kind of dream, not the fantasy kind; it doesn't count as a psychotic thought, since you can't help what you dream about. No one was hurt, even in the dream, but I was allowed at least a modicum of satisfaction, knowing that nobody else would ever sleep in my bed or enjoy my coveted soaker tub with the must-have jets. Knowing that our years of photos together would curl up on the sides and melt and boil before meeting the rest of our earthly belongings as ash in a puff of rolling black smoke above our house.

I don't want to burn it down anymore. I just want what's mine. I tell everyone I'll just be a few minutes. First, I punch in the garage code.

My giant, very expensive tool collection is exactly where I left it in the corner, because everyone knows Reid can't even change a light bulb. He thought the tools should stay with the house, but they're mine. Barry pops the hatch when he sees me waddling out with the toolbox and helps me throw it in the back. I hold up a finger telling them I won't be long, and I go around to the side door where a spare key is hidden in a cactus pot, and I let myself in.

So much of the house is the same. The paintings I bought from art fairs all hang in the same places, the plates I picked out sit dirty in the kitchen sink, a quilt my mother made is draped over the couch. I left so quickly, I didn't take much. He's made it impossible for me to come back. I pull the quilt off the couch with a violent tug and wrap it around my shoulders.

I walk upstairs and hesitantly push open our bedroom door. The satin bedding I got at Nordstrom is still on the bed, with tiny birds embroidered into the sides of the pillowcases. The bedframe and nightstands we bought together are there; mahogany, timeless. Even most of the framed photos on the dressers are the same, except that the ones with me have been replaced with ones of Kimmy. When I open my closet, all of her clothes are hanging there, and I do think about getting the house paint from the garage and flinging it all over the room like a Jackson Pollock. But I don't.

I sit on the bed. It feels as if someone died. There's a hollow flutter between my shoulder blades; the feeling of slipping on a stair, or leaning back in a chair just a hair too far. It feels like falling. I lie down on the bed. I let myself, for just a moment, even though it's almost unbearable.

Across the room, I see a few boxes of diapers and a baby mobile with little moons and stars hanging from it, and it's all confirmed. The house my family was supposed to grow up in belongs to someone else now, and I have no family. Suddenly I don't want anything in here anymore besides my quilt. I numbly walk outside, knowing it's for the last time. It's time to go.

Outside, I head to the waiting van parked on the side of the street when I see my herbs. It's stupid to be triggered by herbs, but they were mine. Each one has a Popsicle stick in the soil with a label like Super Sage and Rockin' Rosemary. I loved to garden, and we said we'd plant these and keep them alive— we'd give them funny names…for our kids. To get them excited about gardening and cooking the way I was. Reid surprised me with them after a particularly hard loss; the last loss we had. It was a sweet gesture of hope, and look at them now…they're letting them die.

Tears stream down my face against my will, and I drop to my knees and begin tearing all of the plants from the ground. I'm sobbing and digging and trying to collect them all in my arms when I see a red flash of light in the darkness and hear some warning shouts from the girls in the van.

A cop has pulled up. I'm certain one of the nosy neighbors called them as soon as they saw me pull up. I don't stop, though. I keep pulling my herbs and trying to save them by not tearing any of their precious roots. I can't stop crying. I can't stop.

"Ms. Abbott," the voice of an officer says, and he actually sounds kind, but probably only because he's witnessing someone having a complete mental breakdown.

"These are mine," I snap, not looking up, just determined not to lose these, too.

"I'm sorry, ma'am. We were informed you assaulted someone

at the Eldorado earlier tonight. There are dozens of witnesses, so I'm afraid I'm gonna have to ask you to come with me."

I don't fight anymore. I don't say anything at all. I'm entirely defeated and exhausted. I hear the click of the handcuffs around my wrists and feel the cold sting of the metal.

"Don't worry! We gotcha, girl," Jackie hollers out the window of the minivan as they escort me into the back of the cop car, and I'm arrested. Headed to jail and not back to The Sycamores where Callum is waiting for me—where right now I am supposed to be doing the unthinkable.

17

ANNA

The next morning, I wake up to a soft tap on my front door. When I open it, I'm surprised to see Rosa standing there, toddler on one hip and a sheen of sweat already forming across her forehead in this insufferable heat.

"Ms. Anna, hi. I'm sorry to bother you so early."

"It's okay, um…is something wrong?" I ask.

"No, well. Yes. It's Cass. She went to jail."

"Uh…okay. Why…what happened?"

"She pushed a girl into a big cake and then broke into her ex's house and pulled all his plants out of the ground," she says, and I try not to laugh, but it sounds absurd.

"Oh, I'm…sorry," is all I can think to say.

"It's just that…" She pauses and glances down to the pool deck, then back to me. I see Jackie fanning herself, and Crystal on her phone. Barry's there, too, holding a Dunkin' Donuts coffee and shifting his weight from foot to foot. "The bond is $500, and none of us have that much money."

And I realize they want me to bail her out. The woman laughing in Henry's painting, who I spend half the night thinking about. It's even more absurd now, but I want to talk to her.

And if she's a captive audience in my car, this might actually be the best possible scenario.

After a cursory Google search, it wasn't hard to find lots of information on Mira Medford, and I had planned to show up at her job this morning. Facebook showed me she works at the Dairy Queen on Park, so I called last night and asked for her, and they said she wasn't in until tomorrow morning. Bingo. I plan to catch her not only unawares, but in public for the best shot of not getting a door slammed in my face and gleaning at least some response or information from her. But Cass is at the top of my list, too.

"You want me to bail her out," I confirm.

"I'm so sorry. She'll pay you back. It's just… I mean, maybe not right away…"

"It's fine," I say.

"Really?" Rosa says, looking surprised.

"Yeah, just give me the info, and I'll do it."

When Rosa turns to give a thumbs-up to her waiting friends, they all break into applause and cheers. I'm a little embarrassed, but I take down the details and head out to the Santa Fe county jail.

As I'm waiting for her to be released after the paperwork is complete, my phone pings with a text from Callum apologizing for being weird last night. I decide to call him back instead of texting because everything in the world seems off to me, and if he realizes he was acting strange, then why? What is actually going on here?

"Callum, hi. Sorry. I'm driving, so I thought I'd just call instead," I lie. "Cass was arrested, so I'm here seeing about bailing her out," I say, testing his reaction.

There is dead silence on the other end.

"Hello?" I ask.

He starts to say something, but his voice cracks, then he

clears his throat and tries again. "Arrested? Wha—what do you mean?"

"Last night, I guess. In the city, at a hotel is all I really know."

Silence again. "Holy shit—for... I mean, what was she arrested for?" he asks with a shaky voice.

I see Cass walking out the glass double doors with a confused look on her face, and I flag her over.

"Sorry, I gotta go. I'll call you back." I hang up and wonder what the hell would make him that concerned for her.

By the time Cass is sitting in my car, she looks pale and shocked that I'm the one who's shown up. I'm probably just as nervous and uncomfortable as she is, really not knowing what to say to her if, in fact, she is my husband's...what? Mistress? Lover? Muse? She has a rough-around-the edges way about her. I would describe her having a delicate beauty until she opens her mouth to speak, and then it's usually curse words or sarcasm accompanied by a grimace—maybe it's just her tomboy demeanor in general that's so incongruous with her looks that it throws me off. She's really quite mysterious.

"How'd you get roped into this shit?" she finally says as I pull away from the county facility parking lot.

"Your friends were...short on funds," I say, and she nods.

"Well, thank you. I'll pay you back a little with every check. I'm sorry I don't..."

"Honestly, don't worry about it. You got my AC fixed, thanks," I say, and the look on her face tells me she thought I was stupid enough not to know she sent Callum to help. "I heard you pushed a girl into a big cake," I say, trying to get her talking.

"The bitch deserved it," she says. "I mean, it was an accident, but I don't regret it. You probably don't know what it's like to be cheated on because Henry was a great guy and all, but let me tell you, if you are threatened in a bathroom stall by the teenager you were replaced with, you'd push a bitch into a big cake, too," she says.

The deep pain she's feeling shows through the almost humorous delivery. It doesn't sound like something a person would say if they're sitting next to the widow of the man they had an affair with. It seems like the last thing they'd bring up, actually, and I immediately start to think I might be wrong about her. Then I get a glance at her phone she's been distracted with since she just got it back, I assume, and notice nine missed calls…from Callum. What the hell? I don't know what to think.

What I am starting to think is that it's more likely something is going on between these two than with Henry, but I jump in anyway.

"I was going through Henry's things, and I saw a painting of you," I say.

"Oh, yeah?" she asks, distracted, texting furiously on her phone.

"Did he paint you a lot?" I ask, and she laughs.

"Fuck no."

"You seemed really happy in that painting. It's a good piece," I say, and she stops texting and looks at me.

"Oh, really? I never saw it. He asked me if I'd sit to be painted, like he asks everyone, and I said 'hell no' and 'why would I wanna sit still for hours without getting paid.' Who the fuck does that anyway? We're not in seventeenth-century England, just take a photo, and he laughed at that and said that I know nothing about art history but that that was fine and to forget the idea because I always look constipated anyway, so no big loss…and I laughed 'cause it was funny. I probably do always look constipated, and he took a snapshot of me when I was laughing. And he said, there, I took your advice, can I paint your portrait from the photo then, and I said it's a free country. That's it. He said I could see it once, and I said 'hard pass.' Does that answer your question or whatever you're getting at?"

"I guess so," I say, because it's a pretty detailed explanation to be a lie.

"I'm a pro at getting to the bottom of what a sneaky snake man is up to," Cass says. "I'm not an idiot. I know you're probing around for something, but you're barking up the wrong tree."

I guess I am pretty surprised she picked up on that. I wasn't accusing her of anything, but I suppose she has spidey senses after whatever it is she's been through.

"Do you know what tree I *should* be barking up?" I ask, feeling like she knows something.

She hesitates, then just says, "No," and goes back to her phone, but there was a split second where I thought she was gonna tell me something.

"Okay, then. Last question. Do you know a girl named Mira?" I ask, and she looks up again.

"A high school kid?" she asks, and my heart starts to race.

"Yeah," I say.

"I mean, no. I don't know her, but there was a Mira who kept parking in the lot at The Sycamores, smoking pot and just hanging out there all the time in the handicap spot, so I had a couple run-ins telling her to get lost," she says, and I feel a nauseous wave come over me.

I just nod, and she's back to her phone, and my heart is in my throat. Holy shit. This girl was at the apartments all the time? Holy. Shit.

When I drop Cass off, she thanks me again in that genuine but resentful tone that I don't exactly blame her for, and then I speed off to the Dairy Queen with trembling hands and a stone in my chest.

I park on the far side of the lot under a shady oak and watch for a little while first. It's one of those smaller stores where the front has a couple large walk-up windows and red plastic tables and chairs out front. There isn't an inside you can enter, so the handful of patrons who are there—mostly families—sit at the tables while the younger kids run wild on sugar highs with Dilly Bars and Blizzards melting all over the place.

When the line dwindles, I see Mira standing at the counter just inside the window. She's picking at her nails and talking to a girl her age who's leaning on the take-out counter and stabbing her straw into a parfait. Mira looks just like Anne of Green Gables but with rounded swimmer's shoulders and a nose ring. She's just a kid. Jesus. I probably shouldn't be here, but it's just a few simple questions. I don't plan to harass her or make her cry or accuse her—nothing like that. It's just a few questions.

I get out of my car and walk up to the window. Her friend moves aside while I order a cup of coffee.

"It's like a thousand degrees out, and this is an ice-cream shop. You're sure that's all you want?" Mira asks, and her voice is unexpected. Very soft and shy—it does not match the sort of person confident enough to seduce a teacher and have an affair beyond her years.

"You're Mira," I say, and she stops cold, my cup of coffee in her hand, and her brows raised.

"I'm Anna. Henry's wife. I think you were a student of his."

She puts the coffee down and tells me it's on the house. "I'm going on break," she says, starting to shut the order window.

"Whoa, wait! I'm sure you heard what happened to him, and I just want to ask you a question."

"Sorry," she says.

"I have…" I quickly sift through my wallet, wishing I had thought of bribe money. "A hundred and nine bucks if you talk to me."

But she closes the window and disappears into the back.

I don't believe it. I came in thinking it was a box to check because, although I've been disturbed by the rumor, it was just a rumor. Cass's statement made it seem like there was more to

it, but maybe not without explanation. This behavior, though...
This is all red flags.

I leave my coffee and go to my car, cussing under my breath,
already exhausted at 10:42 a.m. and not planning on giving up.
I can't force her to speak, so, what? Bring the affair information to the cops and get them to question her, get closer to the
truth that way?

I blast my AC and close my eyes for a few minutes, wishing
I'd taken that coffee. What do I do now?

There's a knuckle tap on my window that makes me leap and
lose my breath for a moment. I roll down my window, and it's
the friend standing there.

"Yes?" I say, flustered.

"Uh... I could use a hundred and nine dollars. I don't know
what your questions are, but I'd talk to you."

"Okay, yeah," I say, a wave of relief washing over me—a
feeling like I might finally have a way to chip away at the first
layer of this thing. Maybe.

She goes to the passenger's side and lets herself in, to my surprise. "I don't want her to see me talking to you."

"Okay, so why is she afraid to talk to me?"

"First, let's get out of here, and I'll need the money up front,"
she says, like a girl who is accustomed to manipulating people
to get her way.

"Sure," I say. I drive a couple blocks to a park where the girl
hops out and lights up a cigarette.

She's a big girl with a tight bun on the top of her head, and I
guess she's wearing a shirt, although I'd call it a bra, with tight
cutoff shorts. She has hoop earrings the size of hula hoops in
each ear, and she sits on a nearby picnic table under a willow
tree and smokes.

"Here." I hand her the cash. "So same question. Obviously
she has a reason to not wanna talk to me, and she knows who
I am, so what's going on? What's that about?" I ask.

"Probably thought you were here to kick her ass. Love her, but the girl is a deep-fried mess. She was obsessed with Mr. Hartley. I told her he was like a hundred and eww, but she didn't care. In pottery once, she kept asking for help, trying to recreate that scene from that movie *Ghost*—you know with the…"

"I know, yes," I say, wanting her to stay on track.

"She showed me the scene a few times. I never saw the movie, but anyway. She had a teacher obsession, like hard-core. She touched him all the time, and he even wrote her up and gave her warnings, and she acted like that was him flirting back. She like, would not stop. At parties where there were real boys, she'd talk about Mr. Hartley, pull up photos of him she snapped when he wasn't looking. Really nutty stuff. It was like she was legit in a relationship with him by herself," she says, and I can't believe Henry never told me any of this.

He was always trying to protect me from stress, from things I couldn't control so as not to worry me about them, but what about him? He needed to talk about this. He needed to process and figure out a plan on how to handle it. Why didn't he talk to me? Maybe there was someone else he was talking to instead.

"So there were rumors at school about an affair?" I ask.

"Well, I mean, yeah, but they died down. He filed a sexual harassment complaint to make sure it was on record, I guess, and she was suspended. Then her parents switched schools because they didn't want the truth to come out. I only know 'cause I'm her best friend, but I'm not supposed to be telling anyone. Anyway, he made sure it wasn't public and that she wasn't humiliated, but thought it was best for her mental health or whatever to go somewhere else and get help."

"So that was it?"

"Yeah, pretty much." She flicks her cigarette into a nearby garbage bin and misses. "I mean, she started showing up at his apartment—it's like this shitty hotel with long-term rentals—

well, I guess you know. No idea how she gets this info except that she follows him. Her dad bought her an old Suburban, and that's when she started tracking him. I went with her a couple times. We'd smoke pot in the front seat and just watch the place. It's a real shitty place, damn."

"You were at his apartment with her?"

"Well, just a couple times when we were hanging out and that's what she insisted on doing. She kind of let it go when she saw him with some woman."

"What do you mean? What woman?"

"Oh, shit. I guess I assumed you were divorced or something since he lived in the ghetto apartments by himself and had a girlfriend," she says carelessly, and I don't explain that he didn't live there or that we weren't divorced.

"What woman?" I ask again.

"Some old woman, dark hair, kinda thin, a long dress… That's all I remember."

"Old, how old?" I ask, my mind reeling, thinking of everyone who lives at The Sycamores.

"I don't know fifty, sixty…"

"Sixty!" I say in disbelief, trying to wrap my brain around who this could be.

"I don't know, old people look the same to me. How old are you?" she asks.

"Thirty-six," I say sharply.

"Well, she was probably around that then—she looked about your age."

"Jesus," I mutter, and take in a deep breath. "So why do you think this old woman was his girlfriend?" I ask, hoping she has an actual reason and hoping she doesn't, all at the same time.

"When we were watching the place, we'd sometimes sit on the lawn chairs by the grills on the side of the building, you know, when the mean apartment manager was gone, and we saw him with this chick. They were kissing, and they looked around like they were making sure nobody saw, and then we watched them go up to his apartment and close the door. Mira was super pissed. Like, enraged, but she started to sort of give up after that and become my normal friend again. So I don't know… That's all I really got. Probably not super helpful, but I'd be pissed, too, if some chick was after my husband," she says, stuffing the hundred and nine bucks into her pocket and standing. "Welp." She shakes some cigarette ash off her top and smooths her bun with one hand. "Later." And then she shoves her hands in her pockets and starts back in the direction of the Dairy Queen.

I suppose I'm grateful for this conversation, because a very big part of me refused to believe Henry would be in love with a student. Even though I feel like I know very little about him anymore, I still know his character, and so I believe this girl's story. It's an explanation that makes sense, and it's time to focus my attention elsewhere. I don't know where yet, but I'm crossing this off my list for now.

On my drive back to The Sycamores, I think about everyone in and out of the place. Dark hair, thin. Cass comes back to mind. Who else fits the bill? Maybe the person doesn't live at The Sycamores, but it feels like they must.

I avoid crossing the pool deck to reach the staircase up to my unit, because the pool girls are all perched in their usual positions with the kids lying about, and I don't want thank-you's or questions or small talk right now. They can talk to Cass themselves. I just want to think. I need time to put this together because I somehow feel like the pieces are all right in front of me, but I'm not seeing them.

I skirt around the perimeter of the building and step quietly up to my unit when I look down and really notice Rosa for the first time. She's easy to overlook because she's so quiet, but she has that mysterious aura about her. Shy eyes, a slight accent, private and polite, and attractive even though she seems to go out of her way to wear no makeup and keep her ropes of long dark hair in a braid behind her back. Long dresses. Thin.

She's the kind of woman Henry would want to try to help. What if he saw the abuse, too, and stuck his nose in? What if that Eddie guy found out about a relationship between Rosa and Henry? Holy shit. My heart starts thumping and my chest blooms with heat. That could make sense. That could fit.

I stare another few moments, unseen by the others, and then turn to go inside, when I see another small package in front of my door. I gasp and take a step away from it, remembering the maggots, and my gag reflex threatens to betray me. I slam my sneaker down hard on top of the box to crush it before anything can crawl out of it, and then kick it aside with a mix of horror and relief.

Out of the corner of my eye, I see Rosa, down below, give me a small smile.

Did she just happen to notice me and was being polite, or is this a threat?

18

CASS

Callum has been texting me since last night. Of course, I get it. I understand it, but I think Anna saw his many missed calls in the car, and that looks bad. We are supposed to be keeping a low profile, and he has no ability to be cool.

I text back that I'm fine and will see him soon in a light, nonsuspicious way just in case. I cannot believe he thought calling me like that was smart. Of course I can't say anything meaningful over text, but I try to give him something—nothing to worry about. Just my ex's psycho girlfriend causing trouble. That's it. I promise, I say back so he has at least some information that lets him know we are not both prison-bound and this isn't about Eddie.

We both know we have to wait until dark tonight before we can make our move, and somehow I have to get through this entire day knowing there's a body baking in the trunk of my car and the night ahead of me will be the hardest of my life.

The girls are playing cards poolside when Anna drops me off, and they start to clap when they see me.

"Girrrrl, you took that bitch down," Jackie says.

"Are you okay?" Rosa asks, cooling herself with a paper fan and pulling out a chair for me to sit.

"Sorry about last night. Yeah, I'm fine."

"Your toolbox is in my van," Crystal says. "I'm taking Amber and Tiffany and their friends to Waterworld later, so you probably wanna get it."

"Sure," I say, and all I really want to do is brush my teeth, take a shower, and cry for a couple of hours, but instead I follow Crystal to her van in the parking lot. For some reason Rosa and Jackie follow, too. When she opens the back doors of the van, I'm taken aback at what I see.

"Oh, my God," I say, my hand over my heart. "You guys did this?"

And Jackie giggles, and Rosa nods.

All of my herb plants are sitting in a neat row on a couple of towels with the roots intact and the Popsicle stick labels still connected to each carefully placed plant.

"The cops already nabbed you," Crystal says. "So we figured we had time to get them before any of the uptight neighbors reported us... Ah, Jesus, don't cry."

But I'm so incredibly moved and undeserving of this kindness that I can't help the tears forming. I dab at my eyes with the hem of my filthy dress.

"I'm not!" I say. "Thank you. Really."

The girls help me carry the little plants to a patch of dirt on the side of the office where I will replant them, and then Crystal is off readying her girls for Waterworld, and Rosa and Jackie escape the midday heat inside their apartments.

I avoid the front office as if that will keep the smell of the stringent bleach and feel of the frigid AC from being real—that Eddie won't be real, and it will all just be a nightmare I had, and I'll laugh at how real it felt. But of course, it is real. I see the AC unit dripping water onto the dirt below the window, and I can only assume Callum didn't think to turn it back down to a normal temperature after he did what he agreed he'd do and moved Eddie to my car. The fact that I'm even thinking about this like it's a normal thing on a to-do list for the day makes my stomach lurch.

I go into my apartment and take a scalding hot shower and throw on cotton shorts and a tank top and sit on the edge of my bed, and it hits me for the first time that I am meant to be starting my new job tonight at the Egg Platter. A bark of humorless laughter escapes me when I realize that is, of course, *not* what I'll be doing tonight, and I surely lost the job. I don't let myself sit and think about it. I take a long deep breath and then push my feet into a pair of flip-flops and head out the door because I have something very important to do before anything else.

When I ring the doorbell to 109, I can hear Mary's labored breathing and heavy footsteps coming to answer it, which makes me think Sinatra is probably not there. But then I hear the sound of quick spritely footsteps, and when the door opens, Frank appears instead of Mary, who makes her way back down the hall to her good chair.

"Hi," he says with a smile like all is forgotten, but I know he won't forget being lied to and left hanging, and it's almost funny that in the midst of all the absolute insanity my life has become, this makes me want to cry, and I care more about making it right than anything else right now.

"Hi there," I say back.

"Grandma Mary is home, you can come in."

"Actually, I came to see you," I say.

"You did?" he asks, fidgeting with the rim of his ball cap and shifting his weight from one bare foot to the other.

"I wanted to apologize for the other day."

"It's okay," he says eagerly. "I can still help you with stuff if you want."

"It's not okay. I didn't forget about you, I promise. Just, some stuff came up that kept me from being there, but I wanted to give you this to make up for it," I say, and he stares, wide-eyed, at the oversize toolbox at my feet that's nearly as big as he is.

"What is it?" he asks.

"You can open it if you want," I say, and he kneels down and clicks the latch open.

His mouth drops open when he sees piles and rows of all the tools a person could ever want. Wrenches and pliers and vice grips. Hammers, screwdrivers, nails, and bolts. He looks up at me with a look I recognize, because I've given it myself many times. He thinks he's being tricked, so he stays quiet and doesn't let himself get excited. It makes me want to cry even more.

The tools are old, and I have everything I really need in the utility closet. So even though I cared about these tools a lot and have an emotional attachment, this is the best home for them to go to.

He stands up and shoves his hands in his pocket, not knowing what the punchline is. "I don't get it," he says.

"They're for you," I say.

"What do you mean?"

"You like to make things and fix things, just like me. And you're gonna need tools for that. I mean especially if you plan to assist me with stuff, right? I can't have an assistant without his own tools," I say, and he just stares at me for a minute.

"These are...for me? To keep?"

"Yes." I smile.

"I don't understand."

"Sinatra! They're for you, okay? It's a gift. Let me help you carry all this in," I say, picking up one end.

I see his eyes become glossy, and he hugs me around the waist as hard as he can. I don't hug him back because I can't get too invested in this kid. I just can't.

"Okay, all right. Let's move her in," I say, and he lets go of me and picks up the other end.

He's chattering to Mary about his tools before we even put

the box down, and he beams from ear to ear. He asks me if I'm sure, and if I'm really, really sure three more times and hugs me twice more before I get back out the door to leave. As I walk down the stone path back to my apartment I remind myself not to get attached, and more important, not to let this kid need me because I'll likely be either dead or in prison very soon, if I'm honest. But which one?

I see Callum sitting at the small bistro table in front of his door with bare feet and a cup of iced coffee. He watches me, and we both know he's fuming, and we also know we need to act normal. No call, no texts. Yeah, that worked out well. He's been *so* great at following the plan so far, so will he keep his cool now? Do I need to remind him that I'm not accustomed to planning the dumping of a dead body, so excuse me if I am not handling it the right way!

"Coffee?" he says, tilting his head just slightly in either direction to make sure nobody is close enough to hear. He doesn't wait for a reply, just hands me a mug so we look casual standing there. I certainly can't be seen inside his apartment. That would be a scandal. The pool girls have nothing better to do than create scenarios, especially if it includes the guys in The Sycamores they consider fantasy-worthy.

"What happened?" he asks, but I know everyone already filled him in. They can't help themselves.

"I didn't plan for that to happen, okay? I'm sorry. Let's just… What time?"

"I don't know. We don't even know what we're doing."

"Six then. Just come to the back door, and we can figure it out. I have a bunch of paper maps in one of the drawers. We can find a route. Just leave your phone in your apartment, you know, for tracking."

"Right," he says. "Okay."

"God, shit!" I say suddenly, a flash of panic making me light-headed. I take a deep breath. I can't believe what I'm saying

"I know," he says. "You should go."

"Yeah." I give him the mug and try to force a smile as I walk away, in case anyone is looking at us.

I get to the office early and open all the windows to air out the smell of cleaner and to make it look normal again so none of the residents start to think something is off. It's almost a god-send that I did lose my mind and get arrested because everyone in the complex has probably already heard about it, so any odd behavior will be chalked up to heartache. I haven't let myself think about Reid or Kimmy since sobering up, and I am doing my best to keep it that way.

I turn off the AC and listen to the buzz of cicadas and relish the warm breeze coming through the screens and making the long curtains dance, even if it is too hot. I sit at the desk and start to open paper maps of New Mexico to get a head start on presenting Callum with a direction to go. We said east, but maybe we can settle on distance.

I think to dig out a couple of flashlights from one of the plastic storage bins, and as I stand to go and find them, I see a figure appear on the other side of the front screen door, and I'm instantly furious that Callum is coming in the front. People can't see him come in and not leave for hours. You never really know who's paying attention around here.

"What the hell are you doing?" I say. The screen door opens, and then I hear something that makes my heart stop.

"I'm not here to answer questions from you. I can't even believe they let you out of jail after what you did," Reid says.

"What the fuck are you doing here?" I say, completely stunned to see him—his clenched jaw and hazel eyes, the clean-shaven familiar face I know better than any other against the backdrop of this shithole apartment office. It doesn't go together. I'm hu-miliated and angry that he's here, seeing me like this.

"You stole shit from the house. What is actually wrong with you? Everyone thinks you've lost it, you know?"

"I'm sure they do. What do you want? What else could you possibly even take from me? You're seriously showing up here... for what? You already had me arrested. That's not enough?" I fold my arms across my chest and keep him stuck in the doorway so he doesn't come in any farther.

"The neighbor's Ring camera saw you put my tools in your trunk. You know how expensive those are? I don't want to have to call the police again to make a second report about this, okay? But I need them back," he says, and I can see past his shoulder and outside where a rectangle of blue light illuminates Kimmy's face as she looks at her phone in the passenger's seat of the Range Rover I picked out with him.

"What in the hell would you need with those tools? All of a sudden after years of not touching them, you need them."

"Listen, I don't owe you an explanation. They're mine. That's all, that's it. Let's not make this ugly," he says, trying to move into the room, but I hold my ground.

"What, you got baby furniture to put together? Cribs and stroller—" I start to say sarcastically, but the look on his face makes me realize that's exactly what he wants them for. "Oh, my God," I say in a whisper.

"I saw your car behind the building when we came in, and I still have a key, so I'm getting my tools out of the trunk. I was trying to do the right thing by telling you first even though I should have listened to Kimmy and just taken them," he says, and I'm frozen.

I don't know what to say to stop him from opening that trunk. My mouth doesn't open, I just feel my heart thump and pinpricks of heat tap across my chest.

Callum materializes from the back and practically falls over he stops so hard when he sees a strange man in the office with me. "What's...going on?" he asks.

"Who's this?" Reid says with an accusatory tone, but also

with a twinge of something I recognize. Jealousy? Maybe not exactly, but something in that category.

I go with this and jump into action. I walk over to Callum with my back to Reid, trying to convey a look that says *just follow my lead* but having no idea if he picks up on it. He's scared out of his mind right now—we both are—so he'll make sure we get rid of Reid as quickly as possible.

I put my arm around Callum's waist, and I can feel him tense.

"This is Callum," I say. "Callum, Reid here thinks some of his things were taken last night and put in my trunk, but I was just about to explain to him that we didn't take my car. We took Crystal's van, so you should ask your neighbor to specify whether this was a Volkswagen trunk or a minivan hatchback."

"Sure, whatever, Cass. I'm going to get my shit out of your trunk," Reid says, and starts to walk away.

Callum and I exchange a look of panic. We follow him around the side of the building.

"I'm telling you to leave the property, so you're trespassing if you don't. You want the tools back, sue me. File a report, but you have to leave, or I can have you arrested, too," I say, my words coming out at a furious pace.

When Reid reaches my car, I hear the beep-beep of the key fob unlocking the doors, and Callum leaps between Reid and the trunk.

"She told you to leave the property," Callum says, and I can hear his voice shaking.

I quickly pull out my phone and start recording Reid. "This is Reid Chapman," I say. "He's a respected real estate broker and father-to-be. Let's watch him trespass on private property after he's been asked to leave and break into my car and other illegal shit."

"Cass," Reid says with an exasperated tone.

"He likes to make a spectacle of me, so let's make sure the world sees the other side of it. Here he is at my place of residence, harassing me," I say, and Callum flashes me a look—raised eyebrows and a slight nod telling me he approves of the tactic.

"Ohhh. I can post this on Insta. I know how you two enjoy having your epic love story out on social media. The slutty waitress and the cheating barfly and their forever love. Heart emoji. This will be a nice addition to your romantic legacy. Or maybe on your real estate website. Do they let you post video links in the comments?"

"Fine," Reid says, flashing his palms and backing away.

"And give me my fucking car keys," I say, and he hands them over and continues backing away, a show he's putting on for the camera.

"You really want the tools that bad, wow. Just wow," Reid says, and then he looks Callum up and down. "Whatever." He walks around to the front of the building. Both Callum and I are still until we hear his car start and pull away.

Callum squats down on the ground and runs his hands over his face. I can't tell if it's in relief or terror, or maybe a mix of both.

"This was about tools?" he mutters. "God, the shit you put me through." He holds his hand to his heart for a few minutes and breathes.

I go inside, grab the paper maps and some bottled water, and tell him we should just start driving and figure it out as we go, but we gotta get out of here. He ducks in the back seat until we are away from the property where any resident could have seen us together.

The drive is long and quiet. I have my window open and relish the small comfort of the night air. The Eagles are playing softly on the radio. We don't say much until about forty miles out into a long stretch of desert and nothingness. And even then, we are both so numb, it's hard to admit what we are really doing and actually figure out the details of how it will go.

"We have to leave all the money with him," he says.

But I already know that, as much as it kills me to literally throw away literal piles of cash. It's dirty and could be traced, and we don't know anything about it or how dangerous it is to keep. "All the IDs stay with him. His phone is at the apartments and won't be connected to anything," I say.

"Good, that's good," he says, and he's just comforting himself now, repeating the facts we already know.

"It's gonna be okay," I say, out of some bizarre conditioning to say stuff like that when people are upset.

"Yeah," he mutters.

We drive into the night, and when we feel certain we are miles from anything—only the open scrub desert of the high planes around us, and after the darkness has swallowed the horizon—we decide to pull off the main road. We drive a short distance and park near a cluster of parched bushes and kill the headlights. The only light is a sea of stars. There are no cars on the lonely stretch of highway, and we are far enough off the main drag that we go unnoticed in the darkness...probably.

You never think about how long it takes to dig a grave. It's not something that would ever cross your mind, and then when you begin, it seems like it will be easy to do. It takes hours. You also don't think about bringing gloves. Rubber gloves for touching the body, yes. Working gloves never crossed my mind. With two wooden-handled garden shovels and bloodied hands, Callum and I dig in the silence and blackness, only the sound of our breath, and metal breaking up earth.

We don't speak often, and when we do it's about how much longer it will take or how much water we brought, and then, when we worry about dawn breaking, we decide that the hole is deep enough, and we are far enough away from anything for the loose earth to be noticed by anyone.

When it's done, we sit on the ground, exhausted. It was a brutal act and traumatic. *Trauma lives in the body*, an old therapist of mine once said, and I didn't really know what she meant. Now I do. The weight of him—the smell, the look in his eyes before he collapsed, the fear—it's a part of me now. It's etched in the story of my life now, and I'll never be the me of a few days ago ever again. I'll never be the me that thought idiot Reid and The Sycamores was the worst it could get. Now I live with all this, and I carry it with me.

I still somehow find myself thinking, just for a moment, about all of the life-changing thousands of dollars in that back-pack we buried along with him, and it makes me sick. Sick because I need it so badly, and even more sick that I let my mind worry about that when a human life is gone, and I'm the monster who did it.

We check the area closely and make sure we leave nothing behind, then I pour what's left in a gallon jug of water over my muddy hands and wash out some of the open blisters. Neither of us acknowledge how foolish we were to overlook this and that we now have evidence on both of our torn-up hands, but we both silently know it.

There is a thin line of orange glowing along the horizon, and it's time to go. On our drive back, we go back over our story—every detail. Where we were Friday night—corroborate the story Callum told Anna, who knows he was in the office for hours, and say I was crying over Reid, which is backed up by my insane behavior the next night. Have stories for where we were tonight. Our phones will show us at home. I was binging a Netflix show—which I actually left on at my apartment just in case they can look at that sort of thing—and Callum was grading papers and watching a ball game on TV. We weren't seen. This will work.

But then, when I pick up my purse to dig for a Band-Aid I hope I might somehow have lost in there some long time ago and could really use right now, my cell phone falls out and onto the floor of the car.

"What was that?" Callum asks at the thump, and when I pick it up with a look of horror on my face, I realize my terrible mistake.

"Oh, my God," he says.

But I already know. I know if we are ever looked at or under investigation because of some piece of DNA we don't yet know we stupidly left behind, my phone records will now forever show me out in the desert for hours right after the disappearance... and if the body is found because of the tracing of those records, my life is over.

19

ANNA

The next afternoon, I meet Monica for brunch as promised after I ran out on her, and I explain what I found. I decide to finally say it—to tell her that Henry was having an affair. When I tell her about the high school girl, and Cass and Rosa, and how I just don't know who it could be or if it's connected to his death—that she still believes was a suicide—she insists we spend the afternoon at The Sycamore's pool scoping out the women there.

I feel like if I were going to tell anyone about Henry's death not being suicide, it would first be my parents and then Monica, but I don't know why I can't do it. I think they would interfere. They would tell me to let the police do their jobs and to get out of this place, and they would probably be right. I'm certain they would assure me that I'm not a suspect, but I know I am. If this all happened here and the affair the police don't know about is connected, I can find more answers being close to this place and these people than they can.

Maybe it's insane for me not to have shared with the police what I found in Henry's journal, but I'm not ready. And if they really have me on their list somewhere as a suspect, there is a lot they aren't sharing with me, too, so before I get further questioned or maybe even accused of being involved, I plan to get to the bottom of it myself.

So Monica and I buy some canned margaritas and a Styrofoam cooler. We put on swimsuits and floppy hats and, for the first time since I've arrived, go down to the pool and lie under a weathered sun umbrella on plastic deck chairs with the others. Monica lays down too many towels with a disgusted look on her face, as if everything is sticky and beneath her standards. Which in all fairness, it is, but she could make less of a scene.

Some of the pool girls begin to peer over when she starts spraying a never-ending hiss of sunscreen until she's lost in a cloud of it. Then she finally sits, adjusts herself comfortably, picks up her watermelon margarita can, and peers around over her giant sunglasses. "Okay, now what?" she asks, and I hand her a piece of paper and sit at the edge of my lawn chair sipping my margarita from a straw.

"It's a map of the apartments, kinda. The mailboxes are all in a block by the front office, so I wrote everyone's names and which unit, then I googled most of them to try to get any background information that might be helpful."

"Jesus," she says, looking at it with raised eyebrows. "Most people are crossed off."

"Yeah," I say. "After you get rid of all the men, face-tattoo guy, David with the cats, Leonard, Gordon, Barry…we got a few others that are no's, like a couple elderly women. Mary in 109, Sylvie in 108, and her." I nod toward Babs who's gliding in the pool on a unicorn floatie and sipping a martini. They've already met.

"Right. So why not these other women—Crystal, Gwen, Tina, and Letty?" Monica asks.

"Crystal is blond, Tina and Gwen… I'd give mousy-brown at best, not dark hair…and Letty. She chain-smokes on her balcony almost constantly. She lights one off the other, and I can't see a world where Henry would have anything to do with that. So we have my top three. Cass, Rosa, and Jackie," I say, speaking in a hushed voice.

"Okay, who's who then?" she asks.

I nod to Jackie first.

"The girl with liquid eyeliner and a Harley-Davidson shirt on," Monica says matter-of-factly.

"She's not on the top of the list," I reply and then point out Rosa. "She is," I say, and Monica stifles a laugh.

"The one who looks like she's heading to a church potluck?"

"She's quiet, pretty, like in that natural way where you can see it, but you wish you could fix her hair and take her shopping sort of way. She's sweet. And she's trapped in an abusive relationship. I could see Henry trying to help her and then connecting. I don't know. I don't know anything anymore," I say, and Monica squeezes my hand.

"Okay, who is Cass? She's in your top three."

I look across the pool deck to the grassy area with the picnic table and see Cass there. She's trying to unravel a garden hose, then after a moment, she's given up and is kicking it, swearing at it, and then she stomps into the front office. "She said something that makes me think it can't be her, so I don't know, but I'm keeping my eye on her," I say. "This is stupid. It could be anyone. I just feel like it's tied to this place."

Monica sighs and hands me back my penciled map of the building, and we both watch one of the kids dump a pack of Ritz Bits into the pool. Babs laughs hysterically at this, and Crystal hollers at the kid and fishes it out with a pool net.

"I don't get it," Monica says, shaking her head. "Oh, maybe I do get it. Who's that?" she asks, perking up and adjusting her boobs in her bikini top. She's looking across to Callum sitting in front of his door in shorts and a T-shirt and drinking a beer. His feet are propped up on a planter with a dead cactus wilted and gray inside of it, and he's scrolling through his phone. Monica being married doesn't stop her from requiring all the male attention she can procure.

"Callum. He knew Henry, kinda," is all I share with her. Of course I don't say that we have being widowed in common and he's somehow helping me keep my head above water even though I don't know him well—just that that deep understanding and unspoken connection has been something for me to hold on to.

Callum stands, shoves his phone in his pocket, and starts walking toward the office.

"Well, let's chat with him. He lives here and knew Henry, maybe he'll be helpful," she says, and I know all she cares about is flirting with him, but before I can stop her, she's calling him over. "Hey, Connor!" She waves to him, motions for him to come over.

"Callum," I say. "But let's not..."

Callum looks over, then behind himself, unsure if she's speaking to him, and hesitantly walks over to us. "Hey, Anna," he says, hands shoved in his pockets, looking like he'd rather be anywhere else.

"Hi, I'm Monica. I'm just getting to know Anna's new—" she looks around and searches for the word "—dwelling," she lands on.

"Oh, okay, nice to meet you," Callum says.

Monica pulls up one of the empty deck chairs next to us and pats it, then she thrusts a can of watermelon margarita into his hand.

"Oh, thanks, but I..."

"You have time. We saw you drinking a beer over there. You're not that busy." She laughs and flips her hair, and her directness, as usual, is overwhelming. She'll find a way for this to be about her helping me get intel, but I know her well enough, and he's presenting a challenge that she loves. All she needs is a smile or a kind word, and she'll feel like she's conquered him and will have satisfied this need—or whatever it is—I've seen her demonstrate again and again.

"Uh, yeah. Okay," he says, and timidly sits, taking the drink from her. That's fine, though, because I actually have questions for him.

"Have you seen Eddie around lately? Since…?" I gesture vaguely to the pool meaning *since you saved his kid and he threatened you and all that*, and for some reason he looks like he'll pass out.

"What? I mean… No, why would you ask that?" he says and the truth is, I want to talk to Eddie because there has to be a connection there with Henry. The drugs, the threats, Rosa. I know Eddie won't tell me anything, but he'd surely at least speak to the widow with innocent questions about her husband. And then I could at least gauge if he's hiding anything or if something seems off. Or maybe he'll surprise me and tell me something, after all. What does he have to lose if Henry is gone and can't give another side to his story?

"I'm just trying to ask everyone who lives here basic questions— trying to paint a picture so I can better understand what happened. I talked to most folks, but I haven't seen him in a few days. I know he's trouble, obviously, but I still need to talk to him."

"Oh," Callum says again, looking nervous as hell. "No, sorry. I haven't."

"Well," Monica says, putting her hands on his forearm when she speaks. "I feel like I've seen you before. Do you do CrossFit? You look like a CrossFitter. I go to Grit Fitness on Everwood. They have that cute smoothy cafe. Do you ever go there?" she asks, her knee grazing against his.

He looks at me briefly out of the corner of his eye, and I try to offer an apologetic expression. "Uh. No."

"Oh, which gym do you go to then?" she asks, sipping her drink through a straw with pouty lips.

"I don't," he says, and he's not only painfully uninterested in giving her the desired attention she's used to getting, but he's also distracted.

"Oh, come on, you must go somewhere," she tries again.

I see Cass walk out of the office with a different hose, and she's doing something with the water valve on the side of the building.

Callum hands Monica the can of margarita. "Thanks. It was good to meet you, but I actually do have some things to do," he says and gets up and walks over in Cass's general direction, although she's off somewhere, pulling the misbehaving hose around the building.

When he's gone, Monica curls her lip and rolls her eyes. "He's such an Eeyore."

"Yeah," I say, agreeing with her in hopes to end the topic of discussion. And it does, because rejection is not something she handles well.

After a couple hours more, we mostly talk about how Steven's mother will finally leave the guesthouse next week and how the mad woman has rearranged all the furniture just to upset Monica and how Katie is starting second grade in the fall, but she doesn't like the teacher who Monica refers to as a cow and can't believe she's giving her kid summer homework. I argue that it's actually an optional summer reading list, but she maintains that the teacher is a mean old cow.

She's lost interest in scoping out the women after she saw my list and descriptions and was quickly bored with the discussion. In all fairness, what is there to say? I'm going on practically nothing but conjecture and wild guesses, and what could she really do to help besides keep me company and listen? By dusk, she's packed up her beach bag and margaritas and heads home to see if her mother-in-law has started dinner for Katie and to see all the ways she pitted her daughter against her today.

When we say goodbye, I already know I'm going to go find Callum. Why is he blowing up Cass's phone? That's really none of my business, and I won't ask, but maybe he'll give something away. I do want to ask about Eddie and Rosa. I also want to tell him what I found in Henry's journals, because, just maybe, Callum knows something—has seen something off he could recall once he knows the truth about Henry's affair.

I'm not one to drink often. Certainly not in the afternoon. Even on brunch days with Monica and the girls, I was usually the one with iced tea, but I find the further I go down this rabbit hole, the more I'm saying yes when people hand me a drink, which is often around here. Now I'm four watermelon margaritas in and probably too tipsy to have a conversation with Callum, but ironically brave enough at the moment to do it, so I grab two beers from the fridge and again show up at his door with a small offering and a request for his time.

I feel like a bit of a jerk showing up uninvited after my friend practically tried to seduce him, and he doesn't look particularly excited to see me when he opens the door. I don't even know how to read the look he has. Almost like he's scared of something. The apartment is hot, and he's been trying to get the AC working.

"Ah, we have something in common then," I say, as he invites me to sit in front of the oscillating fan next to the sofa.

"It can't keep up with the heat," he says. He takes the beer and sits next to me, plucking his T-shirt away from his skin and pressing the cold bottle against his forehead for a moment to cool down.

"I didn't mean to interrupt you," I say, looking at the AC unit on the floor and a few tools next to it.

"I don't know what I'm doing anyway," he says, and we sit in the hot air for a moment or two. The only sound is the crickets outside the open windows and the hum of the fan. A breeze floats through now and then and rustles the curtains but does little to cool the room.

"I wanted to apologize for my friend first," I say.

"It's fine." He smiles.

"Jesus. What happened to your hands?" I say, noticing the abrasions and blisters.

"Oh, nothing. Just when I pulled this unit out the other day, I started to drop it and sort of cut up my hands trying to catch it before it fell," he says.

"Oh, wow, looks painful," I say, and there is something about him that seems different today. A despair that seems almost palpable. A brokenness and a tenseness that I should take as a sign to leave the poor guy alone, but I don't because I'm feeling the same despair and maybe we can help each other.

"Well, anyway. I appreciate you talking to me before, about Henry. It's hard not knowing what happened—how this even *could* happen, so I just need…" I stop and sigh. "I found his journals," I say, and Callum looks taken aback.

"What do you mean?"

"He kept a journal I didn't know about, and he, well, I found out that he was having an affair—not just an affair, but he was in love with someone else."

"Oh, God. I'm sorry," Callum says. "Like a diary, you mean?" And he seems to be confused by this because, fine, not many men I know keep a journal. I can see how it seems out of the ordinary.

"We met in a poetry class actually. He was an artist—a sensitive guy. It's not shocking he'd keep a journal," I say. "I mean, okay, I'm a little shocked to find it, but only because of what was in it. He writes about being in love, and he says he painted the woman, like, a hundred times. That's probably an exaggeration, but the point is, I need to know who she is. I can't find any women he painted more than once. I mean, I know you didn't know him that well, but I thought since you live here, you might, I don't know…have seen something? Seen him with someone?"

"God," he says, sipping his beer and leaning back. "That's

a lot for you to deal with after everything that's happened. I mean, it's tough, because all the pool girls doted on him, he painted all the kids, he was friendly to everyone, so picking out one person he seems closer with… I don't know. I was teaching during the day when he was here, and he was home—with you, I assume—in the evening when *I* was here, so I'm probably the last person who would notice. Did you ask the pool girls? They're here all day and seem to watch everyone."

"Yeah. They couldn't help. I have a theory on why, though," I say.

"A theory as to why the pool girls are not helpful." He almost smiles saying this. "I'd love to hear your theory," he says, and he stands and goes to the tiny kitchen only a few feet away and grabs another beer. That's when I notice six empties in the sink and how fast he drank the one I gave him, and my instinct that he is having a very rough time right now is confirmed. He sways just slightly when he comes to sit back down, and I've only seen him in complete control and being careful with his words, but he seems as tipsy as I am at the moment. I can't fault him for that.

"I wonder if Rosa is the one he was having an affair with," I say, and Callum gives me a wide-eyed look that seems to be a mix of surprise and amusement, and I think he even tries not to smirk.

"Okay," he says. "Go on."

"We know Eddie is a psycho, right? What if Henry was trying to help her and they got close? Then what if Eddie found out about it, and…" I stop.

"And what?" he asks.

And in this moment, I just decide to tell him everything. I need to tell someone, or I feel like the weight of it all will suffocate me. "And what if Eddie retaliated?"

"Anna, I mean… I don't know what…" He starts to gently

try to ask me what the hell that has to do with suicide, and I just say it.

"They think it's foul play. They don't think it was suicide." And I say this as if there is still room for doubt, even though they are certain it was homicide. Maybe I'm not ready to say it with indisputable certainty.

"Jesus. What?" He moves to the edge of the couch, and for a moment I think he starts to reach to take my hand but stops.

"So it makes sense that with his track record, and an affair, that could be possible. I mean, it's just a theory, but it's all I got. God, the more I talk out loud the more I sound like I'm losing it," I say and put my beer on the coffee table, rubbing my eyes with my palm.

"No, God. I mean, what you've been through. I just…can't believe that. It makes sense you'd try to figure out who would ever want to hurt him. I thought it was a closed case, it sounded like. Who would ever guess foul play? Jesus." And then he does rest his hand on my knee. "I'm so sorry. I can't imagine how you feel," he says, and I lay my hand on top of his. I revel in the comfort of someone's touch for just a minute before he pulls away self-consciously. He leans back on the couch and sighs.

"Rosa just seems like the last person I imagine having some illicit affair," he says, in drunken detective mode with me.

"It's the quiet ones that surprise you," I say, and he smiles at this.

"You might be right. But let's say it's not her. I just want to apologize again for bringing up the girl from the high school, so please don't jump to any conclusions there."

"No, I looked that girl up, and she's a redhead. The woman he was having an affair with had dark hair, dark brown or black," I say, and he sits up and furrows his brow but then shifts gears.

"So that's why Rosa," he says.

"Or Cass, maybe," I add, to see if he'll get defensive or give away any clues. "You two seem close. You sure you never saw anything off?" I ask.

"We're not close. Not like that—she was very kind when Lily passed. She cooked the books to give me free rent for a month and had everyone in the complex drop by food for a couple weeks. No one asked her to, she just saw the need, ya know. And then one day, she opened up about her ex and money problems. Then I tried to help her. Just listened and agreed that men are scum. That's really all. I feel like she'd have said something in those conversations where she's bawling about what's-his-face, Reid... She'd have mentioned another love interest, especially if it were more than some random fling. And you're saying love was involved, I just..."

"You might be right. I saw a bunch of missed calls from you on her phone when I picked her up, so I assumed you were close," I say, still fishing for more, for a slipup.

"She asked me to check on her because she was going to some party that night and the ex was gonna be there, so when she never came home or answered my 11:00 p.m. call she asked me to make to save her if she needed an out, I got worried. Like a normal person would. Not anything more than that," he says.

And what he says makes sense, and he doesn't owe me an explanation at all. I just wanted to make sure he's not covering for her in some way. I don't know what way that would be, but the affair has to be tied to Henry's death, so at least it would be a thread to pull on, but nothing. I gotta believe it's not Cass. It doesn't add up.

"What about Monica?" he says.

"Huh?"

"I mean no disrespect, I really don't, but she was rather... forward with me after a couple minutes of meeting her. I think she grabbed my ass when I stood up, actually, so..."

"Oh, God, no," I say.

He quickly apologizes.

"No, I mean. Don't apologize. I totally see why you'd say that. It's just. She's married. I mean she acts like that, but it's harmless. She was like a goofy kid sister to Henry. Honestly, he doesn't really like her. He finds her annoying and kinda self-centered. No. I would never…" But I stop and think about it for the first time.

"Okay," he says. "Fair. Just trying to help. I don't know her, so I'm sure you're right."

"Yeah. I mean. It's not her," I say, and he pushes another beer across the coffee table. I smile at him and take it. He smiles back.

"Sorry," he says.

"Don't be. I don't even know what to think anymore."

"I know how you feel," he says. "Well, in a different way, of course—like it doesn't seem possible that the person you love is gone, and nothing really seems…real anymore. Nothing makes sense. You just get through the day somehow. You don't even know how most of the time. And all you really want to do is sleep, but when you wake up it takes a minute to remember what happened and that this is your life now, and then you have to experience it—go through it all over again like it just happened. I know. I get it."

And he does get it. He's the only one who does—not my parents or my friends or the police. Just him—together in our shared pain. Without questioning it or stopping myself like I might have done without the booze, I reach out, and to my own surprise, I kiss him.

For a moment his body is rigid, and I know I've shocked him, but then he kisses me back, and I grip his shoulders and feel the weight of him press against me. And it feels like I'm doing something terribly wrong, but it also feels like a deeply human response to pain and betrayal, and I don't *care* if it's wrong.

We push against one another as he pulls my shirt over my head, and we hold on to each other like two miserable, lonely people. He kisses me hard and passionately, and then he stops. Just like that.

"God," he says, and I quickly move off him.

"What?" I say. "What's wrong?"

"I don't know what I'm doing. I'm sorry. I just. I can't do this," he says.

"Of course. It's okay," I say, and I feel this knot of guilt forming in my chest. He's not ready for this, and what does it say about me that I am? Of course he's not ready. He's so obviously broken. I would probably feel that way, too, if I didn't know about Henry's affair. Maybe this is more revenge than lust. It doesn't matter; I feel ashamed. I pull my shirt over my head and stand to go.

"I'm sorry," I say, gathering my things, my head buzzing with the drinks and the heat and desire.

He stands and moves over to me. "Please, please don't be sorry. It's just the timing," he says, and I nod.

"Of course," I say again, because what else can I say? "Thanks for talking it through with me. It was helpful," I say, and then rush out the door before I start to cry. And I don't even know why I'm crying. Is it the rejection and humiliation, or the desperate loneliness and longing for someone's touch that I can't have?

When I get back to my apartment, I slam my bag down on a kitchen chair and kick my sandals off as hard as I can, pleased when they smack the wall with a satisfying thud. I sit and stare at the piles and boxes of Henry's things. A thought suddenly materializes out of nowhere.

The police are ordering all of his phone records, and that takes time, they said, and his phone was never found...but why can't I just look at it myself? Why haven't I thought about this before? Probably because when it was a suicide and he was just depressed, it wasn't something I thought would be meaningful. And since learning of the affair, I've been in a tailspin. But holy shit, is there any reason I can't look at his records? We're on the same damn phone plan. Of course I can.

I pull a pitcher of lemonade out of the fridge and try to guzzle a couple of glasses to hydrate and sober up, gather my wits about me, and to cool off from Callum's inferno of an apartment. Then I sit at the kitchen table. I think this will probably be an ordeal and take a while, but all I do is log in and click on the statements from the months leading up to his death, and it's all there. That easy. Unbelievable.

I start to scan through all of the numbers. They don't show up as names on a phone record, of course, so I cross-check them in my own phone. Once I start to plug one of the numbers into my phone, if the person is in my contacts, it will pop up. If not, I google the number.

I start with the few weeks right before Henry died. Mostly it's the phone numbers of a few art studios, a couple clients I know. The pharmacy, a couple of guy friends, way more Pizza Palace deliveries than I would have imagined, and then one number that makes me stop cold.

Monica. The week before he died, he called Monica four times in two days. And she called him five times?

I swallow hard. My heart feels like it's in my throat, and I can hear the blood whoosh between my ears. Why would he ever have any reason to call Monica? They've never had a reason to talk in all the years we were together. They don't even like each other. What the hell does this mean?

20

CASS

The phone was a mistake, fine. Okay. But the plan is to never be in a position where they would even question me. I pour what's left in the coffee maker from yesterday over a cup of ice and take a couple of deep breaths.

They have no reason to think I even know the guy outside of a cordial nod of recognition in the parking lot or something—handing him a package from FedEx in the front office now and again. I can't overreact. Fine, we are probably bad at this and maybe left clues, but I need to stay rational and know that there is no reason for anyone to connect me with Eddie Bacco. There are a lot of bad people he's connected to, and they'll probably chalk it up to some drug-related inside job once they find out who he is. If they even find him at all.

I have to replace the blinds in 106 and patch some drywall in 119, and I told Sinatra he could tag along, so I have to some-how—some-fucking-how—pretend none of this happened and try to act inconspicuous.

As I clutch my coffee and keep my head down when I cross the pool deck to open up the office for the day, I realize that I already look awkward and suspicious. So I lift my head to smile at Babs, who I can hear chattering away near the pool, and then I see something unexpected. Babs and Crystal and Jackie and even Tina and Mary are standing in a cluster, quietly. They're never quiet, and their posture looks bent and strange.

I see Callum walk out his apartment door, lock it, pull his messenger bag over his head, and start toward his car, and then he stops cold when he also sees the group of women. I stop cold when I see him stop cold, and I watch them.

When Mary sits down, I see Rosa is in the middle of this cluster, sitting on her usual folding chair at the card table, but Babs's hand is on her shoulder, and Rosa is crying. Holy shit.

Callum notices me, and we exchange a glance. There is a moment where neither of us knows what to do, but acting normal is top priority, so he clutches the strap of his bag across his chest and walks quickly to his car in the parking lot.

I continue to the front door of the office to unlock it. I drop my keys, and they make a sound that gets Jackie's attention. She looks over and gives me a solemn shake of her head. She stretches out her bottom lip in an expression that reads, *Yikes, something is not good.* I should go over, right? Acting normal would mean taking an interest in this, right? Of course. Yes. So I put my things down, pick up my tools, and walk over to the group as casually as I am able.

"Everything okay? What's going on?" I whisper to Jackie in the back of the huddle, with my best playing-dumb voice.

"Girl," she says and sees my tool bag in hand. "I'll walk with you." And so we head over to unit 119, and she lets the other women console a crying Rosa for a few moments. When we get far enough away, she says, "Eddie's gone missin'."

"What?" I manage to say with a gasp.

"Right? Yeah, it's the craziest thing, too, 'cause he don't call Rosa that much from the road. We always joke that he actually went off to another family, oh that's terrible at a time like this. Sorry. We never say that in front of her anyway. Well, it's been a few days and not even a text. Then she gets something out of his truck and sees his phone is there. *Nobody* leaves their phone behind."

"Oh, God. That's awful," I say, eager for all the information she has.

She continues, "Yeah, but then…oh my God, you won't even believe it. I can't believe it, that's for sure."

"What?" I say, trying to keep the impatience out of my voice.

"Rosa calls the trucking company he works for so she can try to find him—see if something happened. They say they never heard of him! Nobody by that name works there. I always knew he was shady. Sorry, that's inappropriate, but it's true. Lying to her all this time. The guy doesn't even work there. He's just vanished."

"That's…crazy. So Rosa reported him missing?" I ask.

"Yeah. Just this morning," she says, and this is an important point, because Rosa would not report him missing if she knew who he was and what he did. Wouldn't that get her killed by the cartel for drawing attention to his identity? Wouldn't that make her a target? If she was part of it, she would never get authorities involved or close to any of it. I think this is a good indication that she doesn't know who he really is. Maybe he did just lead a completely double life, and she was his cover, unbeknownst to her. Damn.

"That's just awful," I say.

"I guess," she says, opening a bag of donuts from her purse and stuffing one into her mouth. "Sorry, it would be rude to eat in front of Rosa, but I'm starving." And if an opportunity to gossip and eat donuts are what's motivating Jackie to talk, I'll take all the information she'll give me.

"What do you mean, you guess?" I ask.

"Well, of course it's awful. Of course, it's just… Crystal pointed out some injuries, bruises and stuff on Rosa a few times, and I just got the feeling that maybe it was from Eddie.

Now, I can't prove that. It's just nobody's that fond of him. I mean I hope he ain't dead, but if he took off, maybe that's not the worst thing that could happen to her. But you didn't hear that from me," she says.

"Right. Of course. Wow, I don't know what to say. Is she okay? That's a stupid question, of course not," I say.

Jackie eats the last of the powdered sugar donuts from the plastic-wrapped package and dusts off her hands. "She's got us girls, but I don't know. I better get back. Hopefully we get more news." She squeezes my elbow as she goes, then she pauses. "Girl, what happened to your hands? Damn," she asks, and I instinctively pull my blistered hands away, which makes me look suspicious, I'm sure, but it's already done. "They work you too hard around here," she says before I can even answer. Then she's off, and I numbly walk to 119.

I can't tell Callum. No calls or texts, we said. He'll be going nuts all day. I guess that's not my problem. Of course, we knew he'd be reported missing at some point. A man just can't disappear, and they won't know exactly when he vanished. And now it's out in the open that he has a job that doesn't exist, and he's been lying about who he's been with and what he's been doing, this might actually be okay. This *is* okay. Don't panic.

Of course, Callum and I figured out his trucking job was a front, but if he's a liar who goes somewhere for weeks on end, for years, and nobody knows where, well, hell. Anyone could have had a reason to kill him. We don't even know this whole other life he's living. This must take any potential focus off The Sycamores, and me. It *must*.

I try to refocus my attention on behaving normally when I see Frank with some of his new tools in a belt he made himself out of Mary's kitchen apron.

"Morning," I say and tap on the door of 119 before opening it, even though face-tattoo guy gave permission and said he'd be away at work.

"Good morning, Cass. I got here early."

"You did. And you're looking sharp. Ready?" I say, and he nods and goes inside.

There's a hole in the wall next to the front door. I have Frank look at it. "What do you think we do first?" I ask.

"Ummm. We need to make a square around the hole so we can apply a patch," he says. He's been watching YouTube tutorials all week, according to Mary.

"Very close. First, we use a stud finder to make sure we don't cut into any wires, then we do that. Have at it," I say, handing him the stud finder.

"Oh, yeah!" he says, excited about every new thing he learns, and it lightens my heart just a little bit. After we've been working for a while, he sits down on an overturned milk crate and drinks his warm Dr. Pepper, looking pensive.

"Did you know the guy who is missing?" he asks, and I stiffen.

I continue taping the drywall patch. "I did," I say.

"He was kinda mean, but I'm still sad he's missing," he says.

"How was he mean?" I ask, trying to keep my voice casual.

"I don't know. Not nice to people, I guess. Do you think someone killed him?" he asks, and I drop my drywall knife, scarcely missing my foot, but he doesn't seem to notice.

"Why would you think that?" I ask.

"Well, kids get kidnapped, and sometimes they get found, but when an adult goes missing, they usually got killed, right?"

"Well, damn, Sinatra, is Grandma Mary letting you watch too much *Dateline*?"

"*Cold Case Files*," he says. "And it's always the spouse, they say. You think Rosa killed him?" he asks, wide-eyed, apparently just now thinking of this possibility.

"No, I do not," I say, and my heart is racing. I try to keep my back turned and remain focused on my task so he can't see the red blotches blooming across my chest.

"Yeah, you're probably right. She's nice. She gave me Lunchables once. The pizza kind even, and it came with Cookie Dunks, not the turkey, so that was pretty cool."

"You know what?" I say, desperately wanting to change the subject. "You're making me hungry, and I owe you McDonalds, what do you say?"

"Really?" he says, standing up. "But you don't have to do that. Grandma Mary says I shouldn't take up too much of your time while you're working, and I promised I wouldn't."

"You're not at all. You're a great help, so you earned lunch, and we will bring Grandma Mary a McFlurry."

"And Rosa. I bet she could use a McFlurry."

"I bet she could," I say, swallowing hard and wiping my sweaty palms on my denim shorts.

When we get back from McDonald's, a very happy Sinatra riding a sugar high goes to hand out the ice cream we bought, and I return to the front office to find an envelope shoved inside the crack in the door above the doorknob.

I don't know why the sight of it makes me freeze. It's likely someone who got a neighbor's piece of mail in their box returning it to make sure it gets back to the right person. That's happened before. They usually leave it on top of the mailbox block or under the door, but it's not that odd. It just feels off. And I'm suddenly afraid to open it.

I scan the area around me subtly, to see if anyone is watching me. I don't even know why. I just feel watched right now. I'm paranoid, because of course I am. Who wouldn't be right now? I grab the envelope and shove the door open. The room is quiet, and a less aggressive bleach smell still permeates the air.

I sit at my desk and open the letter inside. It's handwritten in block letters. And the words make my heart stop. My trembling hands can't hold the paper, and it feathers to the floor. When I pick it up, I notice a map on the back. I sit down shakily and read it again.

I know where you buried him, the note begins, and tears of frustration and terror form behind my eyes until the paper blurs. It continues:

> If you had paid attention or driven a few miles farther, you would have seen you were not in the middle of nowhere, but just outside a town that's expanding. Where you dug is scheduled for groundbreaking to build a new housing community. Dumb move.

I blink at the paper a few times, and I don't know if I've ever felt so numb. It's like I can't handle one more thing going wrong, and I don't even have the capacity to physically react. My mind races, though—who could know? Who could possibly know what we've done? How? We were careful. Nobody followed us. How the fuck could someone know the location? But here it is on a map. And we were too stupid to see that a town was just beyond where we stopped...

Well, who uses a goddamn fucking map anyway!? I don't know what every dot means! It felt like the middle of nowhere. We'd been driving for eternity. And just our luck that if we'd kept going a few miles, we'd hit some up-and-coming little town center. Fuck!

I stand up and try to breathe, crumpling the paper and throwing it in a fit of rage. Who knows? Why don't they just turn me in? Why would they write this? Is it torture—they want to watch me suffer for what I've done? What does this mean?

I can't tell Callum. He'll lose his mind, and he's already shitty at staying cool. I can handle this. Whoever this is, I can be a step ahead. Does someone have access to my phone? That's the only way anyone could have known, right? There were no cars out there. Who would have access to my phone, though? I pace the floor and wrack my brain for who would do this and for what reason, and I come up with nothing, but I need to do something.

I have to move him. That's all there is to it. I just…I'll move him. I'll do it right this time. I'll leave my phone. I'll tell everyone I'm going to visit my father for a night, and I'll be back so they won't wonder or speculate…and then I'll go north. Yes. We should have done that to begin with.

Durango, Colorado, is only a few hours north—where there are actual green fucking trees and mountains and rivers and a landscape that's not barren. Endless places to hide a body, and not just dirt and clay and flat land. A place that nobody is about to build apartments over. I know a place. I know what I need to do. I don't have time to think. This person could turn me in anytime. I have to be quicker than them.

When Callum returns around three, my car is packed and ready to go. He comes into the front office, poorly imitating a man looking for a package. What a dweeb. Can he really not just act natural in any way?

"Just come in," I say, and he nervously slips inside and closes the door behind him.

"I already heard the gossip between here and the parking lot," he says. "So he's officially missing?" he asks, calmer than I imagined.

"Yes, Rosa reported it." I tell him about Eddie not having a trucking job, and we both agree that can only help us if shit ever hits the fan.

"Well, we knew this was coming. It gave us a few days. Sounds like Eddie already has a lot of suspicion around him," I say.

"And anything they find on his phone from the truck can only be good for us. It's probably horrifying and has nothing to do with us, so I mean. It's falling into place the way we need so far," he says. God, if he only knew.

"Look," I say, stuffing some sandwiches and water bottles

into my red Igloo cooler on the desk. "I have to go see my dad. Just until tomorrow night. He's not doing that well," I say, and I see his face redden and his shoulders tense.

"Your dad," he says.

"Yeah, what?" I say.

"You're not... Are you like, skipping town? Are you..."

"What? What the fuck? No. Yeah, that would look good!" I snap.

"Okay, sorry. Keep your voice down," he whispers, accompanied by a shushing gesture.

"Well, seriously. You think I'm that dumb? Talk about painting a target on my back. Hey, someone suddenly skips town without telling anyone the day this guy goes missing? Sure."

"Okay," he says. "I just didn't expect you to be leaving."

"I'm legit going to see my dad and will be back tomorrow. I already told the residents. Any plumbing emergencies, call a plumber. Anything else can probably wait a half a day."

"Yeah, okay, well, hurry back because if anything... I don't know...happens and we can't call or text, I don't know. I just think we need to stay together."

"Ya wanna come?" I say, knowing there's no way.

"That would look even weirder, so no, but seriously. Come back like ASAP."

"Oh, my God. Callum. I am coming back," I say, and he gives a tentative nod and goes back out the front door, which I lock behind him, and it dawns on me for the first time that what if I don't come back? What if I take the stacks of cash this time— all wrapped in plastic bricks safe inside Eddie's backpack—and just disappear?

I think about it more on the long drive through the desert. I have my windows down and a George Strait song playing from the scratchy radio. It feels a little bit like the apocalypse happened, and I was left behind out here. Dark and deathly silent. I try to stay distracted and switch to the only stations that will come in on the radio. A talk show host gives callers shockingly terrible advice about how to handle their rebellious teenager. I change it to a Jesus station with a preacher giving a sermon. I listen to him for a few minutes talk about how the "wages of sin is death" and decide silence is better than the radio.

I go over my movements in my mind again. I have lined the inside of my trunk with thick sheets of plastic drop cloth and taped it all around the edges so it's airtight. The body is already wrapped in thick sheets and then layers of duct tape. I have garden gloves and rubber gloves. I'm stopping at a mom-and-pop motel halfway back from the Colorado border to Santa Fe and paying cash so I can shower and change, and I plan to leave these clothes in a dumpster somewhere along the way just in case. I don't fully understand DNA, but I'm not taking any chances.

When I drive up to the spot where we buried him, I feel my body start to shake, and the waves of nausea make me grip the door handle and take a moment to breathe and try to calm down.

We're total idiots. Our tire tracks off the main road back here are so fucking obvious. It's clay, and there has been no rain. It's just evidence, hanging out. It's lucky we only left this for a couple days. Nobody driving would have any reason to stop out here, fine. You see some tire marks along the long stretch of highway where people pull off for one reason or another, but now, coming back with new eyes, it looks like we just left a breadcrumb trail right to it if anyone was looking out here— like if someone had access to my phone somehow. Dammit. I don't know what I'm doing. This is insane.

I breathe. I refuse to start crying. I have no choice but to do this at this point. It's so surreal that the edges of everything look almost cartoonish. Nothing feels rooted in reality because it's all too bizarre to be real, but here I stand.

The dirt is soft and loose this time, so it doesn't feel like trying to dig into concrete. It's nothing compared to the labor it took last time, thank God. And I was counting on that fact in order to do it alone. He's not a big guy, and the grave is shallow, but I still don't know how I'll do this; just that I have to.

In the hot night air, I dig in silence again. This time my strength and determination comes from sheer terror. What if one of his cartel guys just pulls up at any moment—thrilled at the opportunity to waterboard someone or pluck out my fingernails with pliers instead of just executing me in a practical efficient way. I move as fast as I can and try to regulate my breathing that's nearing hyperventilation.

He's buried behind a huge cluster of oversize bushes, hidden from the road, so it takes me a moment to register the light I'm seeing is headlights coming from the east, and I start to panic. I will myself not to throw up and leave my DNA all over the damn place. I drop the shovel behind the bushes and rush to my car, which is parked about thirty or forty feet closer to the road—closer than last time. I parked there so, just in case someone came by, it wouldn't look out of place—they would think I pulled off like a normal person for car trouble or a whiny kid or a fight with my spouse or something, but not pulled way out to a suspiciously off-road spot like we did last time because we're complete morons and really bad at this.

I sit in my car and... God. Right, I don't have a phone. I was gonna pretend to be looking up directions or something in case this person stops. And then I see it.

Holy mother of Mary. The short flash of red lights, and then the car pulls over, and it's a cop. It's an actual fucking cop. I'm gonna throw up. I'm gonna throw up right now. I pull a Wendy's cup from the console and puke into what was left of a Diet Pepsi and then shove the lid back on and force back tears before he taps on my window. I need a story, and quick.

"Hey, ma'am. Everything okay?"

"Oh. Yeah. Yes. Everything is super." *Oh, God. Stop talking*, I internally plead with myself.

"You lost? Flat tire?"

"Nope. I'm great," I say... Where's my story? What's my reason?

"Can I get your license and registration?" he asks, and he must see my hands tremble as I hand the documents to him. He disappears back to his car, and what is probably three minutes feels like hours

I am stiff and I am numb. My neck is in knots, and my mouth is so dry I don't think I can speak. I think about opening the door and running. How ridiculous—just the image of me running in the middle of the desert to nothing—with nothing—and a cop right behind me, almost makes me laugh. Or maybe cry. Actually, I think I might start screaming. I have an overwhelming urge to just start screaming like a lunatic and have him take me to a mental health facility somewhere. God help me. What do I do?

I should turn myself in before he finds out. I can tell the truth. We were scared—we...

He comes back and hands me my cards. "So what are you doing out here then, if you don't have a flat or something?"

"Is it illegal?" I ask.

"No. But I just gotta make sure you're not in harm's way. Nobody else with you? No one in the trunk?" he says, and then smiles.

"Oh, like you think I'm being sex trafficked or something. Oh! Yeah, no. My fiancé is actually meeting me here. I know that sounds odd, but we live in different towns. See, I'm in Albuquerque, he's in Amarillo, and did you know they are building a new housing development here?" I say.

He softens slightly. "I did hear that, yes. Upscale, with a pool in every yard they say."

"Yep. So we are early buyers. They're breaking ground soon, so sometimes when neither of us can make the long drive, we just meet in the middle here. We like to lay on the hood of the car and imagine our new life in our new house. It's weird, but it's a really long drive, so you know. It's just nice sometimes," I say, sweat dripping down my back, pricks of heat under my armpits.

"I think that actually sounds pretty nice," he says. "Most of my stops out here are DUIs and speeding, so good on ya. Do you need me to wait with you until he gets here?" he says, looking around as if I could be in danger out here alone.

"Oh, no. Thank you, but I actually still have a few miles to go. I just pulled off to check my directions. It can all look the same out here, just making sure I turn off in the right place," I say, and he tilts his hat and taps the top of my car.

"All right, miss. You have a good night. Good luck on your house."

"Thank you, thanks. Bye," I stutter and close the window. When he pulls away and his taillights fade in the distance, I start bawling until my ribs ache.

Who am I? What does lying so easily even make me? That was almost the end of my entire life as I know it. Now I do scream. I scream as hard as I can until my voice is raw, and I beat my fists on the steering wheel, and then, after enough time has passed, and I'm sure he's not coming back, I get out and get back to work.

The hardest part is digging out a sort of ramp into the dirt—a slope that I can pull him up, the way I can't physically do otherwise. I do get a grip on the loops of duct tape around his ankles, and I'm able to sit on the ground, dig my heels in, and use all of my core strength to pull him up in short bursts of energy. It's exhausting, and it takes more time to fill the hole back in and cover up the slope I dug than I thought, but by midnight, I am back on the road, headed to the Colorado border.

When I get close to my destination, it's almost 5:00 a.m. I remember this place from when I was a kid. South of Durango. We were on our way to visit my aunt who lived there. I was maybe eleven, and we camped near a national park, and it was so beautiful. It was nothing like the flat brown landscape I was used to. I was in awe of the hot springs. I was afraid of them at first when my father told me I'd boil to death if I went in, but after I saw other families in them, I went in, too, and it was like magic. I'd never seen anything like it. It's weird because I remember not trusting my dad the same way after that. He might have been kidding, but it felt like I was lied to because he made me afraid and thought it was funny. I don't why I'm remembering this right now.

We camped in an orange tent, and my mother was still with us then. We roasted marshmallows on sticks until they caught on fire and turned black. My mother said it was unsanitary to use sticks and to get a skewer, but we didn't. We played flashlight tag and watched flecks of white ash float way up into the sky and dance around above the flames, and I had a Care Bear sleeping bag and a walkie-talkie, and we were happy. We were happy then.

I remember the abandoned well, too. When we took a walk through the woods the next day, there was a well deep back in the trees. There was a piece of plywood pushed over the top, and my father told me not to play near it. When I asked why he said because it's a couple hundred feet deep and kids fall in them all the time and nobody can hear them scream. They just find their bones a hundred years later.

I was so afraid of it, thinking about a little girl my age curled up in the cold water on the bottom, her bones cracked and broken as she fell against the stones to the depths. I think about her crying for her mother as her pain and hunger slowly killed her. And then I tried to forget about it—to get the nagging images out of my mind.

I camped there one more time, with my brunch girlfriends who don't speak to me anymore. This time they called it glamping, and we stayed in fancy cabins and drank prosecco by the hot tub and the fire was gas instead of wood. Nothing like that first experience, but it was when we drove in that I remembered that well for the first time since I was a kid. There was a wooden horse fence that seemed to go on for a mile butting up against the two-lane road into the grounds. It made me remember the well. It was next to a wooden fence, and so very early in the morning, I took my mug of coffee and didn't even change out of my pajamas. I just shoved my feet into sneakers and made the hike out toward the main road until I saw the wooden fence, and I followed it.

There it was. As an adult, I realized that it was on the farthest edge of an eight-hundred-acre farm buried under tangles of brambles and ivy. There was no plywood on it this time, no well cap, nothing. I tossed a penny in and made a wish. Then I heard a car whoosh by and made the trek back. That wasn't that long ago. It wasn't that long ago at all. It has to still be there—forgotten and abandoned.

The sun threatens to rise when I find the edge of the wooden fence on a narrow two-lane road. But it's still dark, and I know the trees are thick enough for me to be hidden in them as soon as I can pull the body from the back of the car and into the thicket. The fence and the well are not so far that I can't do this, so I tug his backpack onto my back, knowing the best way in is to make small gains like I did before. Short bursts of energy... grip the tape at his ankles, pull as hard as I can and then stop and breathe, and do it again, inching along.

My back is throbbing, my eyes are blurred with tears, but I keep at it. It's harder to do over uneven ground and roots winding and twigs snapping beneath the weight of him, but I pull and stop and pull and stop until I'm there.

It's just like I last saw it. I look into its endless darkness and say hello, my words echoing back to me. *Two hundred feet deep, bones cracking, child skeletons.* My father's face and laughter come back to me. I will not cry. I have to do what I came here for and get the hell out of here.

"I'm so sorry," I whisper to Eddie. Because he's a real person, and he has a wife and a mother somewhere, and I *am* so sorry. And when he falls, it's just a quiet whoosh. It seems like he falls for a thousand miles until I hear a sound—the crash of a body hitting stone, and I try not to think about cracking bones and ripping flesh...and I know nobody will ever find him.

Then I decide to do something we promised not to do. Before I drop his backpack, I take out one of the saran-wrapped stacks of cash. Just one. I won't use it now, but I might need it. Just one is enough. I have to. Then I drop the pack, and there's a long pause until I hear a tap as it hits the bottom, and I marvel at how thousands of dollars and the IDs of seven men—what is left of the lives of five men—sound as small as my single penny falling.

And then I run as hard as I can through trees and vines, as fast as I can until my lungs burn and my ankles are scratched and scraped from twigs and vines, and my face is streaked with mud and tears. And then I reach my car and drive and drive until I can find a place to erase every trace of this dead man and all of my sins. I think again about just driving—just choosing a direction and taking this money and just never going back.

21

ANNA

The police called to ask me a few more questions again. It's something about Henry's laptop, and I wonder if they will be giving it back to me now—or if they found more secrets that I don't know about.

I sit in my car in the parking lot outside the apartments, wondering if evidence of his affair was on his laptop and if they know, but also watching Cass pull in and park in front of the office.

It's been a few weeks since she went to visit her father, from what I hear via the rumor mill at The Sycamores. She was gone one night and hasn't been the same since she got back, if you listen to the talk. There's lots of speculation on what could have happened, but none of it's good because she's acted like a zombie since that night, although she tries hard to cover it.

She usually parks in back but not anymore for whatever reason. She gets out of the car and just stands there, staring toward the building for a few moments. She looks like absolute garbage. Her face is ghostly, and her hair is limp and stringy. She walks slowly to her apartment door and disappears inside, and I know for certain something is up with her. She knows something. Is the guilt about what she knows getting to her, I wonder?

I think about Monica on my drive to the station, and how maybe I'll find the answers I need on Henry's laptop if they do give it back. At least it's worth sifting through before I accuse my best friend of something I can't take back. I haven't talked to her much since I found the phone records. I know I should have confronted her right away, but something made me wait, so I've dodged invites and made excuses to get off the phone when she calls—just until I know more. She would lie, right? If there were something going on that she didn't want me to know about, she would just lie, so tipping her off to the fact that I know they were in contact doesn't help me. Patience is the only thing that's going to help me.

I have barely talked to Callum in the days since that stupid night, either. We avoid each other and give an awkward nod when we pass one another on the pool deck. I just spend my time scouring every square inch of this apartment—every box, every sheet of paper, every photo—for anything that might put my life back together. So when I get a call that they have information, and it's concerning Henry's laptop, I'm anxious; but at least there's something they found warranting my going back in.

He keeps a file on his desktop that's labeled 2012 tax returns, but inside are all his passwords to social media, email, *everything*, so he has them all in one place when he inevitably forgets them. I have them in a similar file on my phone labeled passwords, but I guess his theory that nobody would ever care to look in his 2012 tax return file is smart. Of course, the police would, though.

The point is, I haven't had access to any of this yet; not his desktop, his social media, email. They casually asked for the laptop so quickly after his death, it was all water through my hands before I could even think about how much I needed it for my own investigation. Not that saying no to them was an option. That list of passwords will open up an entire world to me about what he was really doing—things that the police don't know to look for because they don't know about the affair, so certain interactions may not mean anything to them. But I'll know.

When I get there, I expect to wait for an eternity and then answer different versions of the same questions again from the same detective who thinks he's good at making me feel like I'm an ally and not a suspect, but that's not what happens. I'm ushered into a hallway right away. No waiting. Shit. This is probably bad then, it's not like the other times.

"Ms. Hartley. Thanks for coming down."

I turn to see Detective Harrison walking toward me with quick strides before opening a door and gesturing me in, and I follow him into a little depressing room the way I have done many times before. Four walls, one table, two bottles of water, and a soul-stealing feeling in the air.

"You found all you needed on the laptop?" I ask.

"Yes, and we will be giving it back to you sometime in the near future," he says, and there is a shift in his tone from previous conversations—a lightness or warmth, almost. And I realize that I must not be a person of interest anymore because they wouldn't release this back to me if I were, right? What must they have uncovered for this to happen? "I won't keep you long, but I do just have one question."

"Okay," I say, hugging my purse to my chest, wishing I were somewhere else but knowing I need to suffer through more repetitive questions.

"There was a letter Henry wrote…intended for you," he says.

"What? What do you mean?"

"It's on the desktop of Henry's laptop. So you haven't seen it?" he asks, and I just stare at him, confused, still clutching my bag hard and mindlessly chewing the skin on my cuticle for comfort.

The detective clicks at the keyboard on his tablet and then turns it around for me to see.

It's addressed to me. The thought that it's the last letter I'll ever receive from him doesn't slip through unnoticed. I sit forward and hold my heart.

"We found the same text in an unsent email to you," he says, and I read what's on the screen. Henry's precious words to me.

Anna, I love you. I'm so sorry for all the mistakes I've made. This is me coming clean. I've started writing this letter to you a dozen times. My shame and guilt is overwhelming, and you deserve to know how this all started to unravel.

I quietly pray he doesn't say he killed someone the way he did to me over the phone that last day of his life, because I know he was manic, and it's not true, and they can't think that about him, or they'll start going down some pointless path to find out who or what he's talking about. But when I keep reading, he doesn't say any more about that. It's short. It's cryptic.

Just because I made these choices and caused people pain doesn't mean I don't love you. There is so much I need to tell you, but a letter seems so flat and doesn't do it justice. If anything happens to me, the video on my phone will explain it all. If I know I'm in danger, I'll send it to you. If you find this, it's probably too late. If that's the case, I'm so desperately sorry, and this is all my doing. Watch the video I made. You'll understand what happened when you watch. I love you.

The detective looks at me as he clicks off the screen and closes the computer, and I look back at him. I let out the breath I've been holding and blink back tears.

"He clearly never sent it, and it looks like you haven't seen it before, but do you have any idea what he's talking about? Why he's so sorry? Who he caused pain to?" Harrison asks, and I notice my knuckles are white, and my jaw is clenched and mind is whirling—what video? *Why didn't you just talk to me, Henry? What does this mean!?*

"If I knew that," I say, "why would he need to write a letter and make some fucking video explaining it to me?"

"Right," he says quietly. "So you never got a video, haven't seen it?"

"No! Have you seen a video?" I ask.

"No phone was retrieved, as you know, and phone records obviously don't have that sort of ability, so…"

"So can I go?" I ask, holding back tears but approaching the breaking point.

"You can go," he says, and I get up so quick that the chair falls to the floor behind me, but I keep walking until I break into a sprint when I reach the front doors and until I get to my car.

I sit in the driver's seat and watch fat raindrops start to drizzle down the glass in tiny rivulets. I squeeze my eyes closed and shake my head, steadying my breath. He still loved me. No matter what happened. That's all I care about in this moment.

When I get back to the apartments, I sit in my car and watch the rain bounce off the surface of the swimming pool and notice Babs dancing in bare feet and a sundress, laughing up at the sky like a total lunatic. Can I trust what she told me about Eddie? And could the bad people he knew be connected to Henry? Everyone here is wack, and I don't know what to believe.

The words of his letter repeat over and over in my mind. *What goddamn video, Henry? Why didn't you send it? What the hell happened to you? You knew it was coming. You knew someone was going to hurt you, why, why, why?*

Then I see Cass come out of the office in Wellies and a rain poncho. She picks up some deck chairs the wind tipped over, and she stacks the rest in a pile by the wall so they don't blow away.

And I have nothing to lose anymore. Someone here knows something, and it's time to get answers. I follow her when she goes back in the front door of the office, and I think I literally scare the piss out of her, because she wields a kid-size Wiffle bat from next to the door at me when I startle her.

"Sorry!" I put my hands up, and she simultaneously puts the plastic bat down, apologizing. "That wouldn't do you a lot of good if you really were in danger, you know?" I say.

"Well, God, Anna. Give someone a freakin' aneurism, why don't ya?" She's trying to catch her breath.

"Sorry. Are you?" I ask.

"What?"

"In danger?"

The question drains all the blood from her face, but if she is involved in something and knows about Henry and the people who hurt him, maybe she *is* in danger, too. "What? No," she says, turning her back to fiddle with something, or rather, to hide her face from me. "Can I do something for you? If your roof is leaking, there's a pile of ice-cream buckets in the shed. Standard practice around here," she says.

"I know you're hiding something," I say, and she whips around at this and sort of looks me up and down. Pauses, contemplating something, and then looks me in the eye.

"Did you leave me that note?" she asks.

"What? I don't know what you're talking about."

"Then I don't know what the hell you're talking about," she says back.

"You're acting odd, just in case you don't think anyone notices," I say, and I can tell I hit a sore spot by the way her body stiffens. She sits on the edge of her desk and looks at the floor while I go on. "And I think I know why," I say.

She seems frozen to the spot, not making eye contact, and I think I see her flinch ever so slightly. It's like she's waiting for a punch. "Why?" she finally asks in a small voice.

"Because you know what happened to Henry."

She looks up. "What?"

"You know everyone around here and all the silly chatter and talk. And you act like you're just trying to blend in with the furniture and not stick out or be noticed, but I notice. You're always seeing what's going on. Just like with Rosa that night. Except I happened to be here that time, but the point is, you're like a fly on the wall around here. You see things— maybe things you shouldn't, and that's why you're so scared," I say, and she tries to hide her jaw drop by turning it into a lip snarl and roll of the eyes.

"I really don't know where this is coming from. It was very nice of you to bail me out, and I'm sure you're a nice person, and I'll pay you back, but I think you...you have it wrong. You don't know anything about me, so..."

An explosion of thunder cracks through the air, and the rain beats down on the rooftop so loudly we almost have to yell. Cass closes the front door I left open as the rain floods in. She tosses a couple of swim towels on top of the puddles to dry them. It's quieter now, and we look at one another.

"I don't know you, you're right, but you knew Henry. So I'm here, in front of you, begging you to tell me what you really know. What happened to him? Who killed him? It was someone here. I know it. You know it. Nobody skulks around like you do without a big secret, and you're not good at hiding it, so just...please. What happened to him?"

"What the fuck did you just say?"

"You know what I'm asking," I say.

"Nobody kil— What? He committed suicide. You asked who killed him? You're telling me that somebody killed him? That's not what anyone was told... That's not... That can't be true." And again, as she speaks, just like in the car, there is something authentic about her reaction that doesn't feel manufactured. There still has to be something here— something that makes her act the way she does. I just feel it. I can't explain it, but it's a gut thing.

"You don't have anything for me?" I ask, feeling defeated and so, so tired all of a sudden.

Cass sits in her office chair with her mouth hanging open and blinks a few times. She stares at the floor and then shakes it off and looks at me. "You're telling me you're sure someone killed him. Not a hunch. The police said this? This is for real?" she asks, and her words are careful, like she's putting something together in her mind—connecting some dots. Like maybe she does know something, but with this news, she's trying to figure it out for herself.

"Yeah. And don't tell Tweedledee and Tweedledum out there, please, because I don't want that news all over just yet." I don't even need to gesture to Crystal and Jackie smoking cigarettes under the awning in front of the pool for her to know who I mean.

"I'm so sorry. I had no idea. I thought…we all thought he was so depressed. Everyone said… It made sense, but…" She stops and looks gutted and also sort of shocked, but there's something else, too, that I can't put my finger on. "Jesus. I really am sorry to hear that."

"You're sure you can't think of anything you might have heard?" I try one last time.

"Maybe," Cass says.

"What?" I snap. It's the absolute last thing I expected her to say.

"Just… I don't know anything for sure, but there might be something. No promises. Just maybe."

"Whoa, whoa, what? Tell me what you mean. What the hell does that mean?" I plead.

"I gotta go. I have something I need to figure out first. I'll find you. You'll just have to trust me," she says, pulling her rain hood over her head and opening the door.

"Why would I trust you!?" I call to her back, an angry last attempt at getting an answer of any kind now before I totally lose my mind.

"You wouldn't, but do you have any other people helping? Any other choice?"

"I don't know if you're helping or not," I say, arms folded, completely unsure what to make of this woman.

"Just give me a little time." And then she's gone.

I think about running after her, shaking her, forcing her to the ground, choking the words out of her so she tells me what she knows. But I can't do that, of course. She might have an answer, and maybe she's being honest about that, so what can I do but wait?

I walk through the pouring rain, letting myself get drenched as I hurry across to my unit. The cold air inside the apartment stings as I enter. I pull Henry's terry cloth robe from a hook, and his keys fall to the floor with a clink. I step over them, and I curl up inside his robe on the ugly plaid recliner and just sit a moment, asking myself the same questions with no answers— what video? What is Cass going to do now—what does she think she might know? Who was after Henry? How the hell was he aware he was in danger and not tell anyone? The more I know, the less sense it makes.

I stare across the floor at Henry's dropped keys. His key chain, the one with a tiny rubber duck wearing a scarf, looks broken from here. The little duck looks like it's been strangled because it's bent slightly to the right. I tense. I stand up. Holy crap. I remember now, that I gave it to him because it wasn't really just a duck. The head pops off, and it's a thumb drive.

Oh, my God. It's his thumb drive. I never even thought about this before or remembered it was anything but the key chain I saw every day...until this minute.

I scurry across the floor to pick it. I pop off the duck's head to make sure I didn't remember it wrong like everything else in my life. And there it is, the little metal flash drive. I rush to the table, flip open my laptop, and push in the drive.

It pops up—the 2012 tax file I know houses all of his passwords, and at first I'm beside myself because I know I can scour through every inch of his life, and that answers must be there. At first, this is the biggest break I've had until I see another file, and I realize that I don't even need to look through his emails or Instagram messages. The answer is right in front of me.

A file labeled love blinks at me, and I click on it with nervous fingers. Her face blooms onto the screen, and there she is.

I lose my breath for a moment. Then I stand up, a surreal weightlessness, an electricity, runs through me upon seeing her face. I feel myself shaking as I sit back down and stare at the screen—at photo after photo after photo of Henry's paintings. He always kept photos of them for his records and safekeeping, and so the mystery is solved.

The woman he was in love with lies naked in the first few. Many paintings are just her face; smiling, eating a croissant, sticking out her tongue playfully, or even crying in one. There is one painting of their hands intertwined, and another with her hand over her face and her head hung in sorrow. Many are sensual, some are light and whimsical. All are of the same mystery woman. Dozens and dozens of paintings of one dark-haired beauty.

Okay, I know who you are now. And I'm even starting to understand it, but who's hiding a hundred paintings? Where are the actual goddamn paintings?

22

CASS

In the few weeks since I returned from Colorado, things have been quiet in a way where it felt, maybe deceivingly so, like everything might be okay for a while. Like I could lie low at least for little bit. Until, that is, Anna came into the office.

Callum and I check in most evenings around six when he checks his mail, and I make sure I'm out watering the shrubs so we can have a casual conversation about the weather or maybe any life-altering news, but there hasn't been any yet. He doesn't know about the housing development ground breaking, or me moving the body. I am just grateful every day there is no movement, nothing new to tell each other. No cops, no news trucks appearing in the lot with armed cartel, no body, and no more notes from the mystery person who knows what we did.

Rosa and the pool girls have put up missing posters around town and their days at the card table next to the pool are quieter lately, but they still have a gaggle of children to attend to, so they still sit with sweating mason jars of iced tea and paper fans and watch them each afternoon, playing their cards, but with softer voices and a more watchful eye.

But what Anna said started to make all of the pieces fall into place—the hunch I had. I think I was right about it, and I think I probably can help her find out what happened to Henry, but I'm scared shitless if I'm honest, and there's something I need to do first to make sure I'm safe when the shit hits the fan. And oh boy, will the shit hit the fan if what I am piecing together turns out to be right.

I need a day or two, but I definitely have a piece of information that is going to be hard for her to hear about Henry.

On Thursday afternoon, Frank brings over his checkerboard, and we sit on the concrete slab in front of the office, cross-legged in flip-flops, sipping instant lemonade, and playing the game. While he's plotting his next move, my phone rings.

I stiffen the way I instinctively do now any time there's a knock on the door, a phone ping, a cough next door—pretty much over anything. And when I see it's just Reid calling again, I silence my phone, put it face down on the ground next to me, and smile at Frank who says, "King me."

Reid has been calling a lot lately, and I know it's because he's pissed about his tools and the way Callum made him leave, but those tools are Frank's now, and it's over my dead body that he gets them back. Maybe he's actually trying to sue me the way I told him he'd have to do. I mean, Reid putting together an IKEA crib? Sure, that'll happen. He's just being a colossal, controlling prick, and I refuse to respond. I asked him to hand me an Allen wrench once, and he handed me a torx key, I mean, seriously? Maybe if the crib were made out of LEGO, but there's no way, and he can stay the hell away from us.

I feel a twinge of protectiveness over Frank when I think about this. It also feels good to have maybe finally let go of Reid and his…pregnant, adolescent fiancée. Maybe that's what I needed to see to move on. Maybe I should even be grateful I can put it behind me. And maybe I was getting close to doing so, but it's not helping that he's all of a sudden calling after months of nights where I'd have done anything on earth to see his name pop up on my phone. Now, the fact that it makes me cringe is…progress. *Okay, Reid, you got nothing better to do with your time, and with a baby on the way, than to harass me for the precious tool set? Sure, keep callin', bucko, see how far it gets you.*

I see Callum cross to the mailboxes and call out to him. It's not his usual six o'clock time frame. "Hey," I say, and he sees Frank, too, and comes over.

"Wanna play?" Frank asks.

"Oh, thanks, but I'm headed out. I have basketball at the Y tonight. I'll take a rain check, though," he says, and Frank agrees.

"Is your faucet still leaking?" I ask, because usually we make painfully idle talk at the 6:00 p.m. mailbox check-in, but yesterday, he actually had something new to say when he told me about the faucet dripping at night.

"I think so. I shut the bedroom door now so I don't hear, but I'm guessing so," he says.

"I'll fix it, I promise," I say, and he nods a skeptical *okay* and waves at Frank as he goes to his car.

"Can I help?" Frank asks, and he's so excited, I can't say no. So he rushes off to get his tool belt and meet me there, and I grab my workbag and go over to Callum's apartment and let myself in.

I poke around in some of his cupboards like anyone probably would out of curiosity. Nothing interesting. Just an absurd amount of Hamburger Helper and frozen dinners, and a six pack of beer. I take one and offer him a mental IOU after I do. I look at the bathroom faucet and see it's the one that's leaking, then I nose around under the sink and clear a space to access the plumbing and make room for a bucket in case I need to open the pipe.

My heart aches when I see some of Lily's old hair bands and a curling iron in a plastic bin next to Callum's razors and aftershave. It's hard to imagine her here. She lived a whole life before this place, and then one day she starts to cough, thinking it's a cold and just like that, it's a death sentence. I didn't know her well, but I still think about her and feel the void she left behind in Callum's life.

Now I feel like a snoop and an asshole for being in here, so I go outside and wait for Frank because it's an easy fix, and I don't want to do it without him, and as I do I notice Anna walking over, very surprised to see me here.

"You looking for Callum?" I ask, and her face flushes.

"Yeah, just— I was just gonna talk to him, but…" She seems nervous, and I know she's looking at me for answers—she wants to know what I know, and if I were her I'd want to scratch my eyes out, too, for being cryptic and making her wait, and I can also tell that she likes Callum in some way she probably feels guilty about. I'm no idiot. I can see it between both of them, so I throw her a bone.

"I'm fixing the faucet. He's not here."

I'm not giving anything away just yet. She's just gonna have to trust me because I have something she's going to want to see, but I need to make sure one more thing is in place—a little insurance policy so I don't go down with this sinking ship I somehow got myself on.

"He's playing basketball or something, I think. He'll be back later," I say just as Frank saunters past me, walking inside like he owns the place with his tool belt on.

She looks at me so intensely that it makes my skin prickle with uneasiness. "I actually wanted to talk to you," she says.

"Can't now. I'm on a job," I say. "Sorry, later, though."

"Oh…okay, yeah," Anna says timidly and retreats to her apartment.

I let out the breath I've been holding and feel myself trembling. I squeeze my eyes closed and try to pull myself together while Frank is setting up his things. *I feel so bad for her. Goddammit. I'm really sorry, Anna. I screwed up.*

Frank and I fix the faucet pretty quickly and head back down to our lemonade and checkers. *I know what I'm doing*, I tell myself. I look around out of the corners of my eyes for Anna, but she's nowhere in sight. "This is the right thing to do," I mutter.

"What?" Frank asks.

"Nothing. King me," I say, and he does, but then points past me toward the brick office wall.

"What are those?" Frank asks, having slayed me in checkers twice already and probably bored with the poor competition.

I look to where he's pointing and see the beautiful herbs I replanted against the side of the office, green and thriving. "They're herbs. You can eat them."

"Oh, we used to have herbs, but my mom said you're supposed to smoke them. But she did make brownies once, and they were good even though I felt weird after."

I stare at him, not really knowing what to say and marveling at what he's been through in his young life. "Well, these are different. Smell them," I say, and he squats down in front of the little pots and gently handles each one as if they are precious objects.

He smells them, contemplates, and then smells another. "I can tell this is mint, but I don't know the others," he says.

"This one is my favorite. It's basil. Smell," I say, and he does. He smiles. "Right? Have you ever had pesto?"

"No." He laughs. "What's that?"

"Just the best thing ever, and you eat it with a ton of garlic bread and pasta. I can show you how to make it if you want."

"Like with ingredients like they do on the Food Network? Not frozen?"

"From scratch," I say, and my heart swells when I remember that we grew these for just this reason—so I could teach my kid how to fall in love with cooking and plants and the earth, and now here is this great kid, and he needs me. It's not what I expected, but I can't wait to show him, especially when I see the look on his face and how excited he is. And I can see that it's mixed with a skepticism, or maybe it's fear that I'll forget about it; about him. But I won't.

"Whaddya say? Maybe this weekend?" I say, and he nods.

And just then, I feel a shadow fall over us, and we both look up to see the figure of a man—a shadow, backlit by the sun. I cover my eyes with my hand and squint up at him from the ground. He steps into the shade, and I can see that it's Reid. I scramble to my feet in surprise, and maybe to prepare for war, if he thinks he's gonna tear my herbs out of the ground or sue me or whatever the hell he's here for.

"You scared the shit out of me," I say, because there was a brief second I thought he was a cop coming to take me away forever, the way I fear most moments of every day, but I'm still afraid when I think about him saying anything in front of Frank that might make him feel like his very special gift I gave him could be taken away.

"Who are you?" Frank asks.

"He's nobody, and he's leaving."

"Is this your boyfriend?" he asks, amused.

"Isn't Mary expecting you for dinner?" I ask with a hand on one hip.

"I can take a hint," Frank says, smirking. He picks up his checkers and skips off across the pool deck.

"What are you doing here?" I ask curtly.

"Well, if you'd ever answer your phone…"

"Look. Forget the goddamn tools. I mean, isn't this a little much even for you?" I say, and he looks confused.

"What?"

"You got everything you want. *Everything*. Is this who you've turned into? You're seriously stalking me for some tools you can't even use? I have nothing to give you, Reid. Just leave me alone," I say, feeling a bit of a rush because, for the first time ever, I mean it. I can't believe I told him to leave me alone and

meant it. I almost laugh for just a moment—the feeling of ela-
tion is brief but there. I turn, feeling momentarily light as air,
to go inside the office door.

"Wait. Wha...? I don't care about tools. That's not why I'm
here. I tried calling you. I just need to talk to you."

"Why?"

"It's important, okay?" He looks around subtly and tries to
hide a disgusted expression the way most people do when they
first experience the place in daylight. "Can we just...grab a bite
to eat and talk? Please. My treat."

"Of course it's your treat. You think I got money?" I say,
hard as stone, but on the inside, I'm going through all of the
reasons he would need to talk to me. Has someone contacted
him, thinking I still live at that address? I mean, some of my
mail still goes there by mistake. Has someone threatened him
to get to me?

I must not successfully mask my sheer terror at the thought
of what he might tell me because he snaps his finger in front of
my eyes to bring me back. "Uh...hello? You okay?"

"Fine, but I have things to do, so we have to make it quick.
There's a Super Jumbo China Buffet two blocks down," I say,
grabbing my purse from the hook inside the front door.

"Wait, no. I was thinking Terilli's or The Vine or something," he says, and I don't pause to listen to his restaurant sug-
gestions, I just want to know what he's here for.

"Don't worry, they have booze there," I say and lead the way,
and he helplessly follows behind.

We walk down a hopelessly depressing street—no trees to
filter the relentless glare of the sun, a few boarded-up liquor
stores in between a convenience store with bars on the door and
a check-cashing place, all covered in graffiti. The next block is
an Arby's, a strip mall with some nail salons with hand-painted
signs in the windows, and a Dollar Tree before you reach the
oversize Super Jumbo China Buffet.

Reid hates buffets. They remind him of horse troughs. Oh, well. Here we sit, at a table with sticky vinyl place mats and piles of beige food on our plates. I sip my Super Jumbo soda and wait for the screaming kid behind us to take it down a notch so we can hear each other speak. The kid throwing the fit tosses a hunk of sushi, and it bounces off our table and hits the floor. Reid ducks and curses. Not me, though. I don't flinch. This is the world I live in now.

"So what's wrong?" I ask.

"God, where do I start?" he says.

"Did someone die? Get kidnapped? Were you threatened? Tell me what happened," I ask, overcome with fearing the worst because I already know somebody knows what I did. What if they're coming after him, too?

"God, why are you always so dramatic? Nobody died, for God's sake."

"Then why are we here? You said it was important. Did someone send you a letter or…nobody threatened you?"

"No. What the hell are you talking about? I came to… I just… I came because I owe you…" He stops and looks at his plate.

"What?"

"An apology," he says, and I choke on a bite of egg roll upon hearing this and cough until my eyes water and then spit it into a napkin.

"Jesus," Reid mutters.

"I'm fine," I cough, and just then another kid—a toddler on a leash—wanders his leash-length limit from the booth next to them and stares at Reid, who is very uncomfortable. He shifts in his seat and doesn't know what to do, so he takes a wonton off my plate and tosses it like he's throwing a ball for a dog, and the toddler actually does go and chase it, to my delight and surprise.

"Hmm. So you're gonna be a dad then," I say, not concealing

my sarcasm. Then, "What are you apologizing for exactly?" I keep marveling at the fact that I am saying the words that I'm saying and not melting at the idea of an apology I've longed for. Maybe trauma changes you, or maybe that party made me finally let go of something and see who he really is.

"I just… I know I handled things poorly, and I just want to make peace," he says.

I look to either side of me, then behind me and back to him. "Are you talking to me?" I ask.

"Why do you do that?" he asks.

"What?"

"You're just… I'm trying to say I'm sorry here, and you're always so…"

"What?"

"I don't know. Rough around the edges. Crass. I just want a civil conversation."

"Oh, is that what you want? Do you always insult people in the middle of your apologies?" I ask.

He sighs and leans forward in his chair. "I'm sorry. Let's start over. Maybe we can put a pin in this and meet for a nice dinner somewhere later, get those espresso martinis you like at the Casablanca," he says, and I gasp out of nowhere, startling him.

"Holy shit!" I say, louder than intended.

"What!?" Reid looks around, trying to figure out what I'm reacting to.

"No way!"

"What?" he demands again.

"She left you!" I say, laughing, and then I stop and really look him in the eye. "Is that why you're here? You're not denying it. I was kidding for a second… I mean, I thought I was just being a dick, but…holy shit. That *is* why you're here."

He's annoyed with me, but I'm right. "Can we just—" he starts to say.

"So you want to whisk me off because you think an 'I'm

sorry' and an espresso martini at the Casablanca erases the hell I've been through…for months. Did you see where I live? I walked in on Gordon in 104 eating a plate of linguini on the toilet this morning and found a collection of mannequin heads in an empty apartment closet. I don't even technically get paid. I exist. That's it. Because of you, so are you actually kidding me right now?"

"That's not what this… Look, it's not like that. I just had time to really think through how wrong I was…" he starts to say, and I cut him off.

"Well, what happened? 'Cause last I heard you have an actual human baby popping out of Kimmy's very young pristine vagina and into the world pretty soon, so…" I see his face fall, and he picks the edges off his paper napkin and flicks them mindlessly onto the floor.

"She's been seeing someone—a barista at Starbucks. Named Asher," he says, and I can't help it. I spit my sip of soda back into the cup and belly laugh at this. How could I not? It's not just the karma, it's the whole visual.

"Well, that tracks. You're like twice her age."

"No, I'm not," he says.

"Very close. And the weird goatee thing you're sporting is less snowboarder dude that you're probably going for and more middle-aged pedophile."

"I don't expect you to forgive me," he says.

"I don't. So is Asher gonna raise your baby, too? What the hell, Reid?" I say, waving over the table attendant and ordering a sake, 'cause I feel like I'm gonna need it.

"Turns out it's…" He stops, looking for the words.

"Oooh," I say. "Not yours. I see."

We are both quiet for a few minutes. My sake comes, and I slide it across the table to him. He needs it more. He takes it.

"I had a lot of time to think, and I should have supported your handyman company," he says.

"Um, it was called *Handy Ma'am*, thank you very much."

He doesn't really hear me; he's still trying to make his point. "And I know… I am very aware that, like, having a family was all you wanted—all you were focusing on, and I wasn't, but I mean we tried and I'm sorry it wasn't happening, and that was stressful, and I don't know. It was just a lot, and I fucked up, okay? I seriously, royally fucked it all up."

"Yeah," I say quietly.

"Yeah," he says, too, and sips his sake.

"Well, I appreciate your apology, and I should probably get back," I say, eating one last egg roll because I didn't have to pay for it, then piling my napkin on my plate and sliding my chair back.

"You're leaving?" he asks, a crumpled look on his face.

"I have things to do," I say.

"Okay," he says, hanging his head.

My heart lurches, and I hate myself for going back on all the emotional progress I made thirty minutes ago. "Reid, would you be sorry, would you even be here, if she hadn't left? I mean, what do you really expect? You think I'm that pathetic?" I ask, and I mean, I sort of am. A month ago, this would have been a very different conversation.

"I know you won't believe me. I understand that. I know what you're gonna say…that it's convenient timing that I figured it out all now. That's exactly what you'll say next, because I know you better than anyone… Fine, yes, it sucks that it took going through this to realize what a mistake I made. That's the truth." He tries to take my hand, but I pull it away.

He continues, "I really, really fucked it all up, and I wish you knew how much I— How truly sorry I am."

I turn away from him and look out the window. A couple exits their car, a guy is hunched over his phone at the bus stop. A baby in a stroller screams as a mother tries to console it. Yep. The world goes on whether or not Reid is begging for forgiveness over greasy sweet-and-sour pork at the Super Jumbo China Buffet or banging Kimmy on my custom Arhaus couch. Who woulda thought?

I can't take in what he's saying. I have so many more impor-tant things to think about, but when I think about the safety of my life away from The Sycamores, of the normalcy and se-curity and distance, I want to leave with him right this min-ute and forgive him and never go back to the horror show my life has become. I don't respond, though. I keep my eyes on the couple walking up to the front automatic doors and then look down at my lap. I don't know what to say. I stand to go, and he counters me.

"I don't expect you to say anything. Please, just at least think about it," he says, and then he softly kisses my cheeks and looks in my eyes. "Just say you'll think about it?"

"Gotta go," I say, pulling away from him and walking quickly out the front door.

But I do think about it.

When I get back to The Sycamores, I go into the office. I take a deep breath and blow it out hard with puffed cheeks, then kick my shoes off on the cool floor and try to shake off what just happened and the myriad of complex emotions I have about it all, because I have to stay focused. I have to—

My thoughts stop cold when I see a piece of paper taped to my desktop computer that I know I didn't put there. I walk around the giant wood desk and stand in front of the computer and pull off what appears to be an article clipped from a news-paper. It has an image of a married couple in a small black-and-white photo. I skim what it says.

Tortured, then murdered in their own beds. Ties to cartel.

Then I read the name *Victor Becerra, infamous kingpin*… That's Eddie's real name. Holy mother of shit. It says although he was in prison at the time of the murders, it's still thought that he orchestrated them and many others.

I feel my head get light and tingly, and my body shakes. I turn it over to see a note on the back. Who could have come in here? How did they get in? Who would do this? My thoughts race. Then I read it.

Just because he's dead doesn't mean he can't hurt you. Did you leave fingerprints on the money you took? Be more careful.

A scream escapes my lips before I can stop it, and I cup my mouth with both hands as tears stream down my face.

23

ANNA

What is she hiding? What the hell does Cassidy Abbott know about my life that I don't know myself? It's infuriating. I search her for the tenth time all over social media and for some reason I think new information will materialize, but she hasn't posted a thing in months. I already knew from previous searches that there is little about her anywhere—I mean, nothing aside from the basics—a high school softball victory in the local paper years ago, a small business she started that looks like it didn't go anywhere. Lots of photos of her on Facebook from months back, looking like a completely different person, I might add, in designer dresses—always holding a glass of bubbly or with her arms around a group of other women, who all look like they belong in a Macy's ad.

Now she's here in her Super Mario Brothers overalls, covered in spackle half the time, having lost everything and perpetually acting paranoid. It's weird. Is she hiding from someone? And how does she literally just slam the door on me when I want to talk to her? I'm not waiting around anymore. I need answers. The torture of not knowing, of crafting stories in my mind is boiling over now, so patience is no longer my strategy.

By dusk, I've waited long enough, and Callum should be back by now. There's no way I'm calling or texting him about this. What I found will shock him, and he's the first person I need to tell. Maybe he can help me make sense of the image of the woman I'm looking at.

I nod a hello at Rosa and Crystal who sit quietly in front of Crystal's apartment door on folding chairs smoking cigarettes. Then I walk around the corner to Callum's door again, and I tap my knuckle on the window and call his name. Nothing.

"Hey, Callum," I call and jiggle the doorknob, and I'm surprised when it opens. It's not locked, so either he's home or maybe Cass didn't lock it after she did whatever the hell she was doing there. I look behind me to see if anyone is looking in my direction, and then I call one more time inside the front door and listen. No movement.

"Hey," I say one more time, walking inside, tentatively. I realize he's definitely not home, and I really shouldn't be in here, but for some reason I don't leave. I give the pool deck and parking lot one more quick glance before I slip inside and close the door behind me.

The apartments are all tiny—barely five hundred square feet, since they were converted from a roadside motel. They are almost all laid out the same, too. A tiny galley kitchen to the right of the front door. A small living space straight ahead with a sliding glass door to the back of the building with a small concrete slab to put a grill or something on the first floor, and a small balcony off the back of the second. There is a narrow hall to the left, bedroom on the right side, bathroom on the left.

Mine is almost identical, so as I scan the small area, I try to see if anything is out of place because something is off—it feels eerie, and I don't know why.

The kitchen is clean, no scalded pans in the sink, no beer bottles on the counter. The coffee table still has a few bottles and a discarded T-shirt on it. The air is hot and stale, so he didn't end up fixing his AC. I go down the hall and look at the bathroom from the doorframe. The cabinet under the sink is open, and a pipe wrench is on the floor next to a bucket collecting water from what looks like it was a dripping pipe, but it's dry now.

I open his medicine cabinet. God, I feel like such a crazy stalker. Why am I doing this? There's nothing much there. Razor cartridges, cologne, hair gel. I close it. I should go. I'm gonna go.

I turn off the bathroom light and walk out when I notice his bedroom door directly across the hall is closed, and for some reason that piques my interest. He lives alone. No pets. Why is it closed? Probably no reason at all, and I'm just slowly losing my shit, but I decide to open it anyway.

It's dark and hazy inside, but through the bits of light that seep in from the edges of the closed blinds, I can see that all of the furniture besides the bed is covered in white sheets. It looks ghostly and makes my blood run cold. I think of Lily, and maybe it's some sort of respect—preserving her things or... I'm not really sure what, but that's where my mind leaps.

But my instinct to get the hell out of here is eclipsed by my desire to know what I suddenly feel like Callum has been hiding, because this is weird by any standard. I move to where I imagine the dresser is and grip a handful of the fabric, pulling it off in one sweeping motion, but there is no dresser underneath. There is no couch or bedroom furniture at all.

Against the wall of Callum's bedroom, neatly stacked in rows, are Henry's paintings. Dozens of them, and they all have the same image. His wife, Lily's, face.

When I saw Henry's hard drive and realized the affair was with Lily, I thought I would come to Callum, and we might commiserate together and figure out how this happened and what the hell it snowballed into. I was certain he would be as shocked as I am...but he knew. This whole time; when I cried to him, when I asked about Cass and Rosa and the fucking schoolgirl, he *knew*. He never told me the truth once. He acted shocked about the affair. And all this time, the missing paintings were here. And the affair was with his wife. God help me.

I pluck the sheet off another pile that I initially thought was a recliner or love seat in the corner. More paintings. Mostly gritty candids in this section.

They're all here. Lily with her long dark hair and delicate features. Even severely ill and shockingly thin with shadows beneath her eyes, she was hauntingly beautiful, and he captured it with skill. Henry painted her healthy and laughing with a sundress and a daisy tucked behind her ear, and also in bed with a hospital gown and a gaunt face, and made them both equally stunning. This is the woman he loved—the woman he cared for as she was dying and whom he carried out an affair with, even as she was facing her last days…and Callum knew.

I sit on the floor in front of a painting of her by the pool with sunglasses on, sipping a drink with a bendy straw. She's covering her face with one hand and giving the artist a seductive look. The image steals my breath, and I don't know what I'm supposed to think, to feel. How can I hate someone who's died? How can I hate someone my husband loved? And why didn't Callum tell me what he knew? None of this makes sense.

Suddenly, I hear a key in the lock of the front door. I leap to my feet. There's nowhere to run, so I freeze for a moment and listen. The door opens, closes. A bag, it sounds like, is tossed on the floor. He probably unlocked the door the way he does every day without noticing it was already unlocked, because he doesn't call out or look around the apartment with suspicion. I hear the TV click on and the news anchor's voice fill the space.

I don't know what to do. I think about confronting him and charging out of the room, taking him off guard, but then I keep asking myself how he got all of these and if knowing about the affair means he had something to do with what happened to Henry. What if he's dangerous?

Then I think, no, that's ridiculous. He's lost his wife, he's mourning. What if Henry gave these to him, and Callum knows Henry paints everyone all day and somehow doesn't see the intimacy in these? After all, artists paint subjects in all kinds of emotional states and a variety of moods and poses, and really, what the hell does Callum know about any of that? What if these are what's left of his wife, and he cherishes them, and he doesn't actually know?

I hear footsteps in the hall and I just stand there helpless in the middle of the room, adrenaline coursing through my veins. Then I hear him peeing in the bathroom across the hall, and I turn behind me, looking to see if I can go out a window, and I notice his closet with the door open. A few of the paintings of Lily lean up against the wall inside the closet. My heart almost stops when I see the handful of canvases.

In each painting Lily is nude, stretched out on Henry's bed or in a tangle of drop cloths on the floor of his studio. And each of these paintings are vandalized. In every one of them, her face is slashed through, the canvas destroyed.

Holy. Shit.

My heart pounds in my chest, and I feel the blood rush between my ears. The toilet flushes, and I am terrified he'll come into the bedroom next.

I leap onto his bed and try to unlock the window above his headboard. The lock flips open, but it makes a screeching noise when I slide the glass open, and I know I have to move fast. I push the screen out with my palm, and it falls to the sidewalk below, and then I hoist myself into the window frame. I have to go out headfirst, and I reach around blindly until I feel the ground beneath my palms below the window. I get my hips over the frame and let myself fall into the crabgrass below, safely outside, and run for my life before he sees it was me who knows his secret.

24

CASS

Once I lock myself inside the office, I check the back room and utility closet and peek out the blinds a half dozen times in case whoever left this is still here waiting in the shadows, ready to torture and kill me the way they did to that poor couple in the newspaper. I realize an hour has gone by, and nothing has happened. Nobody is here.

Nobody has a key to the office besides the owner, who doesn't even live in town. Did I leave the door unlocked? Even if I did, the person coming here to leave it wouldn't know that. Okay, maybe I just left the door unlocked, and they were going to slip it in the doorjamb like before until they realized it was unlocked and could really scare me, but damn it. I'm sure I locked it. I remember grabbing my things and locking it as I watched Frank just about make it across the pool deck and home before I turned and went with Reid. I'm sure of it... I think.

When I sit down, finally, and look at the clipping again, and read the note over and over, something strikes me. The words, *be more careful*. The whole thing sounds like a threat on the surface, but then when I think about it...if someone knows what I did and wants to expose me, why aren't they? Or why aren't they demanding something in return for their silence? It's this fact that makes me wonder if this isn't a threat at all. It might be someone actually trying to help me.

They warned me to move the body, they're telling me now that I'm still not safe simply because the main threat of bones being dug up is gone, and telling me to be careful. Is there someone out there connected to this who wants me to get away with it?

I know the first thing I need to do and that is to tell Anna the truth—how Henry is involved in all of this. About how I'm involved in all this and hope she can forgive me. But more important, I hope I can make it right. What she told me last night changes everything. Henry's death wasn't a suicide. It all came together for me in that moment.

I text her. I need to show you something. I'm gonna stop by, and I leave it at that because she deserves to know before I go to the police. I can't live like this anymore. It's about to all come out, and the only way to expose the whole story is to start by turning myself in. I've made a decision.

This is it, I think. Life as I know it is about to change as soon as I set this in motion. I take a breath, pick up my bag, and then…I hear the front door lock click open. This time I'm sure it's locked, because I locked myself in and checked it a thousand times in my debilitating paranoia over the last hour. My whole body stiffens, and my eyes go wide and still. An unrecognizable cry of fear escapes my lips, and then the door opens.

I stumble back in fear and clutch my throat. Then, when I see it's Rosa who lets herself in, I'm so utterly confused by it, I don't know whether to be afraid of her or not. She stands there in her church dress and Mary Janes, but I quickly remember who she's married to and what I've done, and the shy, demure facade crumbles.

"Don't go to the police," she blurts out of nowhere in her usual soft, almost childlike voice.

"What?" is all I manage to stutter out.

"I'm tracking your phone and computer. I know you're probably thinking of going to the police, but you don't want to do that," she says flatly, calmly, like she's telling me a perfectly normal thing.

"You what?" Again, that's all I can come up with in my state of shock.

"Meet me at the bar across the street," she says, slipping back out the door. But I just stare at her with my mouth open. "Five minutes," she adds, and I nod dumbly, and she's gone.

What the fuck just happened? I look out the blinds and see her cross the main road and go inside Donnie's Tavern. Oh, my God, is she gonna kill me? Is that whole place lined with cartel just waiting for me?

She knows. Holy hell. She knew all along? This doesn't make any sense. How could she have a key or know every move I made? And what does this all mean, because I thought I had a plan, and little Rosa just waltzed in and blew everything up. I mean…what choice have I got? I go.

In a corner booth, Rosa has two beers in pint glasses sitting in front of her. She pushes one to me when I sit down, and my mind hasn't yet wrapped around Rosa tracking my phone or drinking a beer or giving me orders, and I just— I'm really stunned into silence, just hoping she hasn't poisoned my drink, because that's how upside down this all feels.

I sit, and she can clearly read every bit of distress and confusion across my face, because she just starts.

"I don't think you should go to the police, Cass, because they don't have any leads. Well, they're connecting it to a couple of the cartel guys he was closest to right now, even though that probably won't go anywhere since they have alibis, but you're nowhere on their radar," she says, and it's like a completely different person I've never met is speaking to me. I know my mouth is still hanging open like a bumbling idiot, but I just can't process this.

"I don't understand," I mumble. "You want me to... You know what happened. You..."

"I do," she says, taking a chug of beer, like a person who suddenly fits in in the belly of a dark bar discussing murder, somehow.

"Um...and you want me to get away with it?"

"You didn't do anything wrong. You can't be punished for what you did. I refuse to let that happen. You saved my life," she says, and I can hear the emotion behind her voice.

"I what?"

"I don't want to go into every horror of what it was like once I found out who he was, but I'll just tell you that by the time I knew, it was too late for me to get out. There was no way out, Cass. None. You got me out, and what happened cannot be traced back to you...or me. We won't let that happen," she says.

"So you were trying to help me... I just... Oh, my God. Okay, but there is no way you could know where we—about the housing community and the groundbreaking..."

"I put a tracker on your car. I learned how to do a lot of things I'm not proud of from Eddie. I happened to see him go into the office that day, and I also noticed he never came out. Eddie gave me a key to the office. He has keys to everyone's apartment, too," she says. "Just in case."

"Just in case what?" I ask, all of my horrific night terrors coming true in my mind right now about all the violent unthinkable things that really could have happened to me in my own locked apartment, in my own bed, and I feel an overwhelming urge to throw up.

"I don't know, he just wanted control, so he did a lot of things like that, so I unlocked the back door during the Friday party that night and saw him. Well, I saw an arm and a lot of blood from where I stood down the back hall, and I heard you and Callum talking about what to do. I heard you saying it was self-defense."

"It was!" I blurt out, needing her to know that.

"I know it was," she says.

"I'm so sorry," I say, staring at the floor.

"Do you not hear me?" she asks. "It's the best thing that could have happened to me—to George, to a lot of people. So that's why I kept tabs from then on because I had to make sure you were careful. No offense, but you're not that good at all this," she says.

A couple of guys at the bar keep looking our way, and I don't know if they're a threat or just your average perv. I can imagine this is how Rosa lives her whole life now, just like me—in fear, wondering if these cartel monsters know something, or even *think* they know something, and are trailing you. One of them stumbles to the jukebox and plays "Neon Moon," and I decide he's just an average perv, and we're fine…but you never really know, do you?

Rosa chugs down half her beer and looks around the bar, looking just as paranoid as I feel, and her dress and hair are so incongruous with this bar and stale beer that I almost want to laugh, but of course there's nothing funny about any of this.

"But you reported him missing?" I say, just recalling the part that seems completely contradictory. Why draw attention to it? Who knows how long he'd have gone unnoticed?

"How the hell would it look if the wife didn't report it? I had no choice. I had to play the grieving widow. Someone at some point, sooner or later, was gonna find out, and if I never reported him missing or tried to find him, didn't shed some tears, I could kiss my own ass goodbye. And I have a kid. I didn't want to have to do that, but…"

"Right. I get it. It's just…there's a lot more to this than you know," I say.

"What do you mean? How much more could there be?" she asks.

"You'd be surprised." I sigh wearily.

"Well, whatever it is, I beg you. Cass, you can't get the police involved. Why would you do that?" she asks with desperation in her voice.

"To protect all of us."

"By going to the cops?" she snaps.

"It's not what you think. There's someone else involved in all this," I say.

"Callum, I know! He won't want you to do that, either," she says.

"I want you to look at something," I say, and I show her my phone.

"What is it?"

"It's not about Eddie. There's something else. Something that changes everything...and makes this all a lot more complicated," I say, and I have her watch a video. A very important video I planned to show to Anna, but Rosa needs to know now.

I see her hand fly to her mouth about halfway through, and she gasps. When the screen goes black, she looks at me.

"So you see what I need to do?"

She nods and squeezes my hand. "Oh, God," she whispers.

"I know," I say, and she stares at my phone for a long time. She meets my eyes with uncertainty.

"This changes things. We'll keep you safe, I promise," I say, and then I get up from the booth, and we exchange a hopeful yet terrified look, and I go and find Anna.

25

ANNA

Shit, shit, shit, shit, shit. I pace my apartment floor with a canned margarita Monica left behind, trying to clear my head and not panic-call anyone. There could be explanations. I can't jump off the deep end here.

First, what do I know? I know he is aware of the affair, and he's got evidence, and he slashed paintings of his wife's body like a sociopath, and those piles of paintings were all there every time I was at his place asking for information about Henry. Oh, my God, I tried to sleep with him. I would have. Oh, my— what if he rejected me because that's what was in the bedroom the whole time, and I obviously needed to be kept away from it? Am I in a horror movie?

Okay, but then what if, just what if, anger upon finding out about the affair made him cut up the intimate paintings in a rage? That was understandable, right? But still, he keeps them all like a creepy doll collection, which is very unsettling. I can't just leap to the conclusion that because he knew about the affair it makes him a killer. That's a big leap. There's still Eddie and drugs and a thousand other possibilities. I have said all along, maybe the affair and his death are not even connected. I need to keep my head on straight here. I need to calm down.

There's a tap at my apartment door, and I jump and lose my breath. Oh, God. Is it him? He didn't see me in his place. It can't be him.

"Hello?" I call a few feet away from my front door, eyeing a softball bat on a shelf and listening for a voice outside.

"It's Cass," she says, and I almost collapse with relief. I pull open the door, and she can see my anxiety immediately.

"Sorry, I didn't mean to scare you or anything. I sent you a message saying I was gonna stop by," she says, and I pull her by the arm to come in and shut the door behind her.

"I didn't get it, I—"

"Did something happen?" she asks as I'm looking through pockets and then my purse for my phone. I pat down my body with both hands.

"Oh, no. I dropped it. Oh, God. Something's very wrong, Cass," I say, feeling the tears trying to push in even though I just said I would keep my head. "I was at Callum's, and I must have dropped my phone when I went out the window. I… Shit. I…"

"Anna, hey, it's gonna be okay. What happened? Why did you go out a window?" she says in this mix of a maternal and take-charge way that catches me off guard.

I turn into a frightened child who can't string a sentence together all of a sudden, because it feels like the weight of all of it is starting to crash down all at once, and my chest hurts, and I can't steady my breath. I tell her about the paintings, and she seems less surprised than I would think that story would merit, but then she sits down across from me and puts her hand on top of mine, which makes me look up at her in surprise.

"We'll get your phone back, and I have something that might explain what you saw. I texted you that I had something to show you. Is it okay if I show you?" she asks gently.

"What is it?"

"It's…Henry." She turns her phone around so I can see the screen. "I sent this to myself when I found it—when Henry was still here—but I can explain why, and I can explain why I didn't say anything about it until now. Just watch first."

And then Henry's beautiful face appears on her phone screen. On Cass's phone screen, of all earthly things. I can't make sense of it, but I have to watch. She pushes Play, and he's talking to me. He sounds just like he did on the phone in that last conversation—desperate and scared. Tears spring to my eyes, and I touch my heart. My hand moves instinctively, as if to reach out to him, but of course he's not really there.

"Oh, God," I whisper upon seeing him start to speak.

"Trying to write this to you seemed so impersonal, and so I want to tell you in person, and I hope I can, but I have this feeling something might happen to me. And if it does, I need to make sure you know everything." Henry's voice spills out of the phone speakers, and my heart aches at the sound. I jab my shaking fingers at the screen, pausing the video.

This is the missing video the cops asked me about.

"Why do you have this?" I snap at Cass, with tears rolling down my face.

"Please, I'll explain. Just watch the whole thing," she says, and I do. I catch my breath and push Play again.

"I'm sorry for what I did. If you're seeing this, you probably figured out that I had an affair with Lily. That I fell in love with her, and that sounds like such a shitty thing to say to your wife—the worst thing. And saying you and I were better friends and grew apart all these years is a cop-out, and I don't want to belittle you. I did this thing, and I do love her, Anna, I'm sorry. But I love you, too. You're my best friend, and I don't expect forgiveness. I destroyed everything. But I decided to end it and to tell you and pray you understood. I think you'd have told me to stay with her and keep caring for her and that you were off to Ibiza, if I know you," he says and smirks just a little bit.

I'm sobbing now, and Cass puts her arm around my shoulder. I keep watching.

"But what you need to understand is that Callum found out about the affair before we could end it and made my life miserable in every way he could. He enjoyed getting his revenge, and I did what he asked. Not out of fear he would tell you, because I planned to tell you, but he made me feel guilty for the stress I put Lily through—how it made her so much worse. So it's my fault she's dead, and I feel like I killed her," he says. He's crying now and has to stop for a minute and press his fingers into his eyes and breathe. Then he continues.

"Callum talked me into giving him my Oxy. I had some I never used for my knee surgery, and he must have noticed it in the bathroom, I guess. He said that they can't afford the pain killers because she needed 60 mg of fentanyl every four hours for pain, and it was like fifty dollars a pill or something. Lily needed it around the clock, and it's the least I could do, he said. I didn't know he wanted a prescription that wasn't traceable to him. I swear to God, I would never have thought that," he cries, and Cass looks away and leans her forehead in her hand for the rest.

Henry looks closely into the camera. "Callum overdosed his wife. He wanted to be rid of the constant burden. The medical bills took all they had, and she was worth a lot more to him dead. There was insurance money he'd get. When she died so suddenly, I knew what happened. I put it together and confronted Callum, and he told me I'd better leave it alone because I was the one having the affair, and it was my name on the oxycodone bottle if I decide to push for a tox report, which they wouldn't normally do since she'd been sick for so long. I'm ashamed I did let that scare me for a little bit, but now I'm going to the police. Today. I told him I was. I don't care if they suspect me. I know I would never hurt her."

He starts sobbing now and it's so heartbreaking to watch, I don't know if I can't take anymore.

"I'm going right now to tell the police everything. I love you, and I hope that still means something to you. I'm so, so sorry. Anna. I'm so sorry," The screen goes black, and I'm sobbing, too, so uncontrollably, I can't even talk. I have to get myself over to the couch and hold my head between my knees and just let it all out until I'm almost gagging from the tears in my throat, my breath catching on my hiccuped cries.

Cass just stays sitting at the table, waiting for me to calm down, knowing I can't—that the loss is too heavy, and I can't have him back to forgive him for not being there that day or not answering the phone at the right time. I'm so goddamn sorry for everything that I can't breathe.

Cass finally comes over because I don't stop wailing. She puts her arms around me, and even though I hate her for keeping this from me, I fall into her, and she lets me sob on her chest until there is no more left. She strokes my hair, and after an eternity, we are both quiet and still.

"Send this to me," I say, and she looks taken aback. She hesitates, but she taps at her phone and sends me a copy of the video.

"It's mine. It was for me," I say quietly, trying not to cry again. "Why do you have this? How the fuck do you even have this?" I say, and she moves away from me. My crying, and her comfort, over. Now the anger starts to surface.

"Can I mix us a drink?" she says, rifling through my cupboards and pulling out a bottle of Henry's vodka.

I don't answer. I just continue to let my thoughts chase each other until my head is spinning, trying to understand, more than any of it, who the fuck Callum really is. It was him. He's the reason Henry is gone, and just when I think I'll explode into full-blown rage, Cass hands me a vodka tonic and sits next to me and starts to explain.

26
CASS

I don't know if I can tell her everything. Will she betray my trust? I owe her most of it, but right now, even though Eddie is going to be our ticket to freedom, I won't bring him into it just yet. All she cares about is answers and justice, and that I can give her without implicating myself just yet.

I take a couple of gulps of the cold vodka tonic, and then I stand because I don't even know if I can look at her when I talk about her husband. The shame is too heavy. But I begin anyway, staring out the front window, looking down at the pool where Rosa and the girls sit. I notice Rosa glance up this way once or twice, probably wondering if I've told her yet.

"I used to do this thing where I'd sort of blackmail guys for money," I say. "Just the terrible, married ones who were out cheating—I'd get a few hundred bucks off them," I say. "I pissed off a lot of people, but I survived that way for a while. And I'm not proud of it, okay, but one day Henry came to the apartments late—he was usually only around during the day. But for some reason that night he was super drunk and sat on the bench in front of the office. I was chatting with him about nothing—a lightning bug flying around or something else meaningless, and then he passed out midsentence. I liked Henry, I didn't plan on blackmailing him, okay, but it was an opportunity that fell in my lap. Literally. So I took a twenty out of his pocket. Again, not proud. I know it was shitty, and I took his phone from his hand. It was unlocked, and he was watching a stupid video, and his phone was just hanging from his hand, so I scrolled through it just to see if I could get any dirt. I didn't want to use it on him of all people, but I kind of collected dirt on people for a rainy day, just in case," I say. "I was feeling pretty desperate back then." And I feel like a hypo-crite somehow, saying the words *back then* since it was not that long ago at all.

"And you found the video," she says. "And you didn't call the police? Like right away?"

Now I'm pacing, keeping my distance because she has every right to start belting on me. I can't say that I would show the same restraint if I were her. "I mean, I was going to," I say. "I was shocked and… God, beside myself. I confronted Callum with it, of course. I showed him the copy I sent myself and said what the fuck, Callum? Of course, but damn it, I mean. It sounded crazy, what Henry was saying. It did sound like a drunk rant from an angry person. Lily was sick, nobody killed her—I mean that's what made the most sense—that a dying woman died, and he was depressed and distraught…and drunk. I didn't want to think this was all of a sudden a fucking *20/20* episode. Occam's razor and all…"

"What?" she says, shaking her head.

"Occam's razor," I repeat. "You know, the theory that says the simplest explanation is usually the right one…"

"I know what it means," she says. "But you said he's on some drunk rant. He doesn't seem confused or crazy, though. He seems…anguished, scared maybe…"

"Okay," I say. "But at the time I took this off him, he was passed out drunk, so I guess I just bought that it was a drunk rant. Callum convinced me it was crazy—he said it was the ramblings of a drunk and very depressed man, and that it was the most far-fetched thing anyone could say. That he had these feelings for Lily, and her death put him over the edge. You have to admit that sounds reasonable. I mean, shit, understand; Callum doesn't come off like a total nut job, we were almost friends. Lily *was* dying, Henry *was*... He said himself he was depressed and on meds for it. And Lily was very sick for a long time. I decided I would give him the benefit of the doubt. A video isn't proof by itself. I didn't ask Henry about it, but I did keep the video. I mean, I wanted to believe Callum, but part of me doubted it, I think. I don't know. I actually tried to put it out of my mind after Henry died because his suicide proved to me, I guess, that what Callum said was true. That he was in a really bad way, and if he was that depressed, he might say a lot of things. I tried to move forward. I had a lot of my own shit going on anyway. That's why I didn't tell you. Suicide, case closed. That was it."

I take another gulp of my drink and stare at the ceiling. It sounds pathetic when I say it all out loud.

"You had this this whole time," Anna says, "and you didn't put together that he might have hurt Henry if what he said in that video was true?"

"No! Why would I? You only told me yesterday that it wasn't suicide! Nobody knows that. Everyone here still thinks it was suicide. When you said foul play, that's when everything changed—that's when I knew I'd fucked up by not bringing this to the police," I say.

"But you still didn't!" Anna says, now pacing the floor herself, looking like she could start punching shit or sweeping all the contents off the coffee table before flipping it over. I can't blame her. She looks at me, then... "What are you waiting for? I'll go, then. There's a psychopath on the loose just living his life, getting away with it!" She raises her voice and moves like she's about to bolt out of the apartment and bring it to the police this very second, and that can't happen. She's muttering, "I knew I should have told them about the affair, about everything. I'm an idiot."

"Anna. Wait! Okay...you have to understand, I couldn't go to the cops. Even if I suspected Callum this whole time, which sometimes I did, my hands were tied."

"Why? Tell me how the fuck this could all happen—why nobody did anything?" she says, running her hands through her hair and pacing but not actually leaving.

"Shortly after I confronted Callum, I did a very bad thing. It was an accident! I can't get into it, but he knows about it, and if I outed him and this video... My life would be over. You have to understand, it was actually life and death for me, so I was silenced. Maybe that's why I kept convincing myself he was telling the truth when I had doubts, because he had a very big secret of mine, and we were...sort of...I don't know. Slaves to each other's secrets."

"What did you do? Is everyone here a goddamn criminal?"

"Listen, I didn't think the video was enough to prove Callum did it. I mean, you tell me then... With no toxicology report on Lily and a cremated body, would you have risked your life to point the finger at him?"

"I don't know, because I don't know what kind of trouble you got yourself into! But if you were trying to blackmail the nicest guy in the world, I can only imagine."

"Really? He *was* having an affair on you! Fine, he was a fucking saint, and he had his reasons, and everything he said... Fine. But give me a break. Carrying on a months-long affair would make anyone question him—self-admitted suicidal tendencies and meds would make me at least maybe believe Callum when he explained it," I say, enraged at being the punching bag over and over again with everything. With Reid and Eddie and Callum and now her. I'm just so fucking done and ready for it to be over.

"Fine. You're right," she says quietly.

"I'm on your side, believe it or not, and if you can give me a couple of hours, I have a plan to nail Callum to the fucking wall."

"How? You said yourself that video is worthless on its own."

"I know what I said. But now I have more than that. I'll be back. Since you don't have a phone for me to call, stay here. Don't talk to him. Just… I want this as much as you do. I need it more, even. I'm not gonna say trust me, but if you can't do that at least please just stay the fuck right here until I come back," I say, draining my vodka tonic and heading toward the door.

She takes a deep breath, closes her eyes and nods in agreement.

"And lock the door," I say as I walk out of 203 and really hope I make it back.

27

ANNA

She's crazy if she thinks I'm going to sit here and wait while she tries to play the hero. It's too late for that. I don't need saving while she finally decides to do the right thing. I'm getting my phone, and I'm going to the police with the video myself. She could be in on it for all I know. Why show me this damning video now? Maybe she's the one who was jealous of Callum, and maybe she's the one who gave Lily the overdose, and they're working together. What the hell do I know?

I had to have dropped it outside the window. I was upside down; it must have fallen out of my pocket. I have to at least look before I do anything else. I need a copy of that video for myself. I don't know where she's going or what she plans to do. I just don't know who I can trust.

It's dark outside now, and nobody is around. The only light is from the sparkling blue of the lights beneath the pool water and a scattering of stars. A feeling of static electricity runs through me as I dodge the sprinklers hissing into life and cross the grassy clearing on the side of the building to slip behind it and look for my phone.

The screen is still on the ground, and I feel a flood of relief because maybe he hasn't gone into the bedroom or noticed the open window. The heat in the apartment is stifling anyway, so he probably wouldn't notice an open window in another room—maybe not until he goes to bed. He's probably tinkering with the AC.

There is only the orange glow of a window next door to Callum's casting a small triangle of light on the grass below his bedroom, and so I have to feel on my hands and knees for my phone. It's damp, and fresh-cut weeds cling to my bare knees as I crawl in the darkness. It has to be here.

Then, suddenly, I feel a sharp pain, and I can't breathe. I can't breathe! I clutch my neck and feel something there—a cord, a rope, something—pressing into my throat. I claw at it desperately, and I try to scream. I open my mouth to scream for help, but no sound comes out. I begin to flail my arms, reaching for anything around me to hold on to or push against. I kick behind me and make contact with something. Someone? But I'm helpless.

I see a constellation of stars behind my eyes, and everything goes black.

When I wake up, it's still dark, and it takes me a few minutes to remember what happened and figure out where I am. We're moving. I hear the soft hum of tires and feel the rhythmic seams of the road beneath me. I'm in the trunk of a car. My head throbs, and it hurts to blink. Is this Callum's doing? Does he think he killed me? I don't know whether to scream or play dead. I don't know how long we've been driving.

Oh, my God. I can't breathe in here. My hands are tied with something, and I can't move. My mind reels, and I try to think of a way out, but how can there be a way out of this? Nobody knows I'm here. I think about what Callum did to Lily and what he did to Henry. And he got away with it. There's no proof beyond a video that's easily dismissed as the ravings of a troubled man.

I scream. I know it's futile, but I need to try to get him to stop. I can't let him get me to where he has planned. I need to stop him—get him off plan, off guard. I start to flail my body and kick behind me. I try to use all my core strength to slam my heels into the back seat so he can feel the impact, but I'm weak. I can't do it. My limbs feel heavy and fatigued. He's given me something to sedate me. I can't kick, it all feels like quicksand. So I scream. I scream until my voice goes hoarse, and finally, after what seems like hours but is maybe only minutes, I feel the car slow and then stop.

Every muscle in my body aches and tenses as I wait to see if he'll open the trunk door. But nothing happens, and I feel tears begin to fall and pool around my cheek, pressed heavy against the dirty carpet of the trunk floor.

I must fall asleep or lose consciousness again, because it seems like hours pass before I hear anything, and then all of a sudden, a click, and the trunk releases and opens. Callum stands there looming over me in the darkness.

He doesn't say anything, which is more unsettling than if he started shouting orders. He's eerily quiet and just shakes his head as he watches me climb out. He sees the fear in my eyes, and the way I cower from him when he takes a step toward me, and he seems not to be enjoying it. He seems almost inconvenienced.

"Goddammit," he says, and I see that we are way out in the middle of nowhere. There's a cliff only a few yards behind me, with the Rio Grande below the rocky fall downward. It's exactly like the place Henry fell—it's exactly like the place he was dumped, I mean. By this monster.

"I gave you every opportunity to get out. Jesus. I left threats at your door, locked you in a storage unit for Christ's sake. I *literally* pushed you away because I didn't want it to come to this." He slams the ball of his hand onto the hood of his car.

Those threats were him. He didn't want me to get close and figure anything out, so he tried to scare me away. I almost ask stupid questions—why did you act like my friend? Why did you kiss me back? Why did you say nice things about Henry? But I know the answer. He couldn't scare me away, so he changed tactics. *Keep your friends close and your enemies closer.* Isn't that how the saying goes?

"I won't tell anyone," I say pathetically.

"I know you won't," he says, and for the first time, that clean-shaven, woodsy cologned, sparkly-eyed guy looks like a totally different person. His eyes look dead, his face ashen and creased. How did I miss this? How did I overlook so many things—in Henry, in Callum…in myself? I tried to see them the way I wanted them to be.

"He betrayed you, I know. I'm sure what happened to Lily was an accident. And whoever hurt Henry—" I stop. I don't know if he found out I saw the video. Cass told him something maybe, but how much? Maybe I can still lie my way out of this and play dumb? I have to at least try.

"You don't have to do this. If you say you didn't hurt Henry, then I believe you. There's no proof," I say, my voice shaking. I stand behind the car, my hands bound behind me, and he sits on a tree stump a few feet in front of me and looks me up and down as if he's deciding how this will go.

"I'm not playing games. I know you saw the video. It's cute, whatever you're trying to do, but I'm not someone you can manipulate," he says. Then he walks to the back seat, and I tense, not knowing what he'll do, but he grabs a beer from a cooler and goes and sits back down. A beer. It's unreal.

"The video doesn't prove anything. There's no physical evidence. He's not here to—" I stop. I switch gears. "A video is not enough, and I wasn't there. I have no proof against you. You don't have to do this."

He smiles, swigs his beer, and stares at me. "That's cute. You know my wife used to say cute things like that—I mean, you know, total fucking lies, to get what she wanted. Do you know I live like a fucking homeless person because all of her medical bills were hemorrhaging our bank account? We used to have a beautiful house and a life and then, bam!"

I jump out of my skin when he smashes the glass bottle to bits to punctuate his sentence.

"And I'd give it all up for her. I was glad to do everything for her, and look what she does to me!" he says, and I wonder for a moment if what he did to her was out of sheer hatred or for the life insurance or maybe some of both, but I guess it doesn't really matter. "Look how I'm repaid," he says.

"It's not fair," I try to agree with him, but my words come out soft and hoarse, and my throat throbs in pain.

"She had weeks left. What I did was a mercy," he says, and I want so badly to say, *Then what was Henry?* but I need to try to make him believe I understand.

"So if that's true, then you don't have anything to run from. You don't have to do this," I say again, and I hear the water crashing against the rocks thirty feet below, and in my panic I try another angle. "Will anyone believe that you were this close to three mysterious deaths with no involvement? Lily was ill, Henry isn't tied to you if we hide that video, but me? You add me, and it's over for you. This would be stupid to do. I told you, they have no proof."

"It's okay. I made sure it was clear how distraught you were over Henry and that you didn't know how you'd go on, and there are suddenly lots of searches for depression and suicide on your phone. I'll make sure the phone is found this time," he says, and then he stands and starts toward me.

"That's fucking stupid," I say, stopping him for a moment.

"That will just show you did it hours before I died. Are you that stupid?" I say with nothing left to lose now, because he's ready to make his move.

"Oh, no. I found little ways to search things each time I saw you. I mean, you wouldn't stop coming over for God's sake. It was really pretty easy. I watched you plug in the very secure Z shape to unlock your phone the first day, and then every time you left your phone sitting at the pool, used the bathroom, whatever... You should look at your history sometime. It's quite interesting...and why do you think you're here? I saw that Cass sent you the video today when you left your phone behind. Pathetic, really. It didn't have to be this way."

My fear in this moment is oddly mixed with such confusion looking at this man who I thought I knew and admired for what he'd gone through—his strength in the face of it all. My God...how could I be so wrong about everything?

And then my life truly flashes before my eyes when he advances on me. It's weird, the things you think about when shock paralyzes you—thoughts that have no business in this moment. A pair of wool mittens with hearts on them I got for Christmas one year, lying in a field of dandelions in South Carolina one summer, leaping through the sprinkler as a kid, with the soft drops falling down around us like cane sugar, running barefoot down our porch steps in a yellow sundress to throw my arms around Henry when he came home from a trip. Henry's beautiful face.

My stomach heaves. My adrenaline surges, and I feel suddenly weak with terror. I don't know what's happening to me, but I have to get away from him. I have to try.

He senses that I shift right and get ready to run, and that's when he grabs me. He plasters a piece of duct tape across my mouth, and I try so hard to fight him, but I'm so weak. Then, he pulls a plastic bag from his pocket—a flimsy supermarket grocery bag—and with one swift move, he covers my head with it, but he doesn't pull it tight. I wait for the air to be sucked from my lungs, but he's just tied a loose knot at the bottom of the bag so I can breathe, but I can't shake it off, either. I can't use my tied hands, so I start to run, but I stumble; I can't see which way to go. I run in circles, and I fall to my knees when I trip on some brush. I can feel the hot blood running down my calf, but I get up again, and I'm disoriented, so I don't know which way the cliff's edge is, and he knows that.

He knows I can't get away, and this guy I thought was a desperate, grieving husband who lost it in a rage of jealousy, maybe just snapped…is something very different than I could have ever imagined. He's a calculating sociopath.

As I sob and try to run away, I fall and become dizzy and turned around, I hear the crack and hiss of a beer bottle being opened, and he sits and laughs. He's watching and laughing at me like I'm entertainment as I hopelessly fight for my life.

And that's when I know I'm dead.

28

CASS

When I called the police station earlier in the day and asked to talk to the detective on the Henry Hartley case, they certainly didn't rush to help me, but of course I didn't tell them what I had. They said I could come in after dinnertime, whatever arbitrary time that is, and he'd be in his office, but that he was out during the day. So after I leave Anna, I drive down with a racing heart and a nauseous stomach to tell them what I have and pray to God it all goes to plan; that I've crafted this all perfectly. That I'm safe.

When I sit in Detective Harrison's office, he gives me a skeptical look when I tell him I think a man named Callum Brooks is responsible for three deaths. I think I even see a smirk, but he keeps a professional demeanor and sits across from me, willing to listen.

I hand him my phone first and let him watch the video of Henry explaining what Callum did to Lily and that he fears for his life. He watches. His cheek twitches a couple of times, I see his Adam's apple bob as he swallows. It's difficult to watch someone bawling and saying how sorry they are for anyone, probably. Even a cop, but he finishes the video and lays my phone face down next to him—I guess it's evidence now.

"Where did you get this?" he asks calmly.

"I'll be honest…"

"That would be a good start," Harrison says.

"I went through his phone one night. He stayed at the apartments I work at. I suspected the affair he was having with Callum's wife." This part is a lie. I had no idea, but I don't need him asking why I go through a guy's phone for no reason. "So one time when he passed out at the pool, I looked at his phone. Shitty thing to do, but I'm nosy, and I sent this to myself. And I know! Before you ask, yes, I did confront Callum, and of course he told me Henry is a depressed, manic guy who couldn't handle Lily's death and is hopped up on meds or drunk or whatever to cope and told me to just think about how crazy what he's saying is."

"So you believed him?"

"I don't know what I thought. I told him I deleted the video and that he was probably right. When Henry died and it was ruled suicide, I thought he probably *was* right, and I tried to put it behind me. But I just found out it wasn't a suicide, and so the other weird shit that happened started to come together," I say.

"Okay, like what?" he asks, and fidgets with the small notepad in front of him. I can't tell by the look on his face if he thinks I'm batty or is excited that all this just dropped in his lap, but I continue on.

"I work at The Sycamores, like I said. I do handyman stuff," I say, and he looks up from his notepad and tries to hide a quick scan, looking me up and down, quickly assessing if that could be true because I sure don't look like it. I already know. It happens all the time.

"Handyman?" he says.

"I like to say handy ma'am, but yeah. Anyway, I'm in everyone's apartments because I set mousetraps and fix clogged drains—that sort of thing, so I work out of the front office, and I have something you might want to see," I say, pushing a thumb drive across the table to him.

"What is it?" he asks, keeping the control. He's not letting me run how this will go, I can tell.

"Hard to explain. But you can see what's on it, and it will explain everything," I say.

While he takes out his laptop and boots it up to plug in the thumb drive, I continue babbling about everyone seeing Callum threaten Eddie by the pool one day and not knowing what they were arguing about, but there was some history between them. I explain that Eddie's wife, Rosa, will tell you that Henry and Eddie were friends, so maybe Eddie knew something or maybe Henry confided in Eddie about the affair—that I'm not sure what the motive was, but everyone at The Sycamores will tell you that absolutely nobody knew who Eddie really was. And they will all confirm this, and Rosa will back up my story.

He's only half listening as he connects the drive and starts to click around on it, but I'm still establishing the points I want him to remember. Then, it's clear when he sees it. He is pretty good at masking his shock, but I see the glint in his eye and the way his eyebrows rise, knowing this is a *holy shit* moment and the "missing cartel guy" is now a "murdered cartel guy," and it's all being accidentally uncovered by this quiet little maintenance girl from The Sycamores who stumbled upon some things she wasn't meant to see.

At least I hope those are the inner workings of his mind. It's what I'm trying to lay the groundwork for anyway. I just hope he takes the bait.

Harrison excuses himself. I can't even imagine all the boots on the ground he's gathering up right now to execute a warrant or whatever it is they'll do next, but he still keeps his composure, trying to get every bit of information he can gather from me.

When Harrison comes back into the room, I already hear the chatter and movement outside the door behind him: scratchy radio communications, urgency, bodies up and moving. He sits down. The laptop and thumb drive have been handed off, and he's remaining calm and slightly placating, if I'm honest.

"So, where the hell did you get this exactly?" he asks.

And I know I'll probably be here a few more hours for recorded statements and questions and all of that. But as I sit here and tell them all they need to know, everything behind the scenes has already been set in motion, so I'm patient. And I know that there is a last little detail they need to find on their own. And when they do, I'll be free.

29

CASS

When I arrive back at The Sycamores, police are all over the place, their red lights flashing like strobe lights in the darkness. The door to Callum's apartment is open, and I see the silhouette of a couple officers inside. Another stands by a squad car on a radio, and yet another is talking to Babs by the front gate. There are a couple more in the front office going through the desktop computer. All to be expected. I park in the lot, and nobody notices me in all the chaos.

I go straight to Anna's apartment. I can't tell her the truth about Eddie, but I can tell her I started to suspect Callum was involved with Eddie's disappearance and there might be some snowball effect at play here. Maybe Eddie knew something he shouldn't about Callum's wife—got himself killed that way perhaps. There's a lot I can't tell her, but I can tell her that it's over, and Callum will be charged. I can finally give her closure, at least.

I knock and she's not answering. I open her door. She left it unlocked, and I call in. Nothing.

Shit. Shit, shit, shit. I see many of the residents gathered on the pool deck, watching, asking each other questions, concerned looks across their faces. Rosa is among them. We agreed she would keep playing the part of the grieving wife and act accordingly as one would…especially if there are cops surrounding the building.

She sees me at Anna's door. I give her a flip of my palms in a what-the-hell gesture, and she shrugs.

This isn't good. Callum's car is gone, and the officer on the radio is talking about "an attempt to locate," and I hear Callum's name.

He's gone. He got away, and they don't know where he is. I feel like my legs are going numb, and my heart beats against my rib cage so hard I feel like I could faint. I hold on to the railing and try to steady my breath—to think. I see Rosa hand off her child to Crystal, who's sobbing for whatever reason, and she takes the toddler on her lap, and Rosa gestures with her head over to the parking lot.

I rush down the stairs and pass through the crowd. I pause a moment and watch the police around his apartment. I see one officer hand another something they have placed inside a clear evidence bag. It's something I recognize—a woman's makeup case, pink, with tulips on it. I close my eyes in a moment of pure relief, and I suck in a deep breath, because I know what it means.

Then I go quickly and meet Rosa behind the building. "She's gone. He has her. My plan was fucking stupid, and she wasn't safe."

"Let's go then," Rosa says, as calmly as ever.

"Where? They could be anywhere. She could be dead already. He has Anna, and he knows she fucking knows. I sent her that video of Henry, so he has everything to lose now if he doesn't get rid of her. Fuck."

"Drive," she orders, so we get into my car and just go, with no plan or direction. I just obey and drive because everything seems to be backfiring already, and I don't know what else to do in this moment.

"Go north on 84," she says, looking at a map on her phone.

"Why? Rosa, they could be anywhere, Jesus!" I slam my fist into the steering wheel and then notice she's turned her phone around and is showing me a red dot moving on her Google map.

"Holy shit," I say.

"Well, how could I know whose car you were going to take when you made your trip to the desert that night? I had to track both of your cars to be safe," she says, and I let out a bark of shocked laughter.

"Oh, my God. Oh. My. God!" I howl.

"They stopped! They're in Diablo Canyon, it looks like. No movement."

"Oh, my God," I whisper as I speed up. The cliffs. He could do anything to her out there. How could I let this happen? "We have to find her, we have to. We have to save her from that..."

I speed over dusty clay roads and know I have no real plan when I get there, except that we outnumber him. I searched his apartment for a gun more than once when I was in there fixing something, and I knew he'd be at work. I never found one, and why would he bludgeon Henry to death if he did have one? No gun. No pills to overdose Anna, because that would be a pattern and a death sentence for him. Two women drugged to death? No. So what is his plan with Anna? I shudder thinking of what he might do to her—how soulless he is and what he's capable of.

I'm praying that we get there in time. We have to get there in time. God, please. And we'll do whatever we have to, to stop him—push him off a cliff, run him down.

"We should probably call the police," I finally say, realizing in my adrenaline-high that I should have thought to do that first, but I've become used to fixing things on my own.

"Call them and explain how we are able to track him?" she

says. "Do you really want to keep connecting yourself to this? They can't know you took time to track his car but didn't turn him in. They'll think you're stalking him, maybe even have reason to set him up. No. We can do this. It's three against one."

Rosa never ceases to shock and amaze me with every new thing she says. She just uttered more words than I might hear from her in a month at The Sycamores. And she's right.

I nod vigorously in agreement, and we drive silently for what seems like hours but in reality is only forty minutes outside Santa Fe. Time seems to slow down as we start to wind through the notoriously rough dirt roads that make you feel like your car is shaking apart—everything rattles as the tires dip into the deep grooves as we trudge up the incline. Rosa holds on to the door, and I'm forced to slow down.

Just when I don't know if my crap car can make it, Rosa points to the dot on her map, and then points just over the next incline and to the right. In seconds, we catch the shape of a car in our headlights. It would be impossible to see anything out here without them, and when we catch the edge of the clearing with our headlight beams, I see a figure standing up. It's Callum. The light captures a pale look of surprise and horror on his face.

He's holding a beer in his hand, and he stands. His features shift from an expression of fear into a forced look of defiance—a man pretending to be in control, because what else can he do?

Rosa and I exit the car carefully, standing still for a moment, trying to take in the scene. Is Anna even here? Does he have a weapon? What the hell is he doing out here?

Then I spot Anna. I know it's her because those were the clothes she was wearing earlier. She's lying on the ground with a bag over her head.

"Oh, God!" I cry hysterically, until I see that she's moving—she's leaning against a rock, barely moving, but she's conscious. There's a wash of relief mixed with such hostility toward him that I can scarcely breathe for a moment. He's just torturing her—teasing her because she has no place to run, and if she tries there are cliffs, and she can't see. He's keeping her without chains, but in an even more inhuman way. In this moment, I hate him more than I thought it was possible to hate another person.

Callum seems to be rendered speechless, because I'm sure he can't fathom how anyone could have known he was here. And he's probably trying to regroup and come up with a way out now.

Rosa looks small and helpless as she takes in the situation. We just rushed to try to save Anna, but now what? Do we attack him, run him over? That's hard to do with Anna hostage, so what's the next move?

Callum looks at Rosa with an expression of bewilderment. "You're a surprise," he says. "I guess she told you what she did to your husband. Or were you in on it together?"

"No," I snap. "She's not in on anything."

"I knew it," he says. "Of course she knew what a piece of shit he was."

"I said, she—"

"There's nothing you can do, Cass. You know what happens if you say anything; you did that to yourself, so I'd get the fuck out of here if I were you," he says, and I hear Anna whimper. He must have her gagged or something, because she's not screaming. But he doesn't shove her in the car and run or go to her to protect her from us. He must think he has me. That's because he knows what I did to Eddie, that my hands are tied and that Rosa was secretly involved, so he has her in a corner, too.

He must actually think that nobody will know he was involved—think there is no proof to the contrary—that all the DNA evidence was cleaned, he could blame this all on me if he really had to.

I mean, I'm sure he thinks that both of us would do whatever we needed to in order to make sure none of this came out, but if it did come out, I know he must have had plans to throw me under the bus. He wasn't the one to kill Eddie, after all; that's true. He just killed innocent people and got away with it. He doesn't even look scared. He's actually laughing right now. I scramble over to Anna.

"It's me. It's okay," I say, so she doesn't think it's Callum and try to run. "It's okay," I repeat, shaking and tearing the plastic in half to pull it away from her face. I pull the tape from her mouth, and she gasps for breath, falling into my arms. He's drugged her. Oh, my God. No wonder she's not screaming and running. Her eyes are dilated, and she's deadweight as I hold her up.

I hold her as she shakes and whimpers, and I tell her it will be okay as I untie her bound wrists, but the dead look in Callum's eyes and the way he's just letting this happen—just watching us without doing anything or stopping us from getting near them—is unsettling to say the least.

When I see Anna has severe cuts on her knees from falling, I put her arm over my shoulder and walk her the few yards to my car. Still, he does nothing.

"He's gonna kill me," Anna whispers, looking wide-eyed to the left of us as we pass Callum, who cracks a beer and sits on the hood of his car with a smirk on his face.

Then, in one swift move, he pulls a hunting knife out of nowhere, stands, and plunges it into the tire of my car, so we're stuck. I hear the slow hiss as the air releases and the rubber shrivels. Then he wields the knife at us.

The three of us back up. We're standing in between the beams of both car headlights as he lunges as if he'll slash one more tire, but then doesn't. Instead he laughs and makes a quick movement of both his hands close to my face as if saying *boo!* and laughs again, reveling in the control he thinks he has.

I don't react to this. I hold Anna tightly to me, and Rosa stands firm on the other side of her like a shield.

"You're screwed," Callum says. "You're not taking her any-where. It's hilarious that you think you will, though, and it's your goddamn fault she knows too much. This didn't have to happen like this. I tried to save you from all this, you know." He aims that last part at Anna, who is trembling in fear.

"I'm screwed?" I say. "Look at you. It's over."

"All you yippy little females comin' up here like she's a chick at a bar I'm trying to take home, and you're gonna cockblock me or something. You're just not smart enough to keep up. This isn't happy hour or playtime, whatever you chicks do. It's too late. Cass had to run her mouth and nose around and now it's too late, so you two can stay here. Hope ya make it through the night," he says to me and Rosa, and then makes his first move toward Anna but calmly, like he's had a master plan this whole time and doesn't need to show any fear.

"You think they won't connect you to killing Henry and Lily if you do this? I gave the cops the video of Henry," I say, and he's not rattled.

"They haven't caught me yet. No evidence. You know that. None. Your word and some video that a hundred experts will say is crazy. No DNA, no tox report on Lily, and no way to get one. No weapon used on Henry, no blood evidence, finger-prints, or proof I ever touched him. So go ahead—tell the cops your big theory and see where that gets you. You're the one in trouble. And you know if you don't drop the hero act and let us go without any drama, I got your big secret ready to tell the world. And if she's here—" he nods to Rosa "—she's in on this with you, and you'll both be found out. You don't really have a choice, do you? And don't worry, they won't find her body. She's suicidal, didn't you know that? She's been through an awful lot."

He makes a mock pouty face and I could actually kill him

right this minute with my bare hands—just rip his face from his skull and not feel bad about it.

"They're looking for you," I say.

"Didn't you hear what I said? They can look for me all they want, even arrest me, but they got nothin'. And it doesn't matter, because the money is coming through in a few days, and I'll be long gone. I'm sure I can avoid them until then. It's you they'll want to question," he says, and I know he means the life insurance money from Lily, and I resist the urge to lunge at him and start clawing his eyes out.

"So does she know what you did to Eddie? Or maybe she paid you to do it, for all I know," Callum asks, still looking at Rosa with a what-the-fuck-are-you-doing-here expression but trying hard to keep an appearance of being in control, like he was expecting this all along. He's starting to look a bit like a trapped animal. He's beginning to realize he's outnumbered and maybe he can't peg this on me or Rosa—she's a wild card he didn't expect and doesn't exactly know how to keep the control now. He's fishing—trying to see how Rosa is connected, so he knows if it helps him that she's tied up in this or if it puts the final nail in his coffin if he lets her get away.

"What is he talking about?" Anna whispers to me, still clinging to my arm as the three of us stand close—a small army, allied against Callum Brooks.

"You expect me to still keep quiet after what you did?" he says. "Sending that video to the police? I mean, it will yield nothing—circumstantial crap, but the point is, you started this. I don't have time for...whatever it is you're trying to do here. You should hope they don't find me, because I have a big story to tell them that you won't like, so I don't know what the fuck you actually think you're gonna gain here." He turns to Rosa again. "She tell you what she did, or is she stringing you along in her web of lies, too?" he asks.

"You killed my Eddie," Rosa says, and Callum gives an exasperated laugh and looks at me like I'm a piece of work. A gust of hot wind blows a cloud of red dust into the air and settles as we all stand, ready for someone to make a move—or run or fight, but nobody does. It's just the buzz of crickets and a soft breeze through the trees that make any sound.

"Get in the car," Callum says to Anna.

I hear her sharp intake of breath next to me as he holds out his knife and points it close to her face.

"No," I say, holding her arm as tight as I can.

"Are you actually insane? You know you're the idiot who brought your phone to the desert where the body is. I've gone over it a thousand times, and that's the only piece of evidence left behind. And then maybe if they use luminol in the office—*your* front office—it will light up like a Christmas tree, so good luck. You got nothin' on me," he says, and I know that he won't tell the police any of that because he doesn't want to connect himself and is just using this information as a weapon.

Also, if he's planning on getting away with taking Anna and making her death look like a suicide, a crime I guess he did get away with once, he won't want to talk to police unless he absolute has to. So I wouldn't be overly worried about the words that are coming out of his mouth, even if I wasn't about to drop a bomb on him.

"They dug up that entire area and didn't find any bodies. Someone must have moved it," I say.

And at first he keeps the smirk on his face, but then it fades, and his eyes flit around as he contemplates whether I'm telling the truth.

"I hear it will be a housing community called Willow Grove," I add, and I watch him take out his phone and quickly search the words I'm saying. I know there are a few images that pop up for Willow Grove—a dirt clearing with big machinery excavating trenches and foundations, with the earth all ripped up.

The color drains from his face. If the body isn't there, then where? Someplace my phone record isn't attached to, that's for sure.

"What did you do with my Eddie?" Rosa sobs.

And I know she's giving him a little taste of what he'd be in for if he was arrested and it went to court—she's giving him the whole act, because he knows she stands firmly on my side.

"What the fuck?" he says. "What did you do?"

"Me? I don't know what you're talking about," I say, and I feel the air shift, and his eyes go dark.

He lunges for Anna with the tip of his knife at her chest, and the blade slices her slightly as blood starts to run, soaking into her white T-shirt. Anna screams, and I grab for her, but her arm slips through my hand as he wrestles her into his grip, and Rosa and I shrink back.

He's flustered now, which makes me think he didn't mean to do that—to actually cut her, and it threw him off, another minor loss of control that angers him. I can't tell if throwing him off plan will help us, or if he'll just come completely unhinged.

"There's another video," I say, speaking quickly.

He's holding Anna with her arm forced behind her back. I see tears stream down her face. She doesn't have the strength to fight him, sapped by whatever drug he's given her. He takes out a zip tie and binds her wrist. He forces her to the ground with a knife at the back of her neck. She gives me a pleading look out of the corner of her eye. This is what he counted on. Anna half-conscious, easily controllable with a knife and zip ties. No blunt force trauma or gun or anything. It needs to look like a suicide, after all.

How did I not see this coming? How could I have left her?

He opens the trunk of his car. He's going to take her, and I have no physical way to stop him. Then he looks to Rosa like he might lunge at her, too, but he doesn't. He keeps his focus on Anna. Is he spinning in his mind what he'll do to Rosa—how he'll keep her quiet?

I step in front of her instinctively to protect her and hurl my next little bomb at him. "The video of you dragging Eddie from the utility closet to the car. I guess the cameras were working that day, after all, and I thought the police might want to see it," I say.

He stops and turns to me, his face red and his eyes wide. "You're lying," he says, but what he doesn't know is that the night I stabbed Eddie Bacco, I also set a trap for Callum, just in case that Henry video that was nagging at me was something—and just in case he betrayed me.

So I gave him my car keys, and he took on the job of moving the body out the back door of the office. Before I went to the ball in Crystal's van that night, I turned on the security camera inside the office. It shows Callum pulling Eddie Bacco by the ankles from the utility closet and out the back door. It stops there because there's no camera outside. But in this time stamped video, I'm in Santa Fe at a charity ball, getting arrested.

"The police are at The Sycamores right now raiding your apartment," I say, and to my utter shock, Rosa pulls out a video she took of the police, less than an hour earlier, to show Callum that it's true.

He glances at it and sees the swarm of police and flashing lights—the open door to his unit—and stares at it.

I give her a subtle, surprised look, and she gives me a tiny confident nod.

"They found ten thousand dollars wrapped in plastic under your sink. It was in a woman's pink makeup case—Lily's, I guess. Pink. With tulips on it. It's the money from Eddie's backpack."

"You killed him and then stole from him," Rosa says, shaking her head in disgust, putting on a show to drive home the hold the two of us together really have over him now.

"That's bullshit. You're… Whatever you're doing…there was no money. We buried it. You? What did you do!?" he snarls. In the cones of headlight illuminating us, I see his face redden and his eyes become narrow and full of fear. He's seething with rage, and I don't know what he'll do next.

Rosa knows that I took the ten thousand out of Eddie's backpack when I moved his body, and she knows that I placed it in the back of a cabinet in Callum's bathroom when I fixed his leaky sink. We told each other everything, and he has no chance against us now.

He leaves Anna slumped against the back tire of the car and rushes at me so quickly I don't have time to run—to move, even—and then he has me. He stands behind me with a knife to my throat. It's so fast it steals my breath. I grab his arm with both hands and scream, but that makes him poke the tip of the knife into the side of my throat, and I'm silent.

Rosa stands frozen, helpless as Callum backs up, holding my body to his, and inches toward the cliff.

I squeeze my eyes closed. I've done a lot of shitty things, and I'm not proud of the way I've hurt people. I thought about just leaving—taking the ten thousand, getting the fuck out and not going to the police. Why be connected to Eddie at all—I could just keep Callum's terrible secret, so I don't destroy my own life. It was a consideration.

Maybe it was penance for all my mistakes, but I had to do what I did and turn him in. It was my only real way out of this anyway, but it wasn't just for my own safety… It was for Lily and for Henry. And most important, for Anna.

I can't see the bottom beneath the rocky cliff because it's cloaked in blackness, but I know it by heart. I've hiked here, camped here, picnicked here, and everyone knows the bottom is death. This is how I always thought it would end—after I learned who Eddie was, the vision of this moment flashed behind my eyes—me with a slit throat, left in a Mexican desert. This is close enough.

I shake violently, but every time I pull his arm to try to loosen it around my neck, he pushes the blade closer, and I can feel the sharp edge and hot blood trickle down my skin. I think about kicking him, but I don't have the leverage, and he could startle and plunge the knife deep into my throat, and that would be it.

Anna is trying to stand up. She gets to her hands and knees, and maybe whatever she was given is starting to wear off. Or maybe she is summoning up strength from somewhere deep inside and willing herself to move. She tries to use one knee to steady herself since her hand are tied, and she gets to her feet, and it startles him—it looks like he didn't expect her to be this coherent, and it's throwing him off.

But all of this happens so fast that it's like a series of flashes—his grip, the knife, my scream—we're inching backward. Anna screams out, "Please, no!" but we step closer to the edge, and he has me now by the back of the collar, pushing me forward, enough distance in front of him that he doesn't get too close to the edge himself. Would he really be crazy enough to do this? Or is he just trying to scare me? Maybe he's just that psychotic—getting caught or not isn't as important as revenge. But if that were true, he would have slit my throat by now, right?

And just when I feel my feet about to slip at the crumbling edge of the rocks, a gunshot rings out. Deafening, it echoes across the valley and stops Callum in his tracks.

He lets go, and I fall to the ground, scrambling to move away from the cliff's edge, grabbing handfuls of dirt and rock, and I crawl my way to safety. I feel my head for blood. It's too dark to see anything, so I feel down my body to see where I'm hit. Am I dead? Maybe this is what death is, and I still think I'm alive for a moment longer as my soul floats away, because I *must* be dead.

It takes me a moment until the ringing in my ears stops, and I realize I'm in fact not even shot, and that's when the panic comes. If he didn't shoot me, who did he shoot? And this all feels like slow motion, but it happens in seconds, and then I hear it...and I see it.

Callum is on the ground, a bullet through his thigh as he writhes in pain.

I can't make sense of what I'm seeing at first. In the beam of my car's headlight, I see Rosa holding a small revolver, and Anna standing next to her with both hands cupped over her mouth in horror.

"Cops are coming, you better go," Rosa says to Callum, who looks up at us in a mix of agony and disbelief.

He has no earthly idea about what Rosa really believes and must be entirely confused about why we'd tell him to run instead of holding him here until the police arrive, now that we have him trapped, but he doesn't wait around to ask questions. He limps, practically crawling to his car, leaving a trail of blood beading on the chalky ground in front of the bright headlight beams, and then he takes all the strength he can summon to get into the driver's seat and speed away from us, leaving plumes of dust in his wake.

"You're letting him go!?" Anna cries, but she doesn't know that he's driving a car tracked with GPS, and he can't evade us. Right now, we need to protect ourselves first.

"Don't worry," is all I say in the moment because there is no explanation for this—no way we should know they were here, and no way we can tell the police how we tracked him without digging ourselves a hole and getting more and more connected to the whole thing. Right now, I'm just the girl who works at the apartments who happened to stumble upon some suspicious things while cleaning. They don't have any reason to suspect me. I'm not the one with a history of killing people or any direct evidence linking me to Eddie, so we need to keep it that way.

Maybe he could have trapped me—stopped me from fleeing from him and away from the scene with that flat tire, but he didn't expect to be the one running away and forgot that this particular "yippy female" can easily change a flat tire, so we need to get the hell out of this place and pretend we were never here to begin with.

Rosa takes a sanitizing wipe from her big purse in the car and wipes down the gun, and me and Anna watch in amazement as she walks over to the cliff's edge and drops it into the abyss like it's something she's done a dozen times before.

"It's Eddie's. I found it in his truck, so the serial number is scratched off, don't worry," she says, and Anna and I are speechless for a few moments. Then it's time to jump into action.

I change the car tire by the light of Rosa's phone flashlight, then the three of us drive down the black dusty road until we can see city lights again, until I hear Rosa say, "He stopped!"

And I pull over and shut the car off. I turn to the back seat where Rosa has been tending to Anna's wound and monitoring her tracker app on her phone to see where Callum is going.

We tell Anna everything. The night it all happened in the front office, how Callum stumbled into the wrong place and how that one moment is the only reason he's not getting away with what he's done to Lily and Henry. We tell her of Eddie's past and the GPS tracker and how I stashed the dirty money in Callum's bathroom and filmed him dragging Eddie's body… and that he's entirely and utterly fucked. And most important, how he's tried to destroy all of us, and we need to stick together.

"We need a reason why we'd know where Callum might be headed. They can't know we were on that cliff or that we tracked him or know anything about Eddie besides the stuff Cass gave the cops," Rosa says.

"Where is he?" Anna asks, becoming more alert the more time passes.

Rosa zooms in on her map.

"If I had to guess," I say, "he won't go to a hospital for his leg. He'll be arrested in seconds if he does that. He'll find a remote hotel or something so he can pay cash and have his car out of view. That's what I would do," I say, and I feel a little sick that a getaway plan comes so easily to mind. A couple months ago, I wouldn't have conceived of something like this.

"Desert Inn," Rosa says. "It's remote—has camping sites and everything. You're spot-on."

"I made out with him," Anna says out of nowhere.

We both turn and stare at her seemingly inappropriate outburst.

"I mean—the point is, we got kind of close. He would tell me something intimate that maybe you two would have no way of knowing, like that he was planning on moving out of state soon—once he got his insurance money, but that he would first stop at—what's it called again?" She stops. "A B&B with a cute name, I think…"

"Desert Inn," Rosa says, and it takes Anna a moment to put together what she's trying to say. Then she gets it.

"Yeah," Anna says. "I'm certain he told me that the Desert Inn was where he met Lily, and it was a place he promised to go back to before he left town—to honor her memory, scatter her ashes maybe."

"So you mention that you know where he might go, and that's the only meaningful place that comes to mind, so you might tell the police that you think he'd go there. Right." Rosa nods, putting it all together.

"And they'll find him there, but they'll eventually search the car and find the tracker and…"

"Untraceable, fingerprints wiped," Rosa says, and Anna and I look at each other.

"No," I say. "We need to go to the Desert Inn."

"Um. No way," Anna says, shrinking into the seat and shaking her head.

"We need to clean ourselves up before we go back to The Sycamores. Rosa is the only one not full of dirt and blood, so she can go to a store, get us some clothes and stuff. Then we get a room so we can wait and make absolutely sure he is staying for the night. He's hurt, so I'm sure he is. He needs to hide right now, but we need to be certain. We need to know which room number he's in. Then we call the police from a landline from the inn, and we say we saw a guy who was hurt—looked like he'd been shot, tell them which room—that it looked shady, and we're concerned. They send a cop. And there he is, just waiting for them like a sitting duck."

"Yes. We need to keep you away from all of this as much as possible—all of us," Rosa says to Anna. "She's right. You telling them you two were close—no. We need to go to the inn."

Anna takes a minute, weighing the fear and trauma against the necessity of this. "When we make the call, we leave immediately, right?" she asks.

"Yes. Of course," I say, and she nods in agreement. She's one of us now.

I hold out both my hands and take theirs, and we all hold each other as tears start to fall, and we just stay right there for a very long moment. We don't have to say it out loud—that we saved each other, each in a very different but life-altering way—but we know we will always be bound together in inextricable gratitude...and by very dark secrets.

30

ANNA

Three months later

When Callum was captured at the Desert Inn that night, I cried with relief. I remember that. But the memory of the rest of that night is all mostly a blur—bits of it are hazy, but the important things will always be imprinted in my memory. We did exactly what we planned.

We cleaned ourselves up in room 209 and waited a couple hours before we knew he wouldn't run, not that night anyway. Then we called in anonymously, reporting something troubling in room 106, and got the hell out of there, each back to our own sad apartments.

The police had gone from The Sycamores by then, and I remember being alone and finally falling into a shallow half-drugged sleep. Then, very early in the morning, word came in from Cass, and I knew there would be a long road ahead of more police and more questions and a future trial and a lot of pain to come, and I was ready to go through it. Anything to get justice for Henry, anything to put that bastard away...and most pressing, anything to protect Cass and Rosa.

It was weeks later when we heard that Callum would be held without bail for his trail, which wouldn't be for months, and I had already closed on our house and left The Sycamores behind.

I'm looking out at waves crashing against the shore of a white sand beach when I receive a video call from Cass and Rosa and the pool girls, the way I do every Friday night, so I can join the poolside barbecue and hold up a Solo cup to join in the cheers and listen to the week's gossip. Barry has a girlfriend who works at the comic book store and collects vintage action figures, Babs bought a wig that makes her look just like Dolly Parton without the boobs, and David's cat had kittens, which he gave to Frank, who named them Alpha, Beta, Gamma, and Beyoncé…and they keep Mary's mice away.

"Look at that bitchin' view!" Crystal said, elbowing her way in front of Cass and Rosa to get a look at the seascape through the windows next to me.

"You in Florida now?" Jackie asks.

"I told you seventy-five times, Ibiza," Rosa snaps.

"Well, what the fuck is Eye-beefa? That ain't a real place. You're makin' it up. But wherever it is, it's cool. Can we visit?"

Rosa takes the phone away from Crystal and moves it away from her.

"Maybe we will visit one day," Cass says. "Anyway, just wanted to be the first to tell you."

"Thanks. I'll be back at some point before all of the trial stuff starts. I'll come and say hello," I say, and Rosa waves goodbye.

Cass gives a tight little smile and nods. "Good. It'll be nice to see you," she says, and then I click off the video and I walk out to my terrace overlooking the cobalt sea and sit on a lounger.

I prop my laptop on my knees, and I watch some kids making a turtle out of sand with plastic shovels and buckets on the beach, and I think of Henry. He was right about this place. After the house sold and the arrest happened, I thought Playa D'en Bossa was the perfect place—the place I always wanted to end up because of a fond memory on spring break years ago. But it ended up being a party town with twentysomethings barfing into garbage cans on the street and marijuana wafting on the coconut breeze, giving me a constant contact high. It's noisy, crowded, young. Fine for college, but it really was just a memory I was trying to save, just like Henry always said.

Did I hang on to this past part of my life so hard that I couldn't see a future as an adult in the real world because I would be letting go of a perceived happiness that was never real?

I was a whiny brat about everything—including expecting journalist jobs to come to me and expecting Henry to never change and always look at life through the same lens we did as college freshmen, and maybe blaming him when he grew up and I didn't. Of course he found love with Lily. It breaks my heart that some of his last words were through tears, afraid that he "killed someone." He truly thought her death was his fault, and now I understand why. I hope he's somewhere beautiful where he is at peace and knows none of this was his fault.

I forgive him. I hope he can forgive me.

Within days, I left party town and found a small rental on the beach where I plan to spend a few more weeks until Monica flies into Palermo, and we eat our way through Italy for a week and discuss what I'm meant to do with my life now.

I felt pretty embarrassed when she explained that the phone calls between her and Henry were because she asked him to help plan a surprise birthday dinner at Giovanni's the next month with all of my old college friends in attendance because she thought it would cheer me up, as I seemed out of sorts in the days before. I'm glad I sought out the truth before exploding on her with accusations and destroying a friendship, but I still feel bad for doubting her and plan to make it up to her in gelato and margherita pizzas as much as I can.

But in the meantime, I've written it all down. Henry wanted me to keep chasing it—keep going after that dream, and I was too paralyzed by rejection to listen. Or maybe I didn't have a story to tell.

So I decide to try again. I tell my story now from the day Henry died: The Sycamores, the missing paintings, Lily, the pool girls, the storage unit, the threats, the affair, Callum, the video—all of it. Of course there are parts I don't tell. Parts I'll never tell anyone.

But I do tell the important pieces—how you don't always end up with the love of your life, but how they can still breathe new life into you and teach you forgiveness and grace.

As I read over my story that starts with a phone call at the gas station on a rainy afternoon and ends on a Spanish island, I whisper to Henry, "This is for you," and then I type in the email address of the editor at the *New York Post* who said she'd consider taking a look, and I say a little prayer, and I push Send.

31
CASS

The headlines sensationalized everything, as they do, and made it sound like I single-handedly was responsible for capturing a serial killer. That's, of course, not exactly how it happened.

The more attention I receive, the more Reid calls and asks to take me out or just to talk. Finally, after things with the police and press started to settle down, he called and invited me to dinner at Maggiano's, my favorite. I declined. He pushed and said it was a celebratory dinner for my bravery and for having the right guy headed to trial because of me. Anytime I hear this sentiment, I feel slightly nauseous, but I agree to go and finally have some closure, I tell myself.

So on a Friday night when the weather has cooled and life has returned to normal, and everyone is doing the usual barbecue by the pool but now in sweatshirts and jackets, I get ready to walk back into my old life for an evening. I cross the pool deck in my favorite sequin mini and Gucci shoes, and Jackie hands me a sagging paper plate with a hunk of corn on the cob on it before she really looks at me, and then says, "Well, shit. I guess you don't want this. The kernels will stick all over your teeth. Where the hell are you going anyway?"

"Nowhere," I say.

"Look, Rosa. She's goin' nowhere. I wish I looked that good goin' to the toilet, but okay, whatever you say," she says and hands a paper plate of hot dogs to Gordy.

Rosa looks up from her card game and raises her eyebrows at me. I look at Mary on a nearby deck chair who also gives me a go-get-'em look without even knowing where I'm going or what I'm getting. Then Frank runs over and throws his arms around my waist and starts listing all the things we did that day to Grandma Mary who listens intently, eating a large piece of sheet cake off a paper plate.

"And a fork got stuck in the garbage disposal, and Cass had to stick her hand down in it, and I told her if it got stuck she'd have a bloody pirate hand, but she got it out and then she gave it to me, and I brought it to eat my potato salad with," he says, delighted, as he takes the bent fork out of his back pocket.

Mary smiles at me and tells him to make sure to wash it first.

Frank looks at my heels and then up at me. "Why are you wearing that? You can't play hopscotch in that. We drew one with sidewalk chalk all the way up to fifty," he says matter-of-factly.

"Oh, cool. Well, I just have a dinner thing tonight, but I'll be back."

"You think in time for hopscotch, 'cause my bedtime's ten on Fridays," he says, a concerned tone in his voice now.

"I'll do my best, promise," I say and then I walk to my car and can feel everyone's eyes on my back because I know I look like someone they scarcely recognize dressed like this. And I feel a sense of guilt, because there's this little nagging part of me that doesn't know if I will come back. I mean, of course I have things here and a job to quit, but I mean really, truly come back, because my other life is inviting me back—my real life.

We agreed to meet for a drink at Reid's before dinner. Calling my house "Reid's" feels odd—as strange and unfamiliar as sitting here in his living room on my own couch like it's a stranger's, in my favorite dress he used to love, drinking a bottle of vintage wine from our collection that I bought myself a couple of years before. There is a sense of uneasiness mixed with longing.

"I thought we'd meet Becca and Drew for a drink after dinner at the Moonlighter if you want," he says as he pours me a glass and meets my eyes. "You look stunning, by the way."

"Why would we do that?" I ask.

"Huh? What?"

"Becca hasn't answered my calls in months—zero contact, and all of a sudden, you like me again so, so does she? Or is it that she thinks I'm famous now?"

"Come on, Cass. That's not fair."

"It's not?" I ask.

"It was a confusing time for everyone." He brushes it under the rug. "I'm sure she'll apologize." He sits next to me and changes the topic. "Cheers. To your incredible bravery and..."

I don't let him finish because the words make me want to gag, so I just prematurely clink glasses and wave away what I know he means as a compliment.

"I know I've said this before, Cass, but—okay, I'm not trying to push you at all, but why don't you think about staying just the weekend and see how you feel?" And he has said that before, and I have thought about it. My own bed, my own TV that doesn't need to be slapped in the right corner.

"I don't know," I say.

"Listen," he says, putting my wineglass down and taking my hands. He looks me in the eye. "I won't make excuses anymore. It wasn't a midlife crisis or you not doing enough or anything like that. It was my utter stupidity, and I will be telling you I'm sorry for the rest of my life because I *am so* sorry. I'll do anything to make it up to you," he says.

I want to believe him. I think about all of the mistakes I've made and what he did seems to pale in comparison, and I think about Henry and what he did and why, and maybe people fuck up, and maybe that doesn't make him a total monster.

"I don't know how to do this," I say. "I don't know how to pretend all kinds of horrible shit didn't happen."

"We don't have to pretend," he says, flashing his palm in surrender and then giving me back my wine as if it's settled. "Just take it a step at a time, think about it." He looks like he might kiss me, so I take my wine from his outstretched hand and stand.

"Well, come on," he says, leading into the kitchen. "You must be starving." I follow him in to see a spread of fancy finger foods across the marble kitchen island.

"You made this!?" I ask, thinking he was trying to impress me because I love cooking.

"God no, catered. I wanted it to be special," he says, and he's trying so hard it's sort of embarrassing. I mean, who actually has appetizers catered in for two people before a dinner out? There are flickering candles and bad elevator jazz playing from built-in speakers, and it's all overkill, but it feels sort of nice to have someone care so much. Is that what this is? Or maybe it's manipulation. Whatever the reason, after almost a year at The Sycamores, it seems like I'm in another dimension. It's so clean, and it smells like cinnamon candles and aftershave instead of dirty mop water and mold. I pick up a cream puff and eat it.

"Holy crap. I'm used to Oscar Mayer hot dogs and baked beans," I say.

"Ugh," he says.

"No, it's actually kind of… I don't know. Rosa makes them from scratch and uses molasses as her secret ingredient. It's…" And then I stop myself and switch gears. "Anyway. It's good. Thanks." I look around the kitchen with my double ovens and pot filler, and I feel like I'm staying in a fancy hotel for a moment. It's so foreign and strange.

Then I think about The Sycamores and never having to go

back and smell tuna casserole or never pulling a hunk of greasy hair out of somebody's drain or staring at the yellow water stain on the ceiling above my bed, and in a way, my heart leaps with joy. He wants me here. This is my house.

But then I keep looking around, and something is happening to me. I feel pricks of heat climb my spine and a cold sweat across my forehead. This is all a facade. I sit on a kitchen stool and take a breath. None of it was really mine. At The Sycamores, I earned every High Life by the pool and the view of the water stain on the ceiling. My skill and hours of hard work got me that.

The only thing left here are pieces of the old me. Everything here is not only *not mine*, but it represents a slow unraveling of myself as I came undone—it represents years of becoming someone so far away from my real self that I was unrecognizable, even to me.

And so even though I never have to go back to the land of misfit toys again if I don't want to, those are the people who... love me? Shit, am I saying that? It's hard to admit to myself that the family I've always wanted, that I always talked about having—isn't Reid and a baby of our own in this single-family home with a media room and tub jets, but is one I already have across town. It's Jackie DJing the party with her *Boys II Men* CDs and Barry giving history lessons on samurai swords that nobody is listening to, and it's Crystal flicking Junior Mints at all the kids like a strange game of dodgeball, which they oddly love.

And it's Rosa who is actually, possibly, my only real friend, and it's especially Frank who's waiting for me—who needs me. Frank, who everyone else has left behind.

I hand Reid my wineglass. "I'm so sorry, but I have to go."

"What?" he says, his face dropping in palpable disappointment. "Please. You don't have to go. Just…"

"I do."

"What about dinner? Are you…"

"I have somewhere I need to be. I made a promise to some-one. Sorry," I say, and I take my heels off and rush out of this house. I literally sprint out of this life I know I'll never see again, and I thought I'd feel the heavy weight of loss and mourn the life I thought I wanted, but that's not how I feel. I feel free.

I drive back to The Sycamores thinking about Frank and how I made a promise to him I forgot to keep, so I park in the back of the office, change into a hoodie and jeans, and come out to the pool deck with all the supplies.

Rosa sees me and throws an arm around my shoulder, pull-ing me into her for just a moment before running after one of the kids, who's taken off with an open can of Budweiser from a table. I sit next to Mary on a lawn chair and pull up a cooler, setting my things on top, when Frank comes over.

"You're back."

"Of course I'm back. I live here," I say.

"What are you doing?" he says, looking at my basil and olive oil and bowls.

"I'm making pesto. I don't know what you're doing," I say, and he beams. I pull up a chair and tap it. He sits down, and I begin showing him how to chop garlic.

Rough around the edges. That's what Reid said I was. And I guess he's right. I guess that's why I fit right in. I don't know how the stars aligned this way, but this is what I was given.

Crystal hands me a beer that she opened with her teeth and sits down in her daughter's Rainbow Brite chair, which she doesn't even remotely fit into. Rosa winks at me as she holds a bucket between her knees and peels the veins from a bowl of green beans, Jackie sings "End of the Road" along with the music, in an emotional rendition with impressive interpretive dance, after a few too many wine coolers.

I think about what I'll do and if the Egg Platter would give me another shot, but now that I'm locally famous, at least for a few more weeks until the next headline commandeers everyone's attention, maybe I can do better than that. Maybe I could really do something on my own.

I give Sinatra an approving nod as he pulls basil leaves from the herb plant he's helped care for. He beams and carefully mixes the ingredients the way I showed him. The kid needs me. How could I go anywhere?

The sounds of evening at The Sycamores that I've grown used to hum all around me—kids laughing, a dog barking in the distance, meat loaf wafting from someone's open kitchen window, a motorcycle revving down the boulevard, and Barry showing Tiffany and Amber how to samurai sword fight with pool noodles.

And I smile because I found my family. Because I'm home.

★ ★ ★ ★ ★

ACKNOWLEDGEMENTS

Thank you from the bottom of my heart to my biggest supporter, Mark Glass. A huge thanks to the absolute best agent in the world, Sharon Bowers, and to my wonderful editor Sara Rodgers.

Thank you to Leah Morse and the whole team at Graydon House…and also Kristen Salciccia, proofreader extraordinaire.

Of course, thanks to my family, Dianna Nova, Julie Loehrer, and Mark & Tamarind Knutson.

A very special thank you Tonya Cornish for her amazing feedback and support on this project, and to retired Omaha Police Department Detective, Tammy Mitchell, for all of the priceless research help. And to all of my dear friends who continue to support my work and cheer me on.

5